she
has
your
eyes

Also by Elisa Lorello

Faking It
Ordinary World
Why I Love Singlehood
Adulation
Friends of Mine: Thirty Years in the Life
of a Duran Duran Fan

Translated Works
Vorgetäuscht (Faking It)
Deshalb liebe ich mein Singleleben (Why I Love Singlehood)

she has your eyes

A NOVEL

the continuation of *Faking It*
and *Ordinary World*

ELISA LORELLO

Text copyright © 2014 Elisa Lorello

Published by Lake Union Publishing, Seattle

www.apub.com

ISBN-13: 9781477848128
ISBN-10: 1477848126

Cover design by Mary Ann Smith

Library of Congress Control Number: 2013941699

Printed in the United States of America

For
Nora Ephron, Larry Leitner, and Jo Ensanian
in loving memory

chapter one

Labor Day weekend

"I'm not saying I'll never marry you," I said. "I just want more time to think about it."

The outdoor thermometer topped ninety degrees as a last-ditch-effort-to-save-summer heat wave invaded the Northeast. David and I bought one of those kiddie pools, the largest we could get, filled it with water from the garden hose, and slouched in it on opposite sides facing each other, motionless, listening to classic rock. Doing anything else produced a sweat.

No doubt the marriage conversation had been prompted by the previous day's barbecue. David and I resumed the Labor Day tradition Sam and I started when we got married. Like Sam had once done, David manned the grill and flipped the burgers and steaks with such finesse he could pass for a celebrity chef. Our guests were a mix of my friends from Northampton University and some of David's friends and clientele from the art world. We covered a catering table with burgers, hot dogs, steaks, salads, chips, cold cuts, platters of veggies, cookies, and, when the time came, gallons of ice cream. Shaded underneath the table sat two enormous coolers of water, beer, sangria, margarita mix, soda, and YooHoo. My brothers Joey

1

and Tony came, set up their amps and equipment on the deck, and played Beatles songs until the cops showed up to warn them about the noise (although the cops put in their own requests and lingered for a while).

The bash had run late into the night. Our friends and family clustered around the deck with citronella candles and Bug-Off spray, talking loudly and finishing off the coolers' contents. Their kids were asleep inside. At one point in the midst of a bout of laughter, I looked at David, who had become so comfortable with my friends, so much a part of their lives and this house. And I was filled with contentment, the kind I'd thought would never return following Sam's death. David had caught my gaze and looked at me curiously.

"What?" he'd asked, as if we were alone.

"This," I said. "This is nice." At that moment, the others disappeared as he took my hand. "I want more of this." I didn't know if it was deliberate, but his thumb traced a path along my ring finger.

When David and I had gotten back together for good last year, after spending almost the entire night making love and promising never to be apart from each other again, we'd negotiated several things in our relationship. For one, we decided to live in his Cambridge, Massachusetts, apartment for the first couple of months before moving into Sam's and my Northampton house permanently. Two, I'd stay on at NU as "visiting faculty" and he'd cut down his hours as an art buyer. Since Sam's death, I had come to see time as a precious commodity to be spent on things other than work (the Italians' pleasure ethic had rubbed off on me), especially since we were in the fortunate position of being financially solvent.

The third, of course, had been the marriage thing.

We'd agreed on a "marriage moratorium"—one year without bringing up the subject, with an option to renew every six months.

"The year isn't quite over yet," I said in the present moment, flicking water at him with my fingers in a teasing way.

"But I figured now's a good time to start talking about it," said David. "So, give me your reasons for not wanting to get married."

I sat up. "Well . . . " I drew a blank. "You've caught me off guard. I haven't had the time to put together my argument."

"I figured you knew it by heart."

"Yeah, but who can construct a coherent thought in this heat?"

"Wanna go inside?" he asked.

Neither of us budged.

"Well, let's start with the practical reasons," said David. "If, God forbid, something were to happen to me, you'd be taken care of if we were married. Legally and financially speaking."

"Aren't I already your primary beneficiary?"

"Yes, but there's all kinds of tax stuff to consider, now and after I'm gone."

"But there's such a thing as common law," I said. "If you've lived with the same partner for seven years or longer, the state considers you married."

"Not in Massachusetts. Or at least not without jumping through a bunch of hoops."

"How do you know?"

"I looked it up."

I wondered when and why he'd taken the time to do such a thing. Perhaps he'd been doing some preliminary research for when the time came for him to make his case?

I ran a cup through the water and dumped it on my head several times.

"OK. So what else?" I asked.

He stared at me blankly.

"Well?"

"I don't know, I just want to," he answered. "I know that's a kid's answer, but I don't know how else to put it. Besides, you're supposed to be making *your* case to *me*. Tell me why you *don't* want to."

My reason was no more substantive than his. "It's not that I don't want to," I said, trying to gauge his body language. He didn't move a muscle, however. "I'm just not sure."

"About what?"

"Why mess with a good thing?"

"You think this is a good thing?" he asked, gesturing between us.

"I do." In many ways I felt like we were already married. We'd grown into each other in ways I'd never expected. Companionship had never been hard for us. David and I had known each other for a little over ten years despite having been out of each other's lives throughout the duration of my courtship and marriage to Sam. But once I'd been truly able to move on following Sam's death, David and I had found a way to be both independent and a couple. Neither of us had a problem traveling without the other, for example. It made our together time even more meaningful. We were good together, and I had come to appreciate life again. Life with him, especially.

But I knew he wanted to make it official. And although I'd just delivered the words "I do" with certainty, they left a dry taste in my mouth. Or maybe it was just the heat. Regardless, officially marrying David would mean closing the door on

Sam once and for all, or so I thought. Although death had already taken care of that, hadn't it?

"Are you not happy, Dev?" I asked.

"I just want more, and I think you do too."

"What's a marriage license going to give us that we don't already have?"

"Proof," he said.

"Of what?"

"That we're a family."

The word *family* struck a chord. I'd never considered the connotation beyond my mom and brothers, or David and his mother and sisters, or Sam and his brother. Sam and I had rarely used the word in reference to each other, and despite our love for our cat, Donny Most, we weren't the type of people to call ourselves "parents" or him "our baby."

So that was it. David wanted us to be a family.

⁓෨෨ෟ෨෨⁓

Later that afternoon I was cleaning up outside, the sun still blazing as I sang along with the Doobie Brothers' "Long Train Runnin'," bopping about as I moved, when I heard someone say, "Excuse me."

I whipped around and before me stood a girl in her mid-teens, judging by her ensemble of Daisy Duke shorts and turquoise Old Navy tank top, finished off with enormous sunglasses and bright pink flip-flops garnished with plastic daisies. Her long, dark chocolate hair was haphazardly tied in back with a scrunchie, a neon purple strand falling loose, like a skunk stripe.

"Yes?" I asked, feeling self-conscious in my denim cut-off shorts hugging my cellulite-ridden thighs and one-piece

5

bathing suit, my hair pulled back like a ballerina's bun, gray at the roots, frizzy from the humidity. Sweat beaded down my temples as well as my cleavage.

"Is your husband home?" she asked.

This question used to throw me for a loop when David and I first got back together because I assumed people meant Sam. I learned to ask for clarification.

"Do you mean David?"

"Um, I think so," she replied.

"He'll be back in a minute," I said. We had run out of ice cream the previous night, and David had a yen to make his own, so he left to buy the ingredients. I invited the girl into the house and offered her a glass of iced tea, studying her features after she removed her sunglasses and trying to place her. We sat at the butcher-block table and she surveyed the kitchen, as if looking for something of recognition. "I'm Andi," I said, extending my hand. She shook it weakly.

"Wylie," she answered, quickly adding, "I'm named after my great-grandfather, or so I'm told."

My curiosity got the best of me. "So, how do you know David?"

"I'd better wait until he gets here."

We sat in awkward silence for what couldn't have been more than five minutes that passed like five hours, when to our relief the screen door *whooshed* open and slammed shut. David, entering the kitchen like a whirlwind, was dressed in carpenter shorts and a white T-shirt, showing off his sculpted physique. The ends of his hair were damp from sweat. I stood up.

"Hey, hon, you're not going to believe what I—" He stopped short when he saw Wylie, who stood up, went right over to David, and took in an eyeful.

"Oh. Mygod." She said the last two words as if they were one. "You *totally* look like me."

David, bewildered, looked at her, then at me, then back at her.

"Do I know you?" he asked.

"I think you might be my dad."

chapter two

Her eyes, I realized. They were the exact same sienna, albeit slightly darker, more feminine than fiery. She wore too much eyeliner and mascara, which made them look less rather than more noticeable. A shimmery, possibly smoky shadow would bring them out. Or perhaps something more subtle.

The three of us sat at the table: David and I together, Wylie opposite us. If she was self-conscious about two strangers staring at her, she didn't show it. Probably because she was looking at David just as intently, inspecting every contour and crevice of his face. His defined cheekbones. Olive skin. Round chin. Dry lips.

The butcher-block table seemed to be trembling until I realized that David was hyperactively tapping his heel on the floor, his knee pumping like a jackhammer.

"I'm sorry . . . I didn't catch . . . ," David stumbled, "your name?"

"It's Wylie," she said. "Wylie Baker. My mom is Janine Baker, although you probably knew her as Janine Salvo."

I took my eyes off the girl long enough to see David frantically searching his memory bank for the woman's name, face, something, anything. He closed his eyes and transferred the tapping from his right foot to his right hand, all five fingertips.

"I don't . . . I'm not sure. You said Janine?"

"No, wait—she told me she went by Jane back then. She said she didn't think you used your real name either."

The color drained from his face, while my stomach lurched. He closed his eyes again, and I thought I heard him say, "Jane," under his breath.

"Wylie, where are you from and how did you find us here?" I asked.

"I live in Connecticut, just outside Hartford," she started. "I was four when my parents—my mom and my stepdad—" she clarified, "were married. Well, I didn't always know this. I thought my dad was, you know, my *dad*. When I was about twelve I started going through photo albums and looking at dates, and I noticed there were no pictures of my dad with me when I was born. So I started grilling my mom and she finally broke down last year and told me that my dad wasn't my real dad. At least not biologically speaking."

"I don't understand how that brings you *here*," said David.

"My mom told me there were two possible choices of men, and she had no idea of knowing which one was my father without a DNA test. She also lost touch with both of them. But I kept grilling her—where she met them, where they worked, how old they were, their names . . . she was especially reluctant to give me names. I think she was embarrassed about not knowing your real name."

"Assuming it's me," he said.

"My sister and I did this massive Internet search about six months ago. The first possibility—I at least got my mom to tell me *his* name—turned out to be an investment banker, bald and pale and looked *nothing* like me. And my mom didn't seem to have much of a reaction; not like with *you*."

Had it all not been so shocking, I probably would've stifled a chuckle—David got a rise out of women regardless of where he went or how he knew them.

"She said you had the looks of a model—or, at least, that my dad did. So I thought, *hey, why not look to see if he's done any actual modeling?* and started Googling male models. Well, that turned out to be, like, impossible. Of course, my mom refused to help. She was pissed that I was looking in the first place, but I was like, 'Mom, this is my *dad*, right? Like, what if he has some hereditary medical condition? I have a right to know.' But I pretty much gave up. And then one day, totally out of the blue, my sister—well, my stepsister, actually—who's, like, a total celebrity whore and addicted to this Hamptons gossip blog, she saw this photo of you at some Hamptons party—"

I could tell David was searching his mental database for the last time he'd been in the Hamptons, much less at a party.

"—and said, 'Ohmigod, he totally looks like you.' So I showed the picture of you to my mom and she *freaked out*, like, 'Where did you get this?' and all that. So I figured I was onto something."

I interjected, "So you think David is your father just because of a photo?"

"Hey, I heard about this woman who found her long-lost daughter after posting her baby picture on Facebook—and the daughter was now *ten years old*! Anyway," Wylie continued, seemingly unfazed, "Google to the rescue. So we found your name under the photo and traced you to this gallery in Boston. I'm telling you, my sister is, like, either going to be a private detective or a stalker when she grows up. So then I called the gallery and asked for you, and they said you didn't work there but they knew who you were. They wouldn't give me your number, though. But at least I had confirmation, went back to Google, and found a picture of the two of you tagged on someone's Facebook page. So then I Googled *your* name," she said to me, "and found out you were a professor, which, after a little more digging, led me here."

My stomach lurched again. "But I'm not listed in the phone book," I said.

"It's not hard," she replied. "You were featured in the local paper. So that narrows down the town. From there you can find someone through property records—it's public information. I decided to take a chance. I figured one way or another you had to know something."

David and I were both horrified, and I couldn't help but feel violated. "How old are you?" I asked.

"Fifteen."

I darted my eyes to David, who was doing the math in his head, I could tell. And judging by the look he was fighting to suppress, it added up.

"Anyway," she said after a beat, "here I am. I wasn't going to come—because, let's face it, it was a long shot—but I really wanted to know for sure."

"Wylie," David started, "putting aside the fact that just because we bear some physical resemblance doesn't mean we're related, do you have any idea how much trouble you're in? What you did is an egregious violation of someone's privacy."

"It's not like I hacked into anything," she said. "It was all public information. And I didn't tell anyone or post your address or anything like that."

"Does your mother know you're here?" I asked.

"Not exactly. She thinks I'm on an end-of-summer trip to Cape Cod with my youth group."

"How on earth did you get here?" I asked.

"Bus, taxi. It's not hard."

"Do you have any idea how dangerous that could be? Besides, if your Google search was that thorough, then I'm sure you would've gotten an e-mail address. Why didn't you contact me that way?" I said.

"Who uses e-mail anymore? Besides, I figured you'd think I was crazy and wouldn't reply. I also figured you wouldn't be the type to throw a young girl into the street."

"That's not the point," said David. "Did it ever occur to you that the Internet is full of lies? And just because someone works at a gallery or is a professor doesn't mean they're automatically trustworthy. Look, Wylie. I think we should call your mother right now and have her come get you."

Wylie was neither deflated nor deterred. "Fine," she huffed. "But will you give me a DNA sample?"

We looked at her, incredulous. You'd think she was asking him for a stick of gum, she was so nonchalant.

"A DNA sample is a very personal thing," I said.

She rolled her eyes. "I'm not asking him for a pint of his blood. I just want a lock of his hair or something."

"Then what?" I asked, taking hold of David's hand under the table, and squeezing it.

"Then I'll take it to some lab and have them compare it to mine. How hard can it be?"

"This isn't *CSI*," said David.

"Well, duh."

"So it's really *not* all that simple. There are legal and ethical issues involved."

"Don't you want to know if I'm your daughter?" she asked.

I looked at David. His face looked frozen, his jaw unable to move.

I spoke up. "Wylie, I'm sorry you went through all this trouble, but you've made a mistake. This is something you need to talk to your mother about. Maybe there's a reason she hasn't disclosed the identity of your father to you. Especially if she doesn't know who he is."

"Oh, *she knows*," she said, a touch annoyed. "She just had no idea how to find you," she said to David.

The color drained from his face again. "Please don't say 'you.'"

"Whatever," she muttered.

"Regardless, it's time to call your mom," I said, more assertive than before.

"Not until he promises to give me a DNA sample."

David smacked the table and rose to his feet, unnerving the girl for the first time. "That's it. You don't come into someone's home, make wild accusations, invade their privacy, and then start issuing ultimatums. It's not going to happen, understand?"

Before Wylie could speak, I interjected. "OK, let's try to remain calm." I turned to her. "I agree with David. If you don't allow us to call your mother, then we'll have no choice but to call the police, and you'll be in a lot worse trouble. Trust me, this is the better option. I'll call your mom, she'll come get you, and perhaps we can settle this matter in a mutually respectful way."

Wylie hung her head. "She's gonna kill me when she finds out I've gotten this far."

"Did you really not think it was going to come to this?" David asked.

She shrugged. "I don't know. I guess I thought you'd be more willing to help."

Wylie recited her mother's phone number as I took the kitchen phone from its cradle and dialed.

13

"Who has a landline anymore?" she seemed to be asking no one in particular.

"Hello?" a woman's voice answered.

"Is this Ms. Janine Baker?" I asked.

"Yes." Her tone immediately turned to one of worry.

I spoke in my professorial voice. "Hello, Ms. Baker. My name is Andrea Vanzant. I'm a professor at Northampton University in Massachusetts." I waited for some kind of acknowledgment from her, but got none. "Ms. Baker," I continued, "your daughter Wylie is here at my home for reasons I'd rather not discuss over the phone."

"Who'd you say you were?"

"Andrea Vanzant. I live in Northampton, Massachusetts, and your daughter is here."

"What is she doing there?"

"She's completely safe, but my husband and I think it would be best if you came to pick her up." The word *husband* came out of nowhere. Seemed to give David a jolt as well.

The teen's mother let out a string of expletives. "Put her on the phone," she demanded, and I handed the receiver to Wylie. I could almost hear her mother word for word. Wylie rolled her eyes and responded mostly in monosyllabic words. The girl's steely resolve baffled me—had my mother ever unleashed on me like that at her age I probably would've fainted dead away. Hell, if I'd ever attempted to pull the stunt Wylie pulled, not only would I have gotten no farther than the Long Island Rail Road, but I probably would've boarded the wrong train and wound up going eastbound to Port Jefferson rather than westbound to Manhattan.

Wylie handed the phone back to me.

"What's your name again?" Janine Baker asked me.

"Andrea," I replied. "Call me Andi."

"I'm on my way now. Keep an eye on her. I don't care if you or your husband have to lock her in a closet."

"I don't think there's any need for that."

"Fat chance. If she's gone by the time I get there, I'm holding you responsible, and I'll sue your ass until you've got nothing but the clothes on your back, you hear me?" She had a thick Long Island accent.

"Absolutely, Ms. Baker. I understand. Thank you."

Wylie smirked after I hung up. "Wow, she is *pissed*."

"She has every right to be," said David.

"She's probably more worried than you realize. Mothers' anger usually stems from worry," I said.

"Do you guys have any kids?"

"No," I answered.

"Then how do you know?"

"We know enough to know that," said David. He seemed mesmerized by her, staring at her with a combination of fascination and anger.

"Your mom's afraid you're going to sneak out before she gets here," I said. "Can we trust you not to do that? It's going to take at least an hour, probably longer with the Labor Day traffic. We don't want to watch you every second. I'd really hate to have to treat you like a prisoner."

Again she rolled her eyes. "I *promise* I won't go anywhere. Besides, I was really hoping I could talk to you; you know, get some background information," she said to David.

He stared at her blankly, but I knew the expression well enough to read his mind: *Are you nuts?*

"Excuse me," he said, and turned to me. "I'm going upstairs." He pulled me out of earshot from Wylie and spoke in a low voice. "Set the house alarm so that it goes off if she tries to leave."

"Really?" I asked. David's adamant stance overpowered my skepticism, however, and he set it himself before shooting up the stairs. I returned to the kitchen and sat at the table again, wondering whether David was going to hide out upstairs for the entire hour. Wylie seemed to be waiting for me to say something.

I'd been dealing with nineteen- and twenty-year-olds for most of my teaching career, thus had mastered a communication model that worked ninety-five percent of the time. The key was to listen to them (*always* listen), but not pull any punches. Additionally, always try to show them the other side, the bigger picture, regardless of whether it was for the purpose of analyzing a text, drafting a piece of writing, or solving a problem. Don't invalidate them, but don't let them get away with murder either. Most of all, remember what it was like to be nineteen.

Did it work with fifteen-year-olds too? I was about to find out.

"Listen, he's not mad at you," I said. "He's just . . . in shock. We both are. I mean, what if some strange guy suddenly showed up at your house one day, completely out of the blue, and claimed to be your dad? And you'd basically gone your whole life having never thought such a thing was possible? You would totally freak out."

"I guess so," said Wylie as she wiped the condensation from her iced tea glass and contemplated.

"And he's right. There are a bunch of legal issues to consider."

"Look, I'm not after your money, if that's what he's worried about."

I shook my head in frustration. "Wylie, this is huge. *Huge.* It's a very, very complicated issue. It's not some Lifetime movie."

16

Rather than display any of the usual teenage body language—rolling eyes, impatient huffs, shrugging shoulders—Wylie hung her head, then picked it up again. Her eyes had grown dark with regret.

I'd seen that look before. Only not on her. A shiver ran up my spine.

"I know," she said. "And I'm really sorry. I probably didn't think this through."

I paused for a moment, allowing the weight of it to sink in for her, and I began to see her actions less as reckless and more as proactive. She'd taken matters into her own hands. Such determination in a fifteen-year-old was admirable, even if her execution was flawed.

I looked at the clock on the wall: a little after four thirty.

"Are you hungry?" I asked.

"Starving."

I went to the fridge and rummaged through the remains of yesterday's barbecue feast before pulling out some grilled chicken, potato salad, corn on the cob, and two hamburger patties. I filled an aluminum pie pan with portions of the chicken and the corn, covered it in foil, and set the oven to 350 degrees.

"Why don't you just nuke it?" she asked.

"Oven heating preserves the texture of the food. But if you're really starving, I can nuke it for you."

She nodded, and I removed the foil, transferred the contents except the two patties to a plate, and placed it in the microwave oven. Then I re-covered the two patties with the foil and placed them into the oven without waiting for it to preheat, knowing how much David hated nuked leftovers. When the microwave oven beeped, I removed the plate and set it in front of Wylie, accompanied by a serving of potato salad, a cold can of Fresca, plastic utensils, and a napkin.

"Thanks," she said.

"Would you mind if I went upstairs to check on David?"

"Sure thing. I can't stand when people watch me eat."

I bounded up the stairs and went into what used to be Sam's study. Shortly after David moved in, we'd replaced the old leather sofas and painted the walls to a woodsy, green-umber hue, maintaining its warmth but more suitable to David's tastes, complemented by several carefully chosen paintings. I'd burst into tears when the sofa came out, having spent many hours on it, especially in the months following Sam's death, but had since made the adjustment, grateful that David kept Sam's stupid bobblehead collection intact and on display out of respect, all encased in glass now.

David was sitting at the desk, typing furiously on his laptop.

"Whatcha doin'?" I asked, feigning nonchalance.

"Writing a very nasty letter," he replied, without looking away from the screen.

"To whom?"

"The President of the United States."

"What for?"

"Drone attacks, unemployment, health care . . . pick something."

"I think his Final Four bracket was way off this year," I said. "That right there is grounds for impeachment."

David stopped typing and looked up at me and I knew I'd disarmed him when he tried to shoot me a dirty look that broke into a twisted grin.

"You suck," he said.

"Because I killed your bad mood? Sorry, hon."

He slid his chair out and motioned for me to sit on his lap. I obliged.

"Christ, Andi. This kid comes out of fucking nowhere . . ."

"I know."

"Claims to be *my daughter* . . ."

"I know."

"And expects me to be all Ward Cleaver."

"I doubt she knows who Ward Cleaver is."

He furrowed his brow and looked at me suspiciously. "How come you're so calm about this?"

"Oh, I'm freaked out, believe me. But the professor side of me is kicking in. It's best not to lose your cool. Besides," I said, pushing a strand of hair away from his face, "I think the magnitude of it is starting to sink in for her."

He took a whiff of my hair before giving me a kiss.

"What's she doing right now?" he asked.

"I fixed her a plate of food. One for you too. It's warming up in the oven."

"That was sweet of you, thanks." He paused for a beat. "You really think it's OK to leave her alone?"

"We've already hot-wired the house; what more can we do? Listen, Dev," I started, shifting my weight. "Is there any possibility that she really is your daughter?"

He pushed me off his lap and stood up. "No fucking way. I was *always* careful."

David's past had, for the most part, stayed there. Few consequences came back to haunt him, and certainly nothing of this enormity.

"There's no such thing as 'always' when it comes to birth control. Maybe something went wrong, something you didn't know about."

He paced across the room. "Andi, this can't be—*she* can't be . . ."

"She has your eyes, Dev."

19

He stopped and turned to me. I looked into his sienna irises, ablaze and frightened, and I knew what he was thinking, knew that he couldn't bring himself to agree with me. *It was possible.* More than possible, even. And if it was more than possible, then what would it mean for him? Not just legally and financially, but emotionally? What would it mean for *me*? For us?

It was eighty-five degrees outside, and I was shivering inside. And not because of the air conditioning.

I sucked in my fear and went back into professor mode. "Let's wait until her mom gets here," I said, and made a feeble attempt at reassurance: "She's probably just a drama-prone kid who's rebelling."

"Why can't she read the Twilight books like everyone else?"

chapter three

An hour never passed so slowly. David and I changed our clothes to something more company-friendly and then ate as we watched TV in the den while Wylie sat in the recliner in the corner, glued to her cell phone, her thumbs tapping away furiously. She occasionally caught David staring at her accusingly, until she finally had the guts to say, "What," in an irked tone.

"I'd better not find anything about this on Facebook or Twitter or whatever," he threatened.

"I'm just talking to my friends is all."

"I mean it," he said.

She got up and demonstratively exited the room, and I followed her into the kitchen.

"Wylie, he's just upset about all this."

"Well, how do you think *I* feel?" she said, tears welling up. "Is he always like this? Because if he is then I don't think I want him as my dad."

"He's really not," I assured her. "He's scared, that's all. Same as you."

"I wasn't scared until I got here."

"Maybe that's a good thing."

"So how come you guys don't have any kids?" Her sudden change in emotion and subject caught me off guard.

"We got together kind of late in the game," I said. "In fact, David and I aren't married."

"Were you married to someone else?"

"I'm a widow."

She gasped. "Wow," she said. "I usually only associate that word with older women. You know, like grandmothers."

The word still rang awkwardly for me too.

"What happened?" she asked.

"My husband was killed by a drunk driver."

There was a time when telling a stranger, or even a friend, about Sam's death felt like the ground was going to open up and swallow me whole at any given second. Panic would flood my lungs and seize my heart. But since his death—four years next month—it had become something I'd learned to live with, like being nearsighted or having a bum knee. I'd grown detached, and not in the grief-stricken, denial kind of way. It was what my former therapist Melody Greene would've called "allowance." However, any mention of him still seemed to summon his presence.

She hesitated before asking her next question. "Were you there? In the car, I mean."

"Nope. I was right here. It was the night of our fifth wedding anniversary. He went to the store to pick up something he'd forgotten to buy and never came back."

Wylie looked down at the table; the purple strand of hair swung across her face. She pushed it away.

"I'm sorry," she said. "My grandfather died last year. He had Parkinson's. You know, the Michael J. Fox disease?"

"I'm really sorry. That must have been very hard on your grandmother and your mom."

"It was my stepfather's father. I guess that means he technically wasn't my grandfather, but I've always thought of him that way."

"I'm sure he never thought of you as anything other than his granddaughter."

Just then David entered the kitchen. "Wylie, I want to apologize. I had no right to be so rude and accusatory, especially since you're a guest in our home."

Her face turned red, and she avoided eye contact with him. "It's OK." The three of us returned to the den to wait out Janine's arrival.

Twenty minutes later, we remained in limbo as the uncomfortable silence saturated the room despite the annoying sports commentators rambling on the TV in the background. "Who's winning?" I asked David in an attempt to break the tension.

"Mets just scored again."

"That's rare," I said deadpan. David returned my teasing with a smirk, and I couldn't help but release a flirtatious smile. For the first time since Wylie showed up, his eyes brightened as he nonverbally responded, and for that split second I think we both forgot she was in the room.

Our mental foreplay was interrupted by a forceful knock, and we both jumped.

"That must be my mom," said Wylie.

My stomach instantly filled with rocks. David's did too, I could tell. Together we walked to the front door and opened it. A woman stood before us. At least five-foot-nine. Frosted hair that was once dark. Her eyes made up the same as Wylie's. Full lips, as if injected with collagen. Thin. Full busted. Tanned. She wore black cotton shorts, a fitted white V-neck T-shirt, and gold lamé sandals. One look at David, and her eyes went

23

from angry to stunned, as if an apparition had appeared. Her jaw dropped. I glanced at David, and could read his expression: he *knew* her. And I could practically see his inner wheels spinning as their past relationship, whatever that encompassed—a one-night stand, a summer romance, a former client in the early days of his escort business—zoomed in front of him like a subway train. The floor suddenly felt wobbly. Yet when I looked down, the surface was perfectly flat.

Wylie squirmed around me to say hello to her mother, and seemed almost pleased to see the mutual reaction, which made me feel downright woozy. *Oh yeah.* This was more than just a possibility.

"Jane," David said in almost a whisper.

"Devin," said Janine.

chapter four

I froze. It had been a long time since I'd heard anyone other than myself or Maggie call David by his escort name. He seemed just as rattled by it. It took a full five seconds before one of us shook out of our trance and let Janine in.

"So," said Wylie, "obviously you two know each other. But how? I mean, when and where did you meet?"

Neither David nor Janine said a word or moved a muscle. Wylie waved her hand vertically between the two of them to shake them out of it. "Hel-lo?"

"Ms. Baker, can I get you something to drink?" I asked, my voice quavering.

"It's *Mrs.* Baker, and I'd better not." It occurred to me that she thought I meant booze.

"A glass of water? Coffee?" I pressed.

David asked for water, but after I retrieved a tumbler and held it out to him, he changed his mind. I sipped from it myself.

David had already shown Janine into the living room, and Wylie followed them. I found myself wondering why Mr. Baker wasn't with her, if he knew Wylie had been searching for her biological father (and why had I not asked Wylie up to this point?), and if he knew Janine was here, or why. Wylie sat, eager to get on with the conversation.

Janine remained standing. "No," she said, the word cutting between us. "I am not going to have this conversation in front of my daughter."

"I'm not comfortable with that either," said David.

Oh, great—their first official parental alliance. I shook off the thought as quickly as it came to mind.

"What?" said Wylie. "Why not?"

"Trust me," said Janine, "you and I are going to talk *plenty* later. But first I want to talk to Devin."

"David," he corrected.

"*David*"—she added emphasis to the name as it fell out of her mouth—"alone."

"So what do *I* do in the meantime?" Wylie sulked.

"You mean you haven't done enough?" said Janine, raising her voice.

"OK, OK—let's just keep calm," said David, putting his hands up as if in defense. "Andi, would you mind taking Wylie into the den while Janine and I talk?"

This time *I* was reluctant to move. I looked at him in protest; he read my thoughts and said out loud, "Please." And yet his eyes seemed to be saying, *I'd rather not be left alone with this madwoman.* Wylie skulked ahead of me back to the den, and I followed her, looking back at David one more time, feeling as if we were about to be pulled apart, and it would be some time before we reconnected.

~ഗ၇၇ၮൣ~

The baseball game had finished, and I surfed the channels mindlessly, too nervous to stop at any one show and too distracted to think about anything other than what was going on in my living room.

"Do you want to watch a movie or something?" I asked.

Wylie shrugged. "Doesn't matter. Whatever you want."

I stopped on a rerun of *Iron Chef*. We sat at opposite ends of the couch and stared at the screen as Bobby Flay filleted a giant sea bass. Wylie ignored her cell phone alerting her to new text messages.

"So what do you think they're talking about?" she asked as Alton Brown gave a brief history of the kumquat.

"I have no idea."

"I mean, obviously they know each other. It was, like, *so* obvious the way they were staring at each other that they'd *done it*."

I tried to delete the mental images that kept popping up of David and Janine in sexual positions. "It seems that way," I said. "But that doesn't necessarily mean—" I cut myself off.

"What?" she coaxed, but I didn't respond. *It doesn't necessarily mean they loved each other*, I had wanted to say, and realized that would be a horrible thing to tell a girl about her parents. And why did it threaten me so much? I wasn't naïve enough to think that David had never loved anyone before me. But the magnitude of this particular union—producing *a child*—resulted in a bond that could never be severed. Maybe I was looking for a way to diminish it.

I never missed motherhood. For as long as I could remember, being a mother was as foreign a concept to me as being a safari guide. Both involved developing keen instincts for navigating the jungle (albeit one was metaphorical in nature) and discerning the difference between friend and foe. Unlike mothers, however, safari guides got to carry machetes.

Aside from the fact that I was technically a virgin until my midthirties, I had always been honest enough with myself to know that I was a little too screwed up for parenting. In fact, both my brothers and I seemed to lack the parenting gene.

When I married Sam, we had agreed that kids were not going to be part of our life plan. As professors we could mentor our students without having to pay their tuition too. Kids didn't fit into our liberal, latte-drinking lifestyle, and the cat filled in just fine when either of us was in a nurturing mood.

When Sam was killed, I was grateful that no child had been subjected to grieving the loss of his/her daddy. Of course, my friends saw it another way—had we had children, Sam would've lived on through them. But his writing did that, I argued.

Besides, I was just plain awkward around kids. Babies cried whenever I held them. Sam (and more recently, David) was the one to whom kids gravitated, and who could blame them? Both Sam and David were naturals; in many ways Sam had been a big kid himself, and I think David's inner child came out every time he got his hands on a set of paints. Without a doubt, Sam would've been a great dad, but he had been even more certain than I (if that was even possible) that our bringing a child into this world was not a good idea.

Not fifteen minutes passed before she blurted, "Ugh—this is *killing* me!" She jumped up and stormed into the other room. I followed, calling after her.

"Look," she said to Janine when she entered the living room, "did you or did you not sleep with this guy?"

"Wylie!" Janine hollered. "How dare you talk to me that way." Her Long Island accent was as thick as Wylie's, similar to what David's used to sound like before he left New York. I guessed she grew up on the South Shore, probably on the Nassau/Suffolk County border.

"Well?" said Wylie.

Janine stood up, crossed the room, and pulled Wylie by the arm. "We're going."

"You didn't answer my question."

"Tough shit. Get your things."

"Can I at least use the bathroom?" she pouted.

"Go," Janine commanded.

I directed Wylie to the bathroom and she stomped off, leaving the three of us in the foyer, even more tense than before. I tried to get a read on what David was thinking or feeling, figure out what had transpired between them, but he refused to even look at me.

"Mrs. Baker," I started; suddenly I couldn't remember what I had wanted to say. "Are you going to be able to drive?" I asked after a pause. "There's a Comfort Inn not too far away."

"We're fine. Listen, I'm sorry my kid intruded on you." Her tone echoed more anger than remorse. "You won't be hearing from us again."

"Isn't that Wylie's decision?" I asked, and immediately regretted it, especially when Janine looked as if she was about to smack me. Even David looked a little annoyed.

"*I'll* make decisions for my daughter. This is *none* of your business."

"Hey—" David interjected. "Andi has been nothing but gracious and polite to you and your daughter all day. And this is *her* home. So I'd say it's every bit of her business."

I could've kissed him at that moment. But I couldn't get past his pronoun choice—*her* home? Not *our* home?

Wylie came back into the foyer, her backpack in tow. "Thank you," she said softly, making eye contact with me for a split second before looking away, as if she were trying to tell me something. I felt a sudden tenderness for her.

"You're welcome," I said to her.

"Come on," said Janine, taking her daughter by the arm and pulling her out the door, neither of them saying good-bye to us.

"I'm sorry," Wylie called out to David, her voice breaking, and I was pretty sure she started to cry. David closed the door behind them.

The house was eerily silent after they left. David exhaled through his mouth and pulled me to him in an embrace.

"I am so sorry, *cara*," he said, stroking my hair, knowing how much I loved when he used the Italian term of endearment.

I held him tight. "For what?"

He didn't answer. Instead he went upstairs, and I knew that was my cue to follow him to the bedroom so he could tell me about his conversation with Janine.

"I'll be right up," I called. After taking the tumbler of water back to the kitchen, I was just about to turn out the light when I noticed a napkin with some handwriting on it.

Wylie had scrawled her cell phone number.

Somehow I knew she left it for *me*, not David. And I was touched by this act of trust, this connection. I felt an inexplicable need to protect her, compounded by a need to protect myself as well, although from what I didn't know. My body felt weak and weary, as if I'd just run a marathon. Hard to believe just yesterday we were so relaxed, so full and content, so *together.*

I folded the napkin, put it into the pocket of my capris, and headed upstairs.

chapter five

When I entered the room David practically pushed me onto the bed, wrestling my clothes off and kissing me hard.

"What the . . ." I tried between kisses.

"Please," he pleaded, "I've been wanting to make love to you all day." Having successfully removed my shirt, he then went to work on my capris.

"Seriously? After everything that's happened, you want sex? Shouldn't we talk first?"

"I promise I'll tell you everything after. Right now I need you. I'll do everything you like," he offered just as he slid his hands behind my back to unhook my bra and crept them up to slip the straps off my shoulders while nibbling on my earlobe.

"Don't bribe me, Dev." I silently chided myself for using his nickname at that moment, but he didn't seem to catch it. Or didn't care.

"Fine, then I'll do everything *I* like."

I couldn't help but laugh and give in to his urgency. We shimmied under the sheets and made love until David let out a loud grunt as he climaxed before falling on his back and taking short, quick breaths. It didn't take long.

"Feel better?" I asked, not meaning to sound so sarcastic.

His breathing evened and he looked at me tenderly, cupping my cheek and kissing me.

"Yeah," he said.

I sat up and turned on the light beside me. "OK then. Start talking."

chapter six

David buried his face in the pillow and let out a dreadful groan, not unlike the sound one makes when faced with getting out of bed at the crack of dawn.

"Come on, you promised," I said.

He propped up two pillows behind him and hoisted himself up against them, the back of his head touching the padded headboard. He then put his arm around me and pulled me to him so that my head rested on his chest. It was a feeling I loved—his torso muscular and rigid, protecting what seemed some days to be a very fragile heart.

David paused, no doubt trying to figure out where or how to begin.

"Janine was one of my first clients—well, sort of. She was a bartender at an upscale hotel lounge in Manhattan, and I was trying to drum up business via word of mouth."

"So instead of passing your card on to others, she used it herself?"

"Pretty much. Said the firsthand knowledge would make her a good spokesperson." He guffawed at the memory, and I could tell he was actually reliving the moment in his mind. "And I didn't charge her, told her that the first date was on the house. I don't know, maybe she misinterpreted that as a real date."

"It *was* a real date," I said, unexpectedly defensive on Janine's behalf. "The fact that you called it a date would imply that it was an actual date."

"I also said it was on the house. Wouldn't that imply something as well?"

"I would've thought you were asking me out as you and not as an escort."

"Um, aren't we getting a little off track here?" he said, impatient. "I honestly didn't think about it at the time, OK? Anyway, she went by Jane back then. And as you know, I never used my real name, not even in the early days."

"Did you find her attractive?" I asked. His expression read, *Don't even try to get me there*, and I knew he was right. And yet, like an idiot, I persisted. "I'm not asking in a jealous girlfriend sort of way"—or maybe I was—"I just want to know. She's not a bad-looking woman if you take away all that eyeliner and tone down the highlights. Besides, you must have liked her enough to give her a free date."

He thought carefully about his answer, weighing his options, I could tell.

"I'll take that as a yes," I said before he had a chance to speak.

"Does it matter? The more important detail is that back in those days as an escort I actually . . . I was offering more than just a date to the party, know what I'm sayin'?"

I knew.

"So you and Janine—Jane—had sex."

"*Protected* sex," he added. "Or so I thought. The condom must've been defective."

"So what happened?"

"A few days later I went back to the hotel to meet a potential client for drinks, and Jane was tending bar."

"Did she say anything to you?"

He hesitated.

"It wasn't a pleasant exchange," he said.

"How so?"

"Keep in mind that I was new at this. I had no idea what the proper escort etiquette was, if there even was such a thing. It's not like Christian or I studied under anyone's tutelage—we made things up as we went along."

This couldn't be good if he was laying out a defense for himself. He seemed to need my prodding. "Continue," I said.

"I acknowledged her at the bar. We flirted a bit and she hinted that she wanted to 'see' me again." He gestured quote marks with his free hand.

"And?"

"And I pretty much told her that she was more than welcome to if she ponied up the money."

I cringed and pulled away for a moment to look at him. "You didn't."

He grimaced. "Yeah, I did. I was a real rat-bastard."

"Did you really think you were having sex with her as an escort, though?" I don't know why I persisted with this line of questioning; maybe because at one time I was the target of Devin the Escort's reverse hide-and-seek game.

"I don't know, Andi. It was so long ago. And you have to understand where my head was at. I was just getting started as an escort; I didn't want a girlfriend. I'm not saying it was the right way to think or behave, but the bottom line is that at the time I pushed her away."

"So what did she say?"

"She threw the drink she was mixing in my face. And let me tell you, that is every bit as humiliating as it looks on TV. And it stings, too."

"Still, I'm not sure you didn't deserve it."

"Oh, I totally deserved it, even though I was mad as hell at her." He paused for a couple of beats. "I never went back to that hotel. We never saw each other again, and she never called. Perhaps she threw away the business card."

I slid out of his hold to use the bathroom as David shook his arm to wake it up. Afterward I donned one of his T-shirts and flopped on the bed, as if gossiping with my best friend at a slumber party.

"So what happened tonight?" I asked.

"Jane—Janine—told me she'd been with one other guy during the two-week period she'd been with me, and she had never quite nailed down the date of Wylie's conception. Probably because she didn't want to know."

"Can you blame her? She'd been reckless—"

"—not with me," he interjected.

"So you thought—and she had no way to get in touch with you or the other guy, presumably."

"But she said she'd always had a feeling it was me," said David.

"Because of her eyes. Wylie's, I mean."

He shrugged. "I guess so. Anyway, Janine said it would be best if we just let it alone, left things as they were. She's happily married, and he's the only father Wylie's ever known. According to her, he's a good guy."

Wylie hadn't said anything one way or the other.

I returned to an upright position and tucked one leg underneath. "David!"

"What?"

"You can't just pretend this never happened! That girl has a right to know who her biological father is. So do you, for that matter."

"Look, Andi—like you said, she's just a rebellious teenager looking for some drama. That she actually found me was a freak coincidence. Besides, the odds of my being her father are . . ."

". . . not the point," I argued. "You can't put the pin back in the grenade. You've got to talk to a lawyer and find out if you're legally responsible for her, not to mention financially. You could owe fifteen years of child support."

"Not if her mother doesn't want me involved," he countered.

I shook my head, irritated. "You yelled at Wylie for making it out to be so simple, and here you are blowing it off as if she got into a fender bender with you or something. This is anything but simple and you know it. I can't believe you're both just trying to sweep it under the rug."

David leaned forward. "What good comes of this? All it does is upset two stable families that have been getting along fine otherwise."

"Still, you think you can act like you don't know you may have a daughter walking around, one who has your eyes and wants to know who her father is? How can you be so selfish?"

"Hey," he threatened.

"You have to *know*," I pressed. "We all do."

"And what about *you*?" he said, annoyed. "You've been adamant all along about not having kids. Why are you the voice of reason in this? You suddenly want a teenage girl in our lives?"

I slunk away from him and stood up. "I seem to be the only one who does at the moment. Look, David, this situation scares me to death. But we have to meet it head-on."

We seemed to be in a face-off, each of us locked into a scowl.

"You gonna come back to bed, or are you just gonna stand there?" he asked me. I felt like pummeling him.

I stayed put.

"Andi, I can't do anything more about it tonight, so will you come back to bed so we can get some sleep? It's been a long day and I'm exhausted."

I was exhausted too.

David extended his arm. "Please? I'm sorry."

I reluctantly climbed back into bed. He folded me into his arms and kissed my forehead, apologizing again. I kissed him one more time; he smelled of cologne and sex.

"I love you," I said before adding, "jerk."

He broke into a grin. "Backatcha," he teased. I turned out the light and we snuggled under the sheets. But I don't think either of us accomplished anything more than the occasional dozing.

chapter seven

We hadn't spoken about Wylie, or her genes, since she'd appeared in the backyard two days ago. Danced around it with banal conversation and feigned preoccupation with the beginning of the fall semester and daily chores. But I couldn't go five minutes without thinking of her, in those Daisy Dukes and flip-flops and purple strand of hair, as a child seeking validation. I couldn't stop imagining her sitting at the butcher-block table, eating more than just leftovers. If I was so consumed with these thoughts and feelings, then what was David going through? And how could he so willingly avoid it? How could I let him?

I entered the study, where David was sitting in the recliner, reading, and I approached the easel in the opposite corner. He had always considered painting to be a hobby, a form of relaxation. When I had asked him why he didn't sell his work, he insisted that he'd be laughed out of the very galleries he'd so successfully managed and patronized. He wasn't "a natural," he insisted. He had begun this latest canvas a few months ago, a Manet-style landscape of the Harvard campus. I studied it, letting my pupils go in and out of focus at the fleeting brush-strokes (a phrase from David's first essay that I'd never forgotten), looking as if they'd been painted with such ferocity, except I knew better. I knew the hand that held the brush and made those quick, darting movements—enough for you to miss them if you weren't looking—in a quiet room (he'd gone to Harvard to sketch the scene and study the light, but preferred to work at home). He set up drop cloths in the space around him, although usually he worked in his Cambridge apartment, having converted one of the rooms into a studio, furniture and flooring be damned.

I suddenly found myself wondering what went through his mind when he painted. Were his thoughts just as quick and darting? Did his mind wander off to his to-do list or e-mail inbox, or did he get the way I do when I write—lost in the scene, in an endless *now*, listening to the voices of characters rather than my own inner voice?

"You like?" he asked, startling me.

"It'll be beautiful when it's done. One of your best."

"If I ever finish it."

"Why aren't you working on it in Cambridge?"

"I like being here," he said with a wink.

"Then why'd you call it '*her home*'?" I asked.

He turned his eyes away from the book and looked at me. "What?"

"The other night when you yelled at Janine for snapping at me. You said, 'This is *her* home.' It's yours too, you know."

"I suppose you like to think of it that way, but the truth is, it's not. My name's not on the title."

I frowned. "That's just a technicality, isn't it?"

"It's a pretty big technicality, don't you think? Look, it's not something I resent—"

I interrupted him. "You could've fooled me just now. . . ."

"I know what this house means to you. It's yours and Sam's. That's just the way it is, and it's OK with me."

"You sure?" I asked.

"It's fine," he said, and went back to reading.

Despite my initial reluctance, David had persuaded me that we'd be happier living together in Northampton than Cambridge. The Cambridge place, for all its luxuries and comforts, didn't have the warmth or charm of the Northampton house, to say nothing of the commute to and from NU, especially during the winter months. I'd worried about how it would feel to have David living in what had been Sam's space—he'd owned the house years before we'd met—worried that David would somehow "replace" Sam as if he'd never been there. But David had told me it was important to honor Sam's presence at all times. A framed photograph of Sam lived in almost every room. And David never seemed to mind if I told stories about Sam; if anything, he encouraged them. In a strange way, Sam was a part of our relationship that was neither intrusive nor threatening. He was neither a third wheel nor a wedge, and I sensed that Sam somehow approved of my being with David.

But at that moment the house being in my name only was no longer OK with me.

Lost in thought and still staring at the canvas, I heard myself speak. "Hey, Dev?"

"Yes?"

I took my gaze away from the painting and directed it at him. "Will you teach me to paint?"

He looked up from his book and peeked over his reading glasses.

"Say that again?"

"I think I'd like to learn how to paint."

He closed the book and rested it on his lap, crossed his arms, and gave me a coy look. I crossed my arms as if to return a mirror image of him, knowing exactly what he was thinking: *Déjà vu all over again.*

"Why do you wanna learn how to paint?" He said this in a teasing voice, as if reenacting a scene from long ago. Hell, why couldn't he ever make things easy for me?

"I don't know," I said. "You make it look so simple, not to mention enjoyable."

He stood up, leaving his book on the chair, and padded to the easel. "It's not, you know."

"Not what?"

"Easy. Or even enjoyable, sometimes. Just like writing."

I frowned. "Still, I think I'd like to learn."

"What kind of painting would you want to do? Still life? Landscapes? Portraits? Abstract? Cubist? Impressionist? Do you wanna use oils? Acrylics? Watercolor?"

"I'll concede to your best judgment," I said, practically bowing to him, disciple to master.

He looked at the easel, then at me, as if he were deep in thought—arms crossed again. "Hmmmm . . ."

I rolled my eyes.

"We'll start you on acrylics and still lifes," he said. "But I want a full commitment from you. No cacking out after two lessons."

"When have I ever not given you a full commitment?" I wanted to retract the words just as quickly as they rolled out of my mouth. He cocked an eyebrow. "Fine, Rembrandt," I said. "Shall we draw up a contract?"

He glared at me, and I feared I'd just crossed a line. David and I almost never talked about our original arrangement, the one that had brought us together aeons ago, prior to my meeting Sam—lessons for writing in exchange for lessons in sex. Partly because it was another lifetime, and partly because we had evolved so much since those days—he no longer the suave escort, I no longer the sexually inhibited professor. But with all that had been happening—Wylie's arrival, the story of how David and Janine met, and memories of Devin and his alluring presence—it was hard *not* to think about it. The contract, however, had always been a sticky matter. We had violated its terms before the ink was even dry, metaphorically speaking, and it had caused all sorts of problems then that seemed insignificant now, given our outcome. And yet, who's to say what would've happened had we followed it to the letter? Would he have asked me out after the seven weeks were up? Or would we have parted ways once and for all? Would he have eventually given up being an escort regardless? If Sam's death taught me anything, it was not to get caught in the hamster wheel of hypotheticals.

Nevertheless, if I had just offended him, he either brushed it aside or pretended otherwise.

"Fine by me," he said, "but you have to teach me something. No sense in bucking tradition." His tone was playful again. Charming, even. Just like Devin the Escort all those years ago. And it occurred to me yet again that I had never really gotten over *him*. He was like a crush that occasionally came out to taunt and seduce me.

"What more can I possibly teach you?" I asked. "You write very well, you know every Beatles song. You even got the hang of two-part harmony."

"I want your grandmother's fried-dough pizza recipe."

He'd taken out the big guns. When Sam and I married, my mom presented me with a box of family recipes. My paternal grandmother used to make almost everything from scratch—bread, pasta, sauce, you name it. She kept a garden of herbs and tomatoes in her backyard, and bought meats and cheeses at the Italian deli around the corner from her house in Queens. She passed away two years before my father did (just as well, because his death probably would've killed her). To this day I remember the smell of her kitchen, and the way our names used to roll off her tongue in her thick Italian accent. She called my brothers *Giuseppe* and *Antonio* (the only one who was allowed to), and placed the emphasis on the second part of my name: *On-dray-a.*

Nothing matched her fried-dough pizza. I'd never actually seen her *make* them—they were always warm and ready and waiting for me when I got home from school and on the days she took care of me. The dough was browned and glossy and robust—never flat—fried in batches before topped with her sauce that she always called "gravy" and four perfect square slices of mozzarella cheese on each one.

At the time I was unappreciative of the recipe box, especially since Mom had paid me a backhanded compliment along the lines of my now having to cook for my husband since I never cooked for myself. I didn't even appreciate that she had picked out the box and each recipe herself, and organized it all for me. Sam and I had made many of the recipes together, trying at least one per week when we were first married. The coveted fried-dough pizza turned out to be the hardest to master—forget *master*; we were aiming for *acceptable*. Getting the dough to the proper size and consistency, not to mention replicating the frying process, was key, and many a batch sacrificed themselves in our attempts.

The first time I made the pizzas by and for myself, sometime after Sam's death (during what I call my "recovery year"), I broke into tears—not because I missed Sam, but because it was the closest I'd ever come to getting them to taste like my grandmother's. And I missed *her*. I missed the simplicity of childhood, wondering if I'd ever really experienced it.

As Sam and I used to, David and I usually alternated cooking duties and occasionally cooked together. And while the experience was never as communal as it had been with Sam, I enjoyed it just as much, albeit it for different reasons. By far, David's favorite dish of mine was fried-dough pizzas—I only made them on special occasions, and I never showed him the recipe, much less let him help me make them. It had become something of a game between us—his attempted bribery and coaxing me to reveal the recipe, even let him watch me on the off chance that he might pick up the procedure. Much like the way I hounded him about the secret ingredient in the hot chocolate he made for me from scratch.

I sighed. "Fine. You win. Just don't tell my brothers. I think they'd hang me for treason."

"Deal," he said, speaking and shaking hands in a professional manner before pulling me into a kiss. "We'll start next week."

I smiled. "Great," I said, and exited the room. I was halfway down the hall when I stopped in my tracks. I had entered the room to have an entirely different conversation, the one we'd been avoiding for days. How did I let him steer it so far in the opposite direction?

Right, blame it all on David. Like I didn't initiate it.

I turned around and poked my head back into the study. He was back to reading his book. "Dev?"

"Yes?" He didn't look up.

I stepped inside. "When are we going to talk about it?"

He stopped reading again and looked at me. "Talk about what?"

I gave him a look that said *You know damn well about what.*

He closed the book and huffed. "Andi . . ." he started in protest.

"It's not gonna go away."

"Andi . . ."

"You're gonna just let it hang there, let *her* hang there?"

"*Andi!*" He pounded his fist on the arm of the chair and stood up. "Enough!"

The word dropped in front of me like a thud.

"*No.*"

I didn't raise my voice when I said it, but the way I said it stunned him. It was as if my claws had come out, and I dug in.

"Enough of *this*," I said. "It's been three days. Now you do something about it. But we're not going to pretend for one more second that nothing happened. We're not going to insult each other like that. And we're not going to insult Wylie by depriving her of knowledge about her biological father."

"You keep speaking as if you know for sure it's me," he said. "Just because she has the same eye color as me."

"*David*," I implored. "She doesn't have the same eye color. *She has your eyes.*"

A wave of terror washed over him, as if the truth finally came to light. His breathing quickened.

"Andi?" He called my name like a child seized with panic. I rushed to him, wrapped my arms around him, and held him tight; he clung to me until his panic subsided.

"I've got you," I assured him.

In that instant, I heard Margot Kidder as Lois Lane say with bewilderment to Christopher Reeve as Superman, *You've got me, but who's got you?*

chapter eight

"No. Way." My best friend Maggie sat frozen in a purple upholstered chair with colorful squiggly prints at Perch after I finished telling her about Wylie. A jumbo blueberry muffin sat between us, untouched.

I nodded my head slowly, letting the news sink in for her.

"She showed up, just like that?" she asked.

"Pretty much," I said. "It's scary to know how easy it is to find someone these days. It's getting so that your average Joe needs a Secret Service detail."

"Pretty gutsy of her, if you ask me."

"I'd say she takes after her mom in that regard. Thing is, there's a chance that David really is her father."

"You really think so?"

I nodded again. "You didn't see her, Mags. She totally has his eyes. Same exact shape and color and expression. I mean, what are the odds that some other guy has those sienna eyes?"

"What color are her mom's eyes?"

"Blue, I think. Not that that's all it takes to claim paternity. But I just have this feeling. . . ." I sipped my vanilla chai. "David's pretty freaked out about it."

"Ya think?" said Maggie, as if I'd downplayed it. After a beat she added, "I can't believe *you*'re so calm about it."

"That's what he said."

"I mean really, Andi. You waited four days to tell me. And you're sitting here over muffins and whatnot. How are you not going apeshit over this?"

"Apeshit" had been one of Sam's favorite words.

"I honestly don't know," I replied. "I can't explain it. Believe me, I'm just as in shock as you and David. And scared too. But . . . I can't put my finger on it. It's like a long-lost puzzle piece that's been found or something. Crazy, I know."

"Wow. You've mellowed out," said Maggie. "So what happens now?"

I shrugged my shoulders. "David has to make a decision about whether he's going to get tested. I advised him to talk to a lawyer."

"What if he does—get tested, I mean—and it turns out to be positive?"

A knot tightened in my stomach. "I have no idea."

⚬⚬⚬⚬⚬

Later that afternoon in the den, I was leaning my back against the arm of the sofa, my legs stretched out before me, with my laptop open when I decided to Google "Wylie Baker." Not much came up other than her Facebook page (her profile photo consisted of her dressed in a hot pink tank top and retro Ray-Bans as she flashed the heavy metal devil sign with her right thumb and pinkie. I couldn't help but roll my eyes, grateful that there'd been no such thing as Facebook, or the Internet, for that matter, during the eighties. There was also a report about a regional swim meet (Wylie placed second) and a student art exhibit in what I guessed to be her school district.

She paints!

I sucked in a breath, and perhaps for the first time felt a wave of honest-to-god panic wash over me.

I heard the front door open and close, followed by David calling my name.

"In here!" I called back, closing the Google window and opening the NU online course management site. He followed the sound of my voice and entered the den, looking slightly frazzled.

"Hey," he said, and leaned down to kiss the top of my head.

"Hey," I echoed, comforted by his presence.

"What're you up to?"

"Just some lesson planning," I lied, closing my laptop and placing it on the end table. "What would you like for dinner?"

He removed his messenger bag from across his shoulder and dropped it by the side of the sofa. He then lifted my legs and sat, pulling them back across his lap.

"You OK?" I asked.

"Talked to my attorney today."

My entire body stiffened. "And?"

"And I'm going to get tested. You're right. It's important that we know for sure. For our sake and Wylie's."

I repositioned myself so that I was sitting next to him and offered my hand. He took it into his own.

"And if it turns out . . . ," I started, the rest of the words stuck in my throat.

"Then we have a lot to talk about. All of us."

We sat in silence for several minutes.

"Dev?"

"Yeah?"

"Gut feeling: Do you think she's your daughter?"

He took at least ten seconds to respond. Stared straight ahead, his eyes dark and distant, gone to an undisclosed location in the recesses of his mind and memory.

"I do," he said softly.

I waited another ten seconds before I asked my next question.

"Do you want her to be?"

He dipped his head, and I tilted mine in an attempt to read his expression. All I could see was sadness, and I wondered if he was thinking about his own father, who, at one time, David was certain that if someone had posed the same question to him about David, would've said no.

"I think so," he said.

"Me too," I whispered back, our hands clasped. My answer surprised me.

chapter nine

I didn't go with David to the lab. The test was neither a slow nor painful procedure, and I suppose he wanted to go it alone.

"We should at least call to let her know you got tested," I said, taking out Wylie's phone number.

"It's a bit premature, don't you think?" he said. "We don't want to get her hopes up."

"We don't want her to think you blew her off either."

"You can call her if you want, but I'm not comfortable doing so. Besides, my lawyer already contacted her, so it's not like she's out of the loop."

I called Wylie's cell phone and left a message on voice mail: "This is Andi. I just wanted to let you know that David and I will have new information for you soon. You can call me back if you have any questions." I recited my cell phone number before hanging up.

She didn't return the call, but an hour later I received a text message: *Thx.*

It was going to take up to two weeks to get the results back. David had tried to persuade me to take a trip somewhere with him, but with the semester already in full swing I didn't want to cancel classes. Instead, he went to Bermuda by himself, and

I didn't protest, although I worried about him every day—what if, God forbid, something happened to him and the test turned out to be positive and Wylie wound up never getting to know her biological father? That I put her well-being ahead of my own in this morbid scenario did not escape my attention—wasn't this the way mothers usually thought?

I was surprised he didn't go to Italy, his usual battery recharger. I guess lying on a beach and frying his brain in the sun was less work than taking in the museums and architecture. The latter seemed way more distracting than the former, however, and I had assumed he left in order to be distracted. But what if he'd really left to think things through? What if he was making plans? If so, what kind of plans would they be?

He returned four days later tanned and seemingly thinner, although I suspected that my eyes were playing tricks on me. No more relaxed, however.

"I missed you," he said when I asked why he didn't stay longer.

"I missed you too," I replied.

He spent the rest of the week painting, reading, and consulting with clients. Every conversation between us seemed forced; David insisted that we not talk about "the situation" until we got the test results. This time it seemed to be more out of strength preservation than denial

⚬ᴏᴏ)૧ᴏᴏᴗ

We were dining out with my friends Miranda and Kevin when David's cell phone vibrated (he usually turned it off in company); he excused himself and made eye contact with me in such a way that communicated it was *the Call.*

"Is everything OK?" asked Miranda, who must have seen the look on my face that I couldn't hide. It was a few days shy of the two-week deadline.

"He's just been expecting a really important call," I explained. "One that can't wait."

Ten minutes later—ten *long* minutes—David returned to the table, his casual demeanor gone.

"So, did you close some big art deal, or what?" asked Kevin.

I watched David feign casualness as he smiled his most charming smile ("the escort smile," I secretly called it) and laughed off Kevin's question, avoiding me this time. "Something like that." But when he sat down, he took my hand under the table and squeezed it hard, downing his wine in one shot with the other hand.

I lost my appetite.

We were silent during the car ride home after dinner. Of course I was dying to know the results, and he was dying to tell me. But who were we kidding? I already knew, and he knew I knew, but it was as if someone had stolen our voices.

Once we were home and in the house, David went to the living room and put a couple of logs into the fireplace, balancing one on top of the other. It wasn't yet cold enough outside to warrant a fire, but I knew he'd been trembling ever since the call. At one point during the preparation, he sat on his knees, staring into the hearth as if the fire were already crackling.

I kicked off my shoes and padded to him, knelt behind him, and kneaded his shoulders as I took a whiff of him and was calmed by his scent. I kissed his cheek, leaning in enough to see him close his eyes and take a deep breath.

"I have a daughter," he said; it seemed we could speak of Wylie only in hushed tones. I sensed that saying it out loud was his way of accepting it. If he said it out loud, then it was real.

I kissed his cheek two more times and moved beside him. "I know," I replied, pressing into him. He put his head on my shoulder, and I could see a solitary tear slide from the corner of his eye.

"All these years, and I never knew."

"How could you have?" I asked.

"I would've done the right thing," he said. "I wouldn't have abandoned her."

"I know." I stroked his hair.

He picked up his head. "What do we do now, Andi?"

I searched for an answer. "I guess we tell Janine and Wylie, for starters."

"No," he said, gingerly touching my chin and turning it to face him. "What do *we* do?"

At first I looked at him, my mind a blank, confused by the question. And then suddenly, like a flash of light or the clang of a bell, the answer became clear to me.

"We get married," I said.

chapter ten

David looked at me, agog.

"What did you say?"

"I said I think we should get married."

"But . . . why?" he asked. He almost sounded suspicious.

I paused for a moment to find the answer. "Because you said it yourself: we're a family, you and me. We have been for a long time. And now you have a daughter. We should make it official, for her sake."

"How do we know she'll be a part of our lives?"

"Because she wants to be. She wouldn't have gone through so much trouble if she didn't."

"What if she changes her mind and hates me? And what about Janine?" he persisted. "What if she refuses to let Wylie see me—see *us*?" he quickly corrected.

"Then we'll deal with that when the time comes. Look, David," I started, and touched his cheek. "Wylie or no Wylie, I love you and I want to spend the rest of my life with you. I didn't think I'd ever say that to anyone ever again—hell, I never thought I'd *feel* that with anyone ever again. But I do and I'm finally ready. I want to get married, Dev. I really do. I want to marry *you*."

I watched him as the words sank in, and he held his breath. "My God, Andi . . . do you mean it?"

I nodded my head slowly as a smile crept across my face; I grew more excited by the idea with every passing second.

"Holy shit," he said barely above a whisper. Then he broke into a laugh as he looked at me, his sienna eyes twinkling as he exclaimed, "Holy shit, Andi!" And he pulled me to him in an embrace so enthusiastic that we both fell over laughing.

chapter eleven

The next day, David called Wylie's cell phone, spoke to Janine to arrange a meeting (she was not happy to hear from him), and we agreed to drive to Hartford to meet them at the end of the week.

The Bakers lived in a typical suburban house: blue vinyl siding, black shutters, two-car garage, and a basketball hoop at the far edge of the driveway. Wylie enthusiastically greeted us at the door, accompanied by her stepsister, Trish (the "celebrity whore," as Wylie had described her), a seventeen-year-old Hayden Panettiere look-alike who practically lit up like a match when she saw David.

"*Wow*," said Trish as she leaned in for a better look. "It's like . . . so in the eyes." David blushed. I then caught her turn aside and mouth *Ohmigod, he is HOT!* to Wylie, who admonished her sister with a glare. Trish excused herself as she grabbed her keys and rushed out the door—I didn't know if she'd been banished by Janine, or if she already had someplace to be. Based on her reaction to David and her complicit role in all this, she didn't seem rattled by the disruption to her family dynamic. Wylie took our coats and led us to the living room, a sharp maroon-and-cream color scheme with paintings of flowers on the walls. David and I instinctively gravitated to the love seat, while Wylie remained standing and waited for her mother.

Moments later Janine entered, dressed in blue jeans and a tight heather-gray jersey top with black sleeves, followed by her husband, who introduced himself as Peter and looked uncomfortable in khakis and a chambray button-down shirt, sweat stains already forming under the arms. Janine carried a tray loaded with cups of coffee and a plate of Entenmann's cookies. She set it on the table in front of the couch before joining Peter there. Despite this gesture of hospitality, she couldn't have wanted us there. Wylie sat on the edge of a rocking chair catty-corner from us.

Following the hellos and introductions, we all exchanged nervous glances, waiting to see who would speak first. I mean, how did conversations like this start? Did you ease in with, *So what do you think the Pats' chances are to go all the way this year*, or did you just come out and say, *And the matching DNA goes to . . .* ? Not that any of us didn't know why we were there.

David broke the silence. "Soooo . . . ," he started, but couldn't seem to find words to follow. He turned to me, as if to ask for help, but I couldn't think of a thing to say. He then looked at Wylie. "Should we maybe just talk to your parents first?"

Wylie objected. "It's my life we're talking about. I have a right to hear every word."

Janine seemed to want to argue to the contrary, but gave David permission to continue.

"Well . . ." David stalled again. He looked at me, then Wylie, then Janine and her husband. "As you know by now from my attorney, the test is positive. I'll be retested if you want, but I don't have any reason to believe the results were inaccurate."

"You had no right to move forward on this after we agreed to leave well enough alone," said Janine. "It's bad enough my daughter contacted you behind my back in the first place."

David shot back, "And you had no right to keep the possibility that I had a daughter from me fifteen years ago."

"Well, you've got another thing coming if you think you're gonna come in here and run the show from now on," she said, getting more combative by the minute. In any other social situation I would've gone English geek on her and told her that the correct expression was "you've got another *think* coming," followed by a history of said expression, and otherwise useless information. And how or why such a triviality popped into my head at that moment, I had no idea.

"I have no intention of interfering with anything," David insisted. "But we all had a right to know—you and your husband, Andi and me, and Wylie."

Wylie, however, misunderstood him. "What, you want nothing to do with me?" she asked, insulted.

"Of course I do," said David to her. "I very much want to get to know you. But this needs to be a family decision—*your* family," he quickly clarified.

Peter Baker sat stoic and silent, seeming to size up David and me—especially David—and I couldn't help but wonder if he was contemplating whether he could (or perhaps should) kick David's ass. He looked to be a blue-collar guy, an electrician or something, and although David had several inches on him in height, I probably would've put my money on Peter.

He didn't seem to be a bad person, however, or a bad father. This had to feel like a sucker punch to him, or worse.

I asked to use the bathroom. Peter pointed past me and gave me directions, speaking in fragments. I went and splashed some cold water on my face, looking in the mirror as I dried off.

I could hear Janine and David lobbing back and forth, but I was unable to make out the words. *Holy shit, is this going to be your life from now on?* I thought, inquiring of my reflection and awaiting her response. But she, too, was clueless. When I came out of the bathroom, Wylie ambushed me.

"You have got to talk some sense into them," she demanded. "Tell them I deserve to have a relationship with my father—my *real* father. Tell them I have rights."

"It isn't my place," I replied. "It's David's and your mom's and dad's."

"You mean my stepdad," she said.

"Was he always your stepdad? I mean, is that how you always referred to him and your sister?"

"No. Not until I found out he wasn't my real father."

I inadvertently let out a sigh. "Look, Wylie. Is your stepdad a jerk or something? Because he seems like a perfectly decent guy to me."

"He's fine," she said. "I mean, I don't hate him or anything like that."

"Do you love him?" I asked.

"Sure."

"It seems to me that he loves you too. I'm sure that he thinks of you as a daughter rather than a stepdaughter. That's what's *real*. Have you considered that maybe your eagerness to know David is hurting your dad's feelings?"

Wylie considered this, seemingly for the first time. "I don't wanna hurt his feelings, and I do love him, but he's just not . . . like, he doesn't *get* me."

"Most parents don't," I said, subscribing to the John Hughes theory of adolescence. "My mother certainly didn't get me when I was your age."

Ugh. I couldn't believe I just used the phrase "when I was your age."

Wylie seemed just as disgusted with it. "I just wanna get to know him, that's all."

"OK," I said, and together we returned to the living room. The discussion halted when we entered, and I piped up. "May I make a suggestion?"

All heads turned to me, and I instantly felt self-conscious.

"This is all overwhelming," I said, stating the obvious, "and I think we need some time to process it. Our lives have just been turned upside down in the blink of an eye. The important thing is not to get caught up in reacting to all the anxiety and uncertainty this is stirring up. We've all got to get to a place where we can make proactive choices, and I don't think any of us are ready to do that right now."

God, was I channeling my former shrink, or what? It was a testament to how much my coping skills had improved in the last four years.

"Andi's right," David said, looking at me, beaming with pride. My heart swelled.

Peter spoke up. "I agree. Maybe we should all just chill out and revisit the situation in a week." He too had a Long Island accent. It'd been a long time since I'd heard that accent on a regular basis, David's and my own having diminished somewhat over the years living in New England.

David nodded. "Fine by me."

Wylie also nodded. "I'm cool with that."

We all looked at Janine, who raised her arms in surrender. "What choice do I have?"

David and I left the Bakers around ten o'clock that night, both of us mentally and physically exhausted, and even though we lived an hour away I suggested we stay in Connecticut rather than drive back to Massachusetts.

"Why?" asked David.

"Because you're either going to be in your head the entire time and the silence will drive me nuts, or you'll be so distracted that you'll get into an accident." I didn't tell him my other reason.

He conceded and we checked into a Marriott, and while David took a shower I took out my cell phone and dialed my mother's number. She answered on the second ring.

"Hello, Andi," she said matter-of-factly, as if she were in the room with me. And before I could say hello, I burst into tears.

"I need you, Mom," I cried. I couldn't remember having ever said those words to her.

chapter twelve

I rented a car and took the Bridgeport ferry to Port Jefferson on Long Island the next morning while David drove back to Northampton alone. David had wanted to come with me, but I insisted my mother would be easier to deal with one-on-one. However, the truth was that I wanted to confide in her and not just break the news.

We met at Danford's for lunch. Always one to make an impeccable appearance, she was dressed in black slacks, a pristine white blouse, and a Chanel red suit jacket. Her hair, styled in the same silver bob she'd worn for years, had grown out since I last saw her over the summer. However, she looked gaunt. Her cheeks looked pale and sunken, even with makeup.

"You OK, Mom?" I asked when we were seated at our table. "You look like you've lost weight."

"I'm on a diet," she said, perusing her menu.

"You've never been an ounce overweight in your life."

"Doctor wants me to cut down on a few things," she said, and resumed exploring her food options. My mother always refused to commit to conversation until the business of ordering was out of the way.

She ordered the seafood Cobb salad and a glass of wine (what was she cutting out? I wondered). I ordered the chicken portobello and water with lemon in a wineglass.

"So what's got you so upset, Andrea?" she asked. "You and David having problems?"

I sipped my water. "Everything's great with David. Better than great. We're talking about marriage."

Mom raised her eyebrows. "Well, it's about time. What took you so long?"

I shot her an annoyed look. "You know what took me so long. Death of a spouse ain't exactly a *West Wing* episode, where someone says 'What's next?' "

"It's clear that you love David. And given that Sam is gone, what's to stop you from being happy?"

"You of all people should know the answer to that. Look—" I cut off the conversation. "There's something else. Something . . . unexpected."

Mom was about to take a sip of wine and put down her glass. "Oh, God, you're not pregnant, are you?"

"No!" I said, darting my eyes to see if anyone overheard her.

"Because at your age . . ."

"I'm not pregnant, Mom. But . . . ," I started, and took in a breath. "David has a child."

She looked at me, shell-shocked. "Say that again?"

"David has a child. A daughter, actually."

She turned angry. "You've been back together for less than a year. Did he cheat on you, or did this happen while you two were apart? Either way . . ."

"No! No, no, no, it's not like that. She's fifteen. It happened before he and I met. He didn't even know. We both found out on Labor Day."

"What kind of woman doesn't tell a man that he has a child?"

"I don't think it's our place to judge her, Mom."

She looked away for a moment, processing the revelation. "A daughter . . . ," she said, her voice trailing off. Then she looked back at me. "How did you find out?"

"She showed up on our doorstep—the daughter, I mean. Her name is Wylie."

"I assume he got himself tested to find out for sure?"

I nodded. "He did. They're sure."

"My God, Andi. What are you going to do about it?"

"That's why I called you. To ask for advice. I mean, I don't think there's anything I can do but be supportive, but I'm afraid."

"Of what?"

I paused to answer the question. "I don't know. I mean, this changes everything. I'm afraid it's going to change *us* somehow. And I have no idea how to be a mother to a teenage girl."

"Assuming you're going to be. Does the girl want to live with you or something?"

"I don't think so. Besides, her mother wouldn't permit it even if she did. We haven't talked about any of this yet. We all just met last night in Hartford. That's where they live."

"You'd better tell David to get a lawyer," said Mom.

"He's already on it," I said.

"I don't know what kind of advice I could give you," she said after our food arrived. "It's not like your father ever came home with an illegitimate daughter."

Something about the word *illegitimate* rubbed me the wrong way. It sounded so politically incorrect, so 1950s. As if Wylie were less than.

"She is not illegitimate," I argued. "She's your average sub-urban teenager with parents who love her very much and have given her a good home. And she just wants to know who her biological father is. More to the point, I think she's at the age where she's trying to find out who *she* is."

My mother took a sip of wine.

I continued, "I just don't want to have the same relation-ship with her that you and I had. I want to do it differently."

"Is this when you once again blame me for everything that went wrong in your life?"

Geez. Why, *why* couldn't my mother and I talk to each other, after all these years?

"I'm done with that, Mom. Let it go a long time ago. But you know as well as I do that we didn't do it right."

"Then why would you want my advice if I was so horrible at being a mother to you?"

"You weren't horrible. You did the best you could at the time. I respect you and want us to be better at this. I really want to know what you think, Mom. I'm finally happy again and I'm afraid of losing it. And I'm afraid I'll fall off the edge like I did when I lost Sam. How do I keep that from happening?"

I caught a glimpse of her eyes—they were glassy. She quickly averted her gaze and focused on her salad as she poked her fork into the lettuce and took a mouthful. Then she fin-ished chewing and dabbed the edge of her mouth with the cloth napkin before returning it to her lap.

"I haven't the slightest idea how to help you, Andi. I'm sorry." She took another bite of salad and pointed to my plate with her fork. "You're not going to eat that?"

I shook my head. "I'll ask them to wrap it up."

We spent the rest of the meal forcing stilted small talk. Mom only got through half of her salad before asking the server to wrap up the remains. She insisted on paying the bill, and we left Danford's and returned to Main Street, walking along the sidewalk and passing the shops and boutiques, taking a peek inside. Pretending everything was OK.

The ferry loomed in the near distance, inching toward the dock.

"I'd better get going," I said. "I don't want to be home too late. David's having a hard time with all of this, as I'm sure you can imagine."

"Are you both sure this girl is his?"

I nodded. "DNA doesn't lie. And you should see her, Mom. She has his eyes."

She became wistful. I guessed she was thinking about my father. She always believed I took after his side of the family when it came to my own looks.

"Andi, I'm sorry I wasn't a good mother to you."

Without warning, the little girl in me pushed her pain and abandonment to the surface, and I felt the sting of tears threatening to escape. I blinked them away quickly. "You lost the love of your life," I said. "In more ways than one."

"I'll think about the daughter situation and try to come up with something helpful."

Her effort spoke volumes. "Thank you, Mom." I leaned in to hug her. The gesture was often one that we both tried to get out of the way as quickly as possible, but this time she received my embrace and returned it. I could feel her hands on my back, pushing in a bit.

"Tell David I said hello. And don't wait too long to marry him. You of all people know how precious time is."

"OK," I said.

I boarded the ferry, locked up the car, and went to the top deck. As the boat pulled away from the dock, I saw my mother standing on the boardwalk next to Danford's, watching me sail away.

chapter thirteen

By the time I got home from Port Jefferson it was about seven o'clock, and I decided to return the rented car the next day. When I entered the house I called for David, but heard no response. Too tired to eat and still without an appetite, I put my untouched lunch into the fridge and slowly dragged myself up the stairs. The downstairs and stairwell were unlit, but I saw a flicker coming from my bedroom in the hallway and was greeted with the soft glow of strategically placed votive candles around the room, emitting a scent of vanilla cake. A towering crystal vase of red roses covered the dresser, their reflection in the mirror giving off the illusion that the bouquet was twice as bountiful. David had fallen asleep on the bed, a hardcover book resting on his chest along with his reading glasses. He was dressed in blue jeans and a maroon T-shirt. My favorite colors on him. He still had the body of a model sculpted from marble, of the alluring escort I'd met ten years ago who'd taken my breath away. His brown hair, more salt-and-pepper, remained full and thick and perfect for running my fingers through.

In short, he *still* took my breath away.

I kicked off my shoes and climbed onto the bed. A red rose rested on my pillow. I gingerly picked it up, pulled it to my nose and inhaled, then moved it to the table, careful to keep it away from the flame. Then, with the same touch I applied to the rose, I slid his bangs to the side. His eyes fluttered and opened, then turned warm upon seeing me.

"Hey, beautiful," he murmured.

"Hey, sleepyhead."

The book and glasses fell to the side as he moved, and he tried to orient himself.

"What time is it?" he asked.

"A little after seven. There was an accident on I-91. Surprise," I said sarcastically. "Didn't you get my message? I left it on the landline."

He yawned and stretched. "Forgot to listen to voice mails." He gave me a look as if noticing me for the first time. "So how was lunch with Genevieve?" he asked. David never called my mother "Mom."

"OK, I guess," I said. He sat up, instructed me to do the same, and massaged my shoulders from behind. "It had its moments."

"Good moments or bad moments?" He kissed my neck as he worked out a knot.

"A little of both, although 'bad' is probably too strong a word. Just"—I searched for a better adjective—"typical, I guess," I said, unsatisfied with the choice. I often had trouble putting together any kind of coherent thought when David was kissing my neck.

"You told her everything?"

I nodded. "Mm-hmm." A soft moan escaped me. "God, that feels good. . . ." I trailed off into a whisper. My eyelids grew heavy. "What did you do today after leaving Hartford?" I asked. "Besides romance up the room to get me laid?"

He chuckled. "What makes you think I was trying to get *you* laid?" I turned to face him in mock offense, only to be undone by his wink. "Not much," he replied. "Made some calls, answered some e-mails, that kind of thing."

I gestured toward the flowers. "Those are beautiful. You buy them for your girlfriend?"

"Nope," he corrected, "my fiancée."

I opened my mouth. "Wha . . ."

David stopped massaging me, arose, and moved to the edge of the bed, where he beckoned me to join him. He then knelt and pulled a box out of his pocket.

"*Mia cara Andrea*," he began, knowing how I melted when he spoke Italian.

I took in a breath and put my hand to my chest, feeling my heart pound.

"Please, please marry me."

Despite all our recent talk about marriage, I hadn't expected anything so formal as a proposal. The last time David had popped the question was Christmas Eve almost two years ago. I had said no, and we broke up for almost a year after that. Back then I was still clinging to Sam, still afraid to let myself love another man, even the man who had taught me to love myself. But in the present moment I could almost see Sam in what was once our bedroom, his and mine, standing behind David and giving me a thumbs-up sign of approval. I could almost hear him say, "Go ahead, sweetheart. It's time."

Shortly after David and I had gotten back together, I moved the engagement ring Sam had given me from my finger to a chain around my neck, and put our wedding bands in a keepsake box that I kept in a drawer beside my bed. The ring David had presented to me the first time he proposed was a hunk of a square diamond on a platinum band—magnificent in its radiance. I had never asked if he kept it. This new one was more like an anniversary band than a traditional engagement ring, yet still dazzled in the glow of the votives.

Moist and misty, my eyes met his.

"You rat-bastard," I said, a tear slipping down my cheek; his expression turned confused for only a second as I laughed. "I was gonna ask you first." And then he understood and released his smile.

And with that I let out a squeal as I hopped off the bed and nearly knocked him over. "Yes," I said as I plastered his cheeks with salty-teared kisses. "Yes, yes, *yes!*"

We knelt in the middle of the floor, maniacally kissing each other and laughing simultaneously, until David grimaced and said, "Fuck, I'm too old to stay on my knees like this!" We clumsily lifted each other up to standing positions, and embraced for a long time, the outside world disappearing with every second. And as our breathing slowed and evened to something more sultry and serene, I took a step back, looked at him fiendishly, and it hit me.

"Ohmigod, Dev, I am *starving.*"

David looked at me as if I was nuts. I bent over to put my shoes back on. "C'mon, let's get some Chinese food." He did a face-palm, shook his head with incredulity, and laughed as he blew out the votives and followed me down the stairs.

"You sure know how to tease a guy," he said.

"I'll let you feed me the dim sum," I said seductively. "Who knows where it'll lead."

chapter fourteen

"So that's it?" said my friend Miranda as I showed off my hand to her at Perch, about a week after David's proposal. Maggie was with us. I had texted them both the day after, but this had been the first chance we had to officially celebrate. "You and David are officially engaged, finally, after all this time?"

"Yep," I said.

"Oh, Andi, I am *so* happy for you!" she said. "You and David deserve it."

"He's certainly been patient," I said.

"Have you told your family yet?" asked Maggie.

"Yep."

Miranda possessed a dazzling, toothy smile worthy of a Colgate commercial as she ogled my finger again. "It's quite a ring."

I held out my hand and admired it. "I think it's perfect. Simple, yet elegant. Totally not something Sam would've picked out for me, but I think he'd like it."

"He would've wanted you to be happy," said Maggie. "I know that's a clichéd thing to say about a loved one who's deceased, but it's true with Sam."

I nodded in agreement. Then I withdrew my hand to my lap and changed the subject without warning. "So, Mags, what's the big news you had?"

She brushed her hand in the air as if to wave off a fly. "Totally trivial in the wake of your recent developments. Classify it under gossip, I guess."

"Ooooh," said Miranda, who couldn't resist an occasional snippet of gossip. "Spill it!"

"Well . . . ," said Maggie as she turned to me and pushed her glasses up the bridge of her nose with her index finger. "Someone from your past is looking for you."

"Did you get this from a fortune cookie?" I asked. And yet, no sooner had I said the words than I filled in the blanks so that I didn't even need her to elaborate.

"You're kidding," I said.

"What?" said Miranda.

"I kid you not," said Maggie. "Ran into him at the symposium Westford-Langley hosted in Boston the other day."

"Who?" asked Miranda.

"How's he looking these days?" I asked.

"Lonely," said Maggie, "but otherwise the same. He's back to clean-shaven."

"If one of you doesn't tell me who you're talking about in the next three seconds, I am going Real Housewife on the both of you and flipping the table over," said Miranda.

"My ex-fiancé, Andrew," I said.

Miranda's eyes widened. "Wait—you mean . . ."

I nodded and finished her thought out loud as I had Maggie's. "Andrew Clark. Dumped me to marry someone else, then divorced her a few years later."

"Played acoustic guitar. Folk music, I recall," said Maggie.

"That right there should've been a red flag," I said. "So, he specifically asked about me?"

Maggie nodded. "Asked how you were, what you were up to, that sort of thing."

"And?"

"And I told him you were doing great. Happy. Writing and publishing and teaching and all that."

"Did you mention David?"

"I thought about it, but something told me not to. Is that OK?"

"Of course it's OK," I said.

"Why would it be so bad if you told him Andi found someone else and is very happy with him?" asked Miranda.

"It's not that it would be bad," said Maggie. "I guess I forgot that he didn't know how Andi and David met."

Ah, Maggie. So sweet, so loving, would give you the clothes off her back in the dead of winter if you asked her to. But she seemed to love the taste of her foot in her mouth, even if just a toe. I was used to it by now, but it didn't make the moment less mortifying. Then again, she probably assumed Miranda knew who David used to be, given that Miranda and I had been friends for so long, and who could blame Maggie for that?

Miranda looked at me, puzzled. "You met in Rome, didn't you?"

When Maggie realized she'd done it again, she gasped and touched my arm apologetically. I directed an *it's OK* glance at her, but addressed Miranda. "The second time, yes. The first time was when I lived in New York. Let's just say it was under unusual circumstances. He was going by a different name back then."

"Was he in trouble with the law or something?" she asked.

"Oh, you might as well tell her," said Maggie. "It's ancient history by now."

My forgiving glance turned into a frosty glare. Now I was genuinely mad at her. I didn't think it was right to tell anyone about David's past without his permission. But I didn't want Miranda to feel as if we were keeping secrets from her, either, or that she couldn't be trusted.

I leaned in as close as I could, and gestured to Miranda to do the same. Even Mags leaned in.

"He was an escort," I said almost inaudibly.

"What did you say?" said Miranda, "something about a quarter?"

"An ES-CORT," I enunciated, raising the volume by a fraction.

Miranda got it the second time. She sat up straight and exclaimed, "*No way!*" before catching herself and going stealth again by leaning in and asking above a whisper, "Seriously?"

I nodded.

"Did you hire him?"

"Sort of," I said. "Not for what you think. I mean, he wasn't exactly *that* kind of escort. I mean, he was and he wasn't. It's really complicated."

Have you ever noticed how "it's complicated" has come to mean, "I totally don't want to have to explain this to you right now"?

"Wow," said Miranda, leaning back in her seat. "It all makes sense now."

"What does?" I asked.

"Last year we were all joking around at the Christmas party and I compared him to Richard Gere in *Pretty Woman*— you know, because he acts so cool and collected and is such a schmooze-boy—and then Kevin made a crack like they should remake the movie and have David play Julia Roberts's part instead, because he's so wicked smooth and handsome. I swear, I thought he was going to deck Kevin. I thought maybe it was just some homophobic thing."

David had never told me about the incident.

"Look, Randa, you can't tell anyone about David. Not even Kevin. Especially not now, with everything going on with this new situation." I had already filled her in about Wylie the day after David got the call. He was OK with my telling them, knowing they were my closest friends.

"I won't tell anyone anything, I swear."

After a few beats, I returned to the subject of Andrew. "So, did Folk Boy say anything else?" I asked Maggie.

"He asked me for your e-mail address."

"You didn't give it to him, did you?"

"No, but I said you were still teaching at NU, and he said he'd look you up through their department website."

I scoffed. "Well, I suppose he would've eventually found me there had he not asked you. In fact, I'm surprised he didn't just Google me."

"Maybe he wanted confirmation," said Maggie.

"What will you do if he e-mails you?" asked Miranda.

"What else?" I said as I finished the last of my moccaccino. "Delete it."

~∞∭∭∞~

Two days later, at home with my laptop and working on a new chapter, I took a break and opened my e-mail inbox. Sure enough, there was an e-mail from apclark22 (his favorite book had always been *Catch-22*). The subject heading was a casual *hello.* As if we were well acquainted with each other. Despite the advance warning, seeing the e-mail handle and the unread message in the inbox rattled me a bit. I leaned in to my laptop, put my fingers to my pursed lips, and stared at the *hello*, as if it were waving at me.

Andrew was even more ancient history than David's escort days. Moreover, the person I was when I was with him and the person I was with Sam (and now David) were so completely different that the former was barely recognizable to me. Knowing all the problems I'd had back then—my struggles with intimacy, low self-esteem, and seeking approval and validation from men instead of myself—had made me just as much of a participant in our demise as his cheating on me. Not to say that his betrayal was justified, but I understood it years later, and was able to forgive him for it.

That said, I still thought he was a clueless idiot.

But what if he had grown since then? After all, wasn't I once a clueless idiot too? David insisted there was a difference between being clueless by arrogance and clueless by circumstance. He had put Andrew in the former category, me in the latter. "You were in pain," he once explained to me. "You'd been programmed to believe something about yourself that wasn't true. Andrew didn't care to know any better."

What if he did now? Didn't he deserve the second chance as much as I had? I hadn't seen him in years, but the last two times we crossed paths—once at a conference (the same one where Sam and I met), and then when Mags and I visited our old stomping grounds at South Coast University, two years after Sam's death—I had treated him coldly. What if he had genuinely been trying to extend the olive branch? Maybe he had my rebuff coming to him—after all, he'd not done a very nice thing to me. But what the hell did I care now? Things had, in the end, worked out well for me. I got to be with men I really loved, and who really loved me. Both of them.

Which meant that I didn't need to hear from an ex who had caused me nothing but pain.

But before the pain, wasn't there love? Before he'd been my ex, he'd been my friend. He'd been even more than that.

I looked at the new ring still getting acclimated on my finger.

I already had everything I needed.

I highlighted the e-mail and clicked on the Delete button.

Are you sure? a message on the screen asked.

I then hit Cancel, logged out of my e-mail account, and shut down my laptop.

chapter fifteen

I couldn't get the damn e-mail out of my head. It kept poking at me, an invisible blinking red light demanding my attention. I knew me—deleting it wouldn't have been an option. It would've haunted me in my dreams. This, however, wasn't much better. I should've read it hours ago.

David could tell I was preoccupied throughout dinner, kept prodding me with questions about my day and classes and my latest novel-in-progress. I responded to each one, but could tell he wasn't getting the answer he wanted. Finally he came out and asked.

"Everything OK, Andi? Your mind seems to be elsewhere."

"Oh, it's just everything that's been going on, I guess." Lying to David never felt good, and the bigger the lie, the more convinced I was he could see through it. The statement in and of itself wasn't untrue—certainly a lot of drama had transpired in a short amount of time—but using it to cover up the fact that my ex had gotten in touch with me, and keeping it from David, was the real offense. Why had I done it?

Again, he wasn't convinced. "Anything you want to talk about?" he asked.

"Not really."

"You sure?"

I nodded. He stood up, crossed to where I was sitting, leaned in and kissed me. Then he held out his hand. "Come upstairs with me for a sec. I wanna show you something." I looked at him, uncertain, and he beckoned me again. "Leave the dishes; I'll do them later."

I took his hand and he pulled me from my chair. I followed him up the stairs and down the hall to the guest bedroom. The room had always been sparse with decoration, although Sam and I had painted the walls a taupe color with white trim. The full-size mattress was dressed in neutral-toned bedding occupied by Raggedy Ann and Andy dolls that Sam had bought at a yard sale back when we were dating—he had called them Raggedy Sam and Andi. A single bookcase leaned against one wall (filled, of course), and a chest of drawers countered the opposite wall.

I looked at David, confused. "What? I don't see anything out of the ordinary. I thought you were going to show me a new painting or something."

"What do you think of making this Wylie's room for when she visits?"

I stiffened. "Dev," I started, but he continued.

"We can let her pick out a color—she doesn't seem to be the taupe type—and deck it out any way she wants. Put in a TV or stereo, perhaps, some extra storage. . . ."

"Whoa, Dev—slow down. We don't even know if Janine is going to let that happen."

"She can't legally forbid me from seeing my daughter. I'll take her to court if I have to."

He spoke in a threatening tone I'd never heard before. Like a lion protecting his cub.

"These things take time. You can't expect to have a relationship with this girl overnight."

" 'This girl' is my *daughter*, Andi."

"I know that," I said, feeling like a child who'd just been reprimanded.

"And why not? She's the one who came to me, remember?"

"Because a few weeks ago you didn't even want to get tested, just wanted this whole thing to go away. Now you're redecorating rooms?"

"I'm not afraid anymore. I want her in my life and I want to play some kind of role in her life. I want us to be *a family*."

"She already has a family. She has a mother and a father who love her. We can't swoop in and threaten that."

"You're the one who sounds threatened," he said.

I glowered at him. "I have been nothing but supportive of you throughout this or—" I censored myself from saying *ordeal*. "—*situation*, David. How dare you get all righteous on me."

"I don't see why you're giving me such a hard time about this."

"I am not giving you a hard time. I am trying to be reasonable. You obviously can't see clearly right now."

"Who's being righteous now?"

David followed me as I walked into the hallway and down the stairs, my footfalls heavy. I paced around the living room before moving to the kitchen; the house suddenly felt small and cramped.

"Look," I said, "you know I'm supportive of you and you know I want you to have a relationship with Wylie. But you can't just go in all gangbusters and expect everyone to line up behind you. Sam and I never had children not because we didn't get around to it, but because we didn't *want* to. You yourself were worried about how Wylie's presence was going to affect us. Well, I'm uncertain about that too. We've got to slow down and talk about these things. Who's going to make decisions for or about her—you and Janine, or you and me, or both? Who or what will I be to her—a stepmother? A friend? Her biological father's wife? Does this now mean that I come second in your life?"

He took a step toward me. "Andi, no. How could you ever think that?"

"Because," I said as tears stung my eyes. "Because it's possible."

"OK, maybe I jumped the gun a bit with the bedroom. But you are very much a part of this. I am not going to shut you out, I promise."

A dread like no other filled me as soon as he said the words.

I spied the dirty dishes on the table. "I'd better do those," I said.

"No," said David, "I said I'd do them. Why don't you go upstairs to the study? I promised you a painting lesson, didn't I? We can start tonight."

We hadn't even mentioned our impromptu arrangement since its conception, much less acted on it. "Not tonight. I've got some work to do." Another lie of sorts—not that I didn't have work, but none that couldn't wait until tomorrow. This was turning into a bad habit.

His eyes turned dark with disappointment. "Well, let's make it a standing weekly appointment, like we did last time." He was referring to our escort arrangement. *What the hell had I been thinking?* I wondered. *Then and now?*

"Sure," I said, unenthused. I climbed the stairs to my office, the room next door to the guest room, filled with even more trepidation as I imagined it as Wylie's room, with music blasting from behind the door and pounding through the adjoining wall, shutting us out yet taking full advantage of

David's desire to make up for fifteen lost years. I tried to imagine another person in the house—in *Sam*'s house—vying for David's attention and getting it.

As usual, David was right—I was threatened to the core. It had seemingly snuck up on me when I wasn't looking, like a virus.

Closing the office door and putting on my own music, I went to my laptop, logged in to my e-mail, and clicked on Andrew's *hello*.

chapter sixteen

Dear Andi,

I ran into Maggie the other day and she told me all about you.

(Nice. Make it sound like Maggie spilled her guts willingly when I know it was the other way around. What, you think my best friend doesn't talk to me?)

She said you're doing great, and I'm so happy to hear that. I'm doing fine as well. I'm singing and playing solo now, doing small gigs at coffee shops and the like. I never had the gift your brothers have,

(way to suck up)

but I've always enjoyed interacting with an audience, even if just a few people, and telling stories through my songs.

Speaking of stories, I read the novel you co-wrote with your husband and really enjoyed it. You did an excellent job creating a flaw-less voice; I couldn't tell where he left off and you picked up. There was a genuine inti-macy, not only between the characters but also in the writing, as if Sam was still alive and you actually collaborated. But I

suppose if you've been with someone that
long, it's not hard. The intimacy especially
touched me.

(You don't know the half of it. . . .)

I know I blew it with you. I cheated on you
and you have every right to keep hating me
for that. I don't think I ever truly apologized to you. If there's anything I wish I
could do over in my life, it would be the way
I treated you. Maybe it's too much to ask,
but I really want to make things right with
you. Is there hope for that?

Even if the answer is no, I would love to
hear from you.

Best,
Andrew

I read the last line twice, my heart pounding so loud I
could hear as well as feel it. In an instant it all came back to me:
meeting Andrew at South Coast University; falling in love;
dating; his proposal at some dive during one of his shows (he
serenaded me with a song he wrote just for me and revealed a
ring on a leather band hanging from the capo on the guitar's
fretboard); waiting, waiting, waiting to have sex; my denial of
his withdrawal from me; his confession that he slept with
Tanya, was leaving me for Tanya, marrying Tanya . . .

Despite my being so devastated back then, Andrew's
dumping me was the best thing that had ever happened. Without it, I never would've moved back to New York, never
would've met David, and subsequently never would've met
Sam, although I'd like to think that meeting Sam would've
been what the district attorneys on *Law & Order* called

"inevitable discovery." I would've been married to Andrew, however. I wondered: *Would I have left Andrew for Sam had it worked out that way? Would Sam have tried to steal me away? Would we have had an affair?*

I could no longer fathom being married to Andrew. The very thought was as foreign to me as being married to some random stranger.

But could I be his friend?

I hit Reply and typed:

```
I don't hate you, Andrew. And there's noth-
ing to "make right." You're forgiven. But thank
you for apologizing. That means a lot to me.
For a long time I didn't want you to be
happy. But when you lose your own happiness
and think you'll never get it back, you real-
ize just how cruel it is to wish that on an-
other person. I'm sorry for that, and I hope
you are happy now.
                                        Andi
```

```
P.S. Thank you for buying the novel. I had
come across the unfinished manuscript about a
year after Sam was killed. Didn't seem right
to keep it in a drawer. Also didn't seem
right to take the credit for it. It felt like
a collaboration.
```

And then, my fingers poised on the keyboard, I ignored my gut as I typed three more words and hit Send.

I logged off, shut down my laptop, and went to bed.

Hours later and unable to sleep, I crept downstairs so as

not to disturb David. I watched mindless TV, the volume so low I could barely hear the voices. It didn't matter—those three words were echoing inside my head, like a gong banging the side of my brain, to the point that I thought it would drive me insane. *How could I have been so stupid?*

The three words I'd typed were `Keep in touch`.

chapter seventeen

"You didn't," said Maggie as I sat in her office at Smith College, my head down on the desk, lightly banging it as I told her about my reply to Andrew.

"I did," I moaned.

"Why on God's green earth would you tell him to keep in touch?"

I picked my head up. "I don't know. David and I had gotten into a tizzy earlier."

"A 'tizzy'?"

"Yeah."

"What's a tizzy?" she asked.

"Not quite a fight, but a little more heated than a disagreement. Worked up. I was feeling threatened by this whole situation with Wylie—would you believe he wants to redecorate the guest room for her? I mean, one minute he wants to sweep the whole thing under the rug, and the next minute—"

"Whoa—focus, Andi."

"Can I just say the devil made me do it and leave it at that?"

"No, you can't. Sounds to me like you knew exactly what you were doing."

I put my head down and moaned again. "He was being so contrite and remorseful and I felt sorry for him."

"Did it occur to you that maybe he was putting you on and got the exact reaction from you that he wanted?"

I rested my chin on my arms and looked at her. "It did, actually. But even if he wasn't, what's the harm in finally letting him off the hook? As it turned out, staying with Andrew would've been worse than being dumped by him. He and Tanya did me a favor."

"There's nothing wrong with forgiving him," said Maggie. "But resuming communication with him is thirty-one flavors of wrong."

"It was one e-mail," I protested—or, to be more accurate, rationalized. "Now that he got what he wanted, he probably won't bother with a follow-up."

"What makes you so sure that's all he wanted?"

She had a point; he did say he "wanted to make things right" with me. But I had pretty much shut that down, so he couldn't possibly be ballsy enough to pursue anything else, could he?

Then again, I'd invited him to.

"Mags, I know you didn't tell him about David, but did he ask you if I was seeing anyone?"

"No. But if he had, I would've told him you were. Maybe he was too afraid to ask the question. And let's face it: even if you weren't with David, I probably would've lied and said you were with someone just to piss him off."

"Really?" I said, troubled by this admission. "You would've lied to him?"

"Wouldn't you?"

I didn't have to ponder the question. "Yeah," I said, just as troubled by my own admission.

I wasn't teaching classes that day, so I went home to find David working in the study. He took off his reading glasses when he noticed me in the doorway.

"Hey," he said.

"Hey," I replied as I entered the room. "I didn't think you'd be home today."

"Didn't sleep well last night."

"Me neither."

"I know."

I sank into the sofa and reflexively yawned. "I'm sorry about the tizzy," I said.

David joined me on the sofa and pulled me close to him. "Me too."

"I should've been more supportive."

"You've been monumentally supportive," he said. "I was being a self-absorbed jerk."

"No, you weren't."

I closed my eyes and rested my head on his shoulder. One of the safest places to be. We sat quietly for a bit, the only audible sound being our breathing. I hadn't even realized that I dozed off until the ringtone of David's cell phone jarred me awake. I flinched and clumsily moved away from him as he reached for it, checked the caller ID, and sprang up, his joints popping.

"Hello?" he said, followed a second later by an uncharacteristically shy yet eager, "Hi!" followed by, "No, I'm glad you called."

And then I knew: *Wylie.*

Every muscle in my body tightened as David motioned to me and then the door, which was his way of asking me for privacy. The gesture rattled me, making me feel like he'd just asked me to exit more than the room. He closed the door behind me as I left, which unnerved me even more. I retreated to my office and back to my laptop. I logged into my e-mails, and didn't even allow myself to admit that I was *hoping* it would be there until I saw it: Andrew's reply.

Hi Andi,

   I can't tell you how happy I was to get your e-mail. Was even happier to see that you've forgiven me. I certainly don't deserve it. I really would like to keep in touch with you, if that's OK. Maybe I've been nostalgic lately, but I miss our conversations from the good ol' days. How are things at NU? Do you like it there? Same old, same old, at SCU.

   Anyway, it would be nice to hear from you again.

                                        Best,
                                        Andrew

   I snuck down the hall and could hear David speaking in muffled tones behind the closed door of the study. I didn't like the feeling of being shut out.

   Returning to my office and the e-mail, I reread it as my memory replayed the conversation with Maggie. *What makes you so sure that's all he wanted?* Every fiber of my being was screaming at me to listen to Maggie. And yet, one little lone voice was inviting me to give Andrew the benefit of the doubt. Hell, maybe it was Andrew's voice. Hadn't he started out like this—Thoughtful? Attentive? Interested? He wasn't always a slimeball. Or had he been on his best behavior all that time before he cheated on me, and slimeball was his true Crayola color?

No, I decided. He was never a slimeball. Did he cheat? Yes. Did he betray me? Yes. Did he hurt me? Absolutely. Did he have Sam's depth and sensitivity? No. But then again, neither had David. When he was Devin, he'd been insightful, thoughtful, even, but aloof. Not like now—so much more present, so open, so willing to let me in, even if it left him wide open to be hurt. If David could evolve, why couldn't Andrew?

But David wasn't letting me in. Not at this moment.

Once again, I found myself typing a reply.

```
Hey Andrew,
NU is great. I'm technically not tenured
anymore—had left and then returned part-time
after Sam died. I say "technically" because
everyone in the department treats me other-
wise. It's not a large department, so we all
know each other, and I guess everyone got
used to me as being tenured. Fine by me; all
the perks and none of the hassles. I teach
one, sometimes two classes per semester,
upper level. I don't have much to do with
first-year writing anymore, but I'm still a
rhetoric girl at heart.
Just so you know, I'm getting married
again. My fiancé's name is David and I've
known him for about ten years. We met when I
moved back to New York (after you and I broke
up), then reconnected a little over a year
after Sam died. We had a rocky go of it for a
while, but things are solid now.
Hope you are well. Take care.
                                        Andi
```

Elisa Lorello

There. That ought to do it. No open-ended invitations to write back, no leading him on, straight and to-the-point. Not even a greeting. Mags was right: Reopening the lines of communication with an ex was playing with fire. Especially since David and I got engaged after I'd been resistant to marriage for so long.

I was about to add a P.S. saying I'd changed my mind about keeping in touch when David entered the room, and in a knee-jerk reaction, I clicked Send rather than Save.

"Sorry I kicked you out, Andi, but I have good news. Wylie is coming up for a visit next weekend. I spoke to Janine and she gave the OK."

I stared at him, stunned. "Did you think to consult with *me*?"

"I didn't see the need. We have no plans to go anywhere. And you didn't tell me anything was coming up. Come on, Andi, I thought you and I were on the same page!" he said, impatient. His tone was beginning to grate on me.

"We *are* on the same page," I said, a bite to my voice, "but I still like to be consulted about these things. We consult each other about far less important things."

His face softened. "You're right," he said. "I'm sorry. I should've asked you."

"How is she going to get here?" I asked.

"We're going to split driving duties. They're going to bring her here, and we're going to take her back."

"Doesn't it make more sense for us to drive to Hartford and spend the day with her there?"

"Wylie specifically asked to come here."

"Why?" I asked. Something about her request didn't sit well with me. Then again, perhaps it wasn't too far a reach. Wylie was a teenager, after all. Spending time in a different place was probably an adventure to her, a form of escape. Maybe it was her chance to see where and how David lived, whether it was worth pursuing a relationship with him. And me.

"Does it matter?" said David. "I'm just happy she wanted to, and Janine said it was OK," he reiterated.

"I'm kind of surprised she did. She was so resistant when we met with them in Hartford. What happened to 'revisiting the situation'?"

"This *is* revisiting the situation," said David. He gave me a look one that I'd never before seen and couldn't read at all. Its unfamiliarity terrified me.

"What is it, Dev?" I asked.

He shook his head slowly, condescendingly. "Nothing."

"Are we on the same page?" I asked. "Because if we aren't, we'd better get there fast. There's a lot of change taking place, and we can't get married in the midst of chaos. We need to talk about this."

His sienna eyes pierced me—dark, searching, as if he wanted to say something. He turned away for a moment, but when he turned back to face me, he wore a different expression altogether. Cool, collected. Business-as-usual. *Devin's* look. So not comforting.

"Everything's fine," he said, and abruptly changed the subject. "So, your grandmother's fried-dough pizza? You owe me a cooking lesson."

Sharing secrets with my husband-to-be was the last thing I wanted to do at that moment, which terrified me even more.

chapter eighteen

October

I don't know who was more jittery, David or myself. We were outside, waiting for a car with Connecticut license plates to pull into the driveway. I sat on the stoop with my Kindle, but couldn't even get through one screen page without having to read it several times. David, meanwhile, paced in front of me, his arms crossed more out of nerves than the morning New England chill. You'd think we were both seeing Wylie for the first time, but I knew what this visit was really stirring up: It was the first time we were seeing her as *family*. As David's teenage daughter.

So when Peter Baker's black pickup truck pulled in and she emerged from the cab, her backpack in tow, for some reason I was momentarily taken aback. Instead of Daisy Dukes and flip-flops, she wore skinny jeans with black suede boots, and a candy-apple red jacket with faux fur–trimmed collar and cuffs. I suddenly felt very frumpy and unimpressive in my gray carpenter pants, long-sleeved black T-shirt with retro No Nukes logo, nubucks, and faded denim jacket. My hair had been uninspired lately, an indecisiveness to grow it out or cut it short, and the same chestnut color I'd been dyeing it for years. David, of course, looked suave and stylish as always in dark blue jeans, oxfords, a mocha-colored mock turtleneck, and a leather jacket so buttery smooth you wanted to lick it.

Peter emerged in tan chinos and a white button-down shirt, no jacket. He pulled Wylie's overnight bag from the back of the cab and carried it by the strap rather than use the pull-handle and wheels.

David met them halfway, me a couple of steps behind him. He extended his hand to meet Peter's, who took it with all the warmth of a brick wall. And who could blame him? He was dropping off his daughter—*his* daughter—into the hands of strangers. Worse still, *at her request*. The enormity of his gesture pummeled me like a boulder and nearly crushed me. I put a hand to my chest and forced out a couple of deep, slow breaths.

"I'd like to know what your plans are for this weekend," said Peter to David.

David seemed taken aback for a second. "We were originally thinking of going to Boston, but we'll probably go into town instead." This was news to me; we had decided on Boston. Something in Peter's handshake and tone must have rattled David. Perhaps he felt the same crushing boulder.

"I'd like to be informed if your plans change. And Janine and I would like Wylie to check in with us—once tonight and once tomorrow."

Wylie rolled her eyes, but David promised, "We'll make sure she does. And I'll keep you informed."

Peter turned to Wylie, and the color drained from his face, as if he were seeing her for the last time. "If you change your mind, just call and I'll come get you. Doesn't matter what time it is."

It sounded like something a father would say to his little girl at her first sleepover. Maybe that's what it felt like to him.

"I'll be fine," said Wylie, almost impatient.

This was wrong. *Peter* was Wylie's dad, not David. David and I were intruders, interlopers, thieves.

Wylie dropped her backpack and opened her arms. Peter hugged her close, and I studied him as he did. His hair, the color of sandpaper, was short and uneven. A five-o'clock shadow hugged his chin, the kind that existed no matter how closely one shaved. When he released her, Wylie lifted herself on her toes and kissed him on his cheek. "Thanks, Daddy." I caught him swallowing his emotion.

Just as he was about to return to his truck, I piped up. "Peter, thank you so much for allowing Wylie to stay with us. For *trusting* us." I took an extra step forward, as if David and Wylie disappeared, and it was just the two of us in the driveway. I wanted to reach out to him, assure him he was going to get his daughter back. I wanted to tell him, *I know how you feel.* But did I? I hadn't raised a child and then turned her over to some woman who shared her DNA. But he and I were on the edge of this. We were outside, on the margins, looking in. I extended my hand and locked him in a gaze. His irises were watery blue. "*Thank you,*" I said again, hoping somehow the words would decode the jumbled message I was trying so hard to send.

He seemed to comprehend, and I felt solidarity in our handshake when he accepted it. For a second he gave me a look that said *I trust* you. *Not him. You.* From that moment, I felt a weighted responsibility to Peter Baker.

We watched him get into his truck, back out, and drive down the street. When he was out of sight, David and Wylie looked at each other. To hug, or not to hug? I had never seen David this befuddled. He wound up giving her a pat on the arm. "How was the ride?"

She shrugged. "OK, I guess."

"It's nice to see you." I said, and took hold of the suitcase handle. "Here, let me get that for you."

"Thanks."

David wrung his hands for a moment as he frantically searched for something to say, and came up with, "You hungry?"

She shrugged again. "I guess so."

"We can do Italian," he suggested. "Or would you rather get a burger?"

"David, it's only eleven o'clock," I pointed out.

He scratched his head. "Sorry." He paused to consider options. "There are some cute shops on Main Street in Amherst. Wanna walk around and check 'em out?"

"There's also Emily Dickinson's house," I offered. "You know, the poet?"

David sought Wylie's approval before giving his own. Wylie shrugged. "Whatever you guys want to do is OK with me. I mean, I guess we could check out those shops." She paused for a beat before asking, "Can we go to Boston?"

"Your dad didn't seem too keen on it," I said. From my peripheral vision I caught David furtively slip me an irked look for answering on his behalf. Or maybe it was because I referred to Peter as her dad. I clamped my mouth shut and felt self-conscious, as if I'd just been commanded to shut up.

"Ever been to Boston?" asked David.

"My parents took me along the Freedom Trail the summer before middle school," she replied. "I was bored beyond measure."

David laughed in a forced effort. I watched him in awe, wondering why he was so bumbling and fidgety, why schmooze-boy wasn't taking over.

We took Wylie's suitcase inside, freshened up, and left for Amherst less than thirty minutes later. We sauntered up and down Main Street, in and out of the shops and boutiques and Starbucks, exchanging bits of shy small talk along the route, mostly in the form of questions:

"Do you want to go in there?"

"If you want to buy anything, let us know, OK?"

"Do you like kites?"

"I smell waffles."

The weather was perfect—sunny and mild and cloudless, the azure sky complemented by golds and reds and oranges of the foliage. College students abounded at every turn, and I ran into three students, two of them from the previous semester. "Hey, Professor Vanzant!" they called and waved. I smiled and waved back and returned their greeting: "Hey!" One of them even crossed the street to tell me that he'd submitted a short story to an online magazine and it had been accepted. I beamed and congratulated him. Running into students, past or present, filled me with validation and well-being, a sense of being at home in my skin.

"Wow," said Wylie. "You're, like, popular here."

"Andi is a *great* teacher," said David. His pride made me feel even better. "Her students love her. In fact, she taught me everything I know about writing."

All the walking worked up our hunger, and we decided on a café that made pita wraps. When we sat at a table, a shot of something worse than silence stunned each of us into submission, as if we'd become paralyzed not only in our tongues and throats, but also our brains. I could see the look of panic both in David's and Wylie's eyes, not doubting that it was in my own as well.

However, I was the first to break free of it. *This is stupid*, I thought. "Just breathe normally, folks," I said as I picked up my wrap and bit heartily into it. I followed with a yummy sound and licked my fingers that had caught some of the spilled contents. The earnest gesture broke David's spell, and the muscles in his face softened. I read a note of gratitude, as if for the first time he was glad I was there. They each imitated me by picking up their own wraps.

"You know, I always loved the idea of baking your own bread," said Wylie, "but I'm *horrible* at cooking. So's my mom. She *hates* it."

"I used to be the same way," I confessed.

"What changed?"

"Being married to someone who enjoyed it. His enthusiasm rubbed off on me, and it became a thing we did together."

It took her a moment to realize that I wasn't talking about David. "Oh, you meant the other guy—I forgot his name," she said.

I nodded. "Sam."

"Right. That's really nice," she added. But whereas Wylie's eyes expressed interest and attention, David's turned dark.

I paused for a few beats, trying to think of something to say to comfort David. I pointed to him, but was struck dumb when it came to addressing him—what should I call him? After the interaction with Peter, *Dad* was completely out of the question. And yet, calling him *David* seemed just as inappropriate. But I was out of alternatives, and it was the better of the two. "David is a good cook." I took a gulp of ginger ale in attempt to wash out my discomfort, although this was one of those rare times I wished for a stronger elixir. David took a swig from a bottle of iced tea. He seemed equally bothered by the lack of a proper moniker, and in the end I concluded that I'd made things worse.

Wylie leaned in to her straw and took a sip of Coke. And then she noticed the ring on my finger. "Wait—are you two engaged?"

David took my hand. "Sure are."

"Since when?"

"'Bout two weeks ago," I replied.

She frowned. "Did you not want me to know?"

David dropped his head. "You'll have to forgive me, Wylie. I'm just not sure of my footing here. None of us are. That's why I invited you to visit with us. I want us to get to know each other, so we can feel comfortable sharing such things. Andi and I really want you to be a part of our lives, and vice versa."

Wait—*he* invited *her*?

Her eyes darted to me, as if seeking my confirmation. I blinked rapidly and nodded, but I knew my expression was betraying me, and I knew she knew as well.

"Well, congratulations, I guess," she said. "I hope you'll at least invite me to the wedding."

"Are you kidding?" said David. "We want you *in* the wedding."

Where had *that* come from? Not that I wouldn't want to invite Wylie—but for her to be a part of it? I hadn't even begun to consider such details for my own family and best friends.

Things were happening way too fast. I couldn't get the look on Peter's face as he turned his daughter over to us out of my head, couldn't stop feeling as if we were doing exactly what Janine threatened us not to do—swooping in and taking over. I couldn't stop feeling as if this was all *wrong*.

I could barely look at the pita wrap, much less swallow another bite.

The conversation quickly turned casual, peppered with bits of entertainment gossip and stories about Wylie's high school and David explaining his work to her. They became engrossed in a conversation about painting, especially when David started in on the Impressionists. It was like sitting with two Red Sox fans talking about the game and not being able to get a word in edgewise. She seemed to be genuinely interested in his explanation of Manet's color contrast. Or maybe she was already trying to please her father. Either way, I couldn't hold it against her. David's passion always lured me into his aura, like a mosquito being lured into an ultraviolet light, and then he'd zap me with his electric smile. Even at that moment, I could feel the pull of his sienna eyes, the music of his voice, the rhythm of his words and his breath, and knew I was already done for. Wylie would be next. It was inevitable. Moreover, having those same eyes, I knew she was capable of doing the same to him.

✺

We got back to the house by late afternoon/early evening, and I realized that I had forgotten to turn my cell phone back on (I always turned it off when we went out to eat). When I did, I found a terse voice mail from my mother. I called her back, and she picked up on the first ring.

"Hi, Mom," I said.

"Where were you?"

"In Amherst with Wylie. She's staying with us for the weekend." I was trying to speak nonchalantly, as if this were something we did every Saturday.

"Wylie? The daughter?" my mother asked. "Already? Aren't you rushing things a bit?"

I dipped into another room, out of earshot from David and Wylie. "It's what he wants," I said. "We both do. And they should get to know each other."

"Are you sure she's not some golddigger?"

"Mom!"

"Not her personally. I mean maybe her mother is putting her up to it."

"I've met her mother. Trust me, she's not putting anyone up to anything. And I told you, Wylie just wants to know her real father. I want that for her too. It's something I never had at her age."

"It's not like your father wasn't around at all before he died."

"But I didn't *know* him. And I never felt understood or appreciated by him. I know you don't like to hear me say such things, but that's how I felt."

The line went quiet for a few seconds before she resumed the conversation and changed the subject. "I called to ask you to come over tomorrow and stay overnight. Your brothers will be here too."

"Sorry," I said. "Can't. Next weekend, perhaps?"

"It has to be tomorrow."

"Why?"

"Because it does. It's hard enough getting your brothers to stay in one place for more than a week or two, and I've got several appointments in the coming week."

"What, are you running for election?" I quipped.

"Please, Andi!" Her tone was pleading rather than admonishing. It was a tone I'd never heard from her before. "I really need you here. I'm sorry to take you away from David and your weekend, but this is more than an invitation."

Every muscle in my body tightened. "Mom, what's wrong?"

"I'll even pay your ferry expenses, if you want."

"Never mind that. I'll be there tomorrow, OK?"

I heard what sounded like a sigh of relief. "Thank you, Andi. I'll see you tomorrow."

That was my signal to say good-bye. I put the phone down and went back to the den, but no one was there. I could hear voices coming from upstairs, and traced them to the study, where Wylie was sitting at the desk, a full-color, enormous book of Manet paintings spread open before her, and David standing behind her, pointing out depth-of-perception points. She looked enthralled. He looked changed.

"Excuse me, Dev?" I asked. They both looked up. "David," I corrected. "I'm sorry to interrupt you, but could I speak to you for a moment?" I diverted to Wylie. "Excuse us, please."

I could tell he was disappointed that I'd just disrupted the moment and broken the fledgling bond between them. We stepped into the hallway. "What?" he said slightly above a whisper, a snip to the word.

"My mother called. Something's wrong," I whispered back. "What is it?"

"She wouldn't say over the phone, but I have to go to Long Island tomorrow and stay overnight."

"What do you mean you *have* to go? Didn't you tell her we have Wylie here this weekend?"

"Of course I did, but she practically begged me."

"Don't you teach on Mondays?"

"So I'll cancel. Missing one day of class in the semester doesn't kill anyone."

David brooded. "She's going to think you don't want her here," he said of Wylie, pointing to the other side of the wall and trying not to raise his voice.

"Look, this is *my mother* we're talking about. She doesn't ask me for anything unless she really needs it. I don't know what's going on, but she needs me, and I'm not saying no to her."

He shook his head and muttered, "Fine," as we reentered the room.

I willed a smile and said to Wylie, "I was just wondering what you wanted for dinner, or are you still stuffed from lunch?"

"Whatever is OK," she replied.

"We've got a ton of leftover Chinese food in the fridge. That OK?"

"Sure, whatever," David said, waving his hand as if to swat me away, and with that I was exiled.

Later, after dinner, Wylie offered to help me clear the table, no doubt to give herself a break from David, who had been practically hovering over her all day. While he went back to the study to find more books that she might like, she handed me each plate and glass as I rinsed and transferred them to the dishwasher.

"So I was wondering, why'd you call him 'Dev' before?"

Damn. She'd heard.

"It's just a nickname. He hates 'Dave,' so we kinda settled on 'Dev' instead."

"Does everyone call him that?"

"It's something only *I* call him. You know, like a pet name." I could hear the possessiveness in my tone, wishing it wasn't outing itself and hoping she wasn't perceptive.

"Because I heard my mom call him *Devin* the night you came over. So I was wondering why he used another name."

Oh God. How in hell do you explain to a kid that the father she's never known used to be an escort?

"I think at the time he wanted to keep his work life and his personal life separate," I replied. "Kind of like authors who use a pen name."

"What did he do?"

Please, please, please don't ask me this!

"Umm . . ." I started, but came up short. What was I supposed to say? Sales? Public Relations? *Ask your father? Ask your mother*? I didn't want to lie to her, but telling her the truth was certainly out of the question.

"Well, um, he was a consultant of sorts. But art was always his passion."

Fortunately she dropped the subject and moved on to her next question. "When you two stepped out of the room before, did you have a fight about something?"

I almost dropped a glass. "I have to see my mother tomorrow. She lives on Long Island, which means I'm going to stay there overnight. I know it's bad timing, but it's important."

"And he's mad at you for it?"

"We both feel bad about it. This is your visit, after all. And I'd like to spend some time with you. But my mother wouldn't have asked if she didn't have a good reason."

"I'm sorry," she said. An expression of worry and guilt accompanied her words.

As if on its own, my hand reached out and gently touched her arm. "No. No, Wylie, it's not your fault. This was . . . unexpected. My mother and I have a difficult relationship."

The second those last words slipped out, I regretted saying them. *Why* had I said them?

"How come?" she asked.

"We always have. I don't know why. I mean, I know now, but . . ." I stalled for an explanation and a chance to crawl out of the hole I was digging before it caved in on me. "Anyway, I'm the one who's sorry to leave you this weekend. I hope there'll be others."

"Sure."

"I guess it'll be nice to have some one-on-one time with—" I stalled again. "With David."

"My mom will *love* that," she muttered. "She and I haven't been getting along at all lately."

I wanted to ask why, but the question felt too prying. "It's your age," I offered instead. "Most girls don't get along with their mothers at this age. It'll improve once you're out of high school and on your own. Besides, you're both going through a lot of change right now. Change is hard. And she's afraid of losing you, that's all."

"I'm not going anywhere. I mean, sure, I'm *here*. But I'm not, like, dumping them for a new family."

"She'll see that in time," I assured her. I had to assure myself too. "But in the meantime, that's what it feels like to them. Your father especially. This is incredibly hard on him. Painful, even. He must feel like you don't want him anymore."

"That's silly. I just . . . I need to do this right now."

"I'm sure he understands that. But, Wylie, you've got to see how much he loves you. Enough to let you do this humongous thing. Heck, he *drove* you here himself. Do you realize how loving a gesture that is? How courageous?"

We finished cleaning the kitchen in silence.

"I can see why your students like you," she said after a bout of contemplation. "You get people to see things in ways they didn't before, without making them feel stupid."

"Thanks," I said. "That's nice of you to say."

"I could tell when you saw them today that you really like being a teacher."

"I love it," I replied.

"English isn't one of my best subjects—it's not that I don't like it—" she quickly backpedaled, and I smiled. People always felt the need to apologize for not loving words as much as I do. But before I could tell her that, she continued without a pause, "I just don't get it most of the time. I never seem to know what my teacher wants. And my essays . . ." She made a gagging face. "Forget it."

I couldn't help but laugh. "You're not the first one to tell me that. Unfortunately, I think school ruins English for a lot of students."

"Totally! It's like, can we make this any more boring?"

"Don't even get me started on the five-paragraph essay," I said. "Are they still teaching that?" I was enjoying this conversation. And she seemed to be equal parts surprised by and pleased with my validation.

"I was thinking that maybe you could help me," she said.

I stopped what I was doing and looked at her. She seemed so open and innocent at that moment, and I was moved by it. I felt an instant connection unlike one I'd felt with anyone else. Was it as a friend? A teacher? An aunt? A mother? All of the above? I had no idea. Maybe it was acceptance—she wanted *me* in her life as much as she wanted David. She was asking, inviting me in. And I wanted in, I realized. Maybe that's what David had felt when he was so eager to make a space for her here. Hell, he probably felt it tenfold.

I smiled. "I would love to help you, Wylie."

Her eyes sparkled, and their familiarity was almost too much for me to bear. "Really?"

"Sure. Maybe we can make a standing appointment. You know, like tutoring. I'll come to your house once a month, or something like that—if it's OK with your parents, that is," I quickly added.

She frowned quizzically. "Why wouldn't it be?"

"Well . . . ," I started, but couldn't finish.

She didn't wait for me. "Do you, like, have Shakespeare memorized and stuff?"

I laughed. "Hardly! I hated Shakespeare growing up. All throughout college and grad school too. Didn't get it. I mean, I have an appreciation for him now, but I'd still rather see *The*

Social Network than read *Julius Caesar*, or even watch it onstage."

Wylie lit up. "Ohmigod, I *love* that movie! Jesse Eisenberg is such a hottie."

I laughed again. "The writer is pretty cute too."

The puzzled frown returned. "What writer?"

It occurred to me that she thought I was referring to one of the film's characters. Before I could clarify, David came into the room and announced that he'd found another art book for Wylie.

"Hey, guess what? Andi's gonna help me ace my English class!" she said.

David peered at me, then returned his attention to Wylie and smiled. "That's great." He couldn't have sounded less enthused. "Come on," he said, excusing the both of them, and practically pulling her away.

"Thanks for helping out," I called out as she left the room.

Wylie had gone to the guest room around ten o'clock. She bade us good night, although she wore earbuds attached to her smartphone and rummaged through her backpack. I retreated to David's and my room, got ready for bed, checked e-mails and found another one from Andrew. I silently groaned, logged out without opening it, and shut down my laptop.

Thing is, a part of me was glad to see it.

chapter nineteen

David joined me in bed. Typically he snuggled with me and kissed me good night, but this time he didn't even brush up against me.

"So far, so good, don't you think?" I said. "I mean, you two really seem to be hitting it off."

He didn't answer.

I couldn't take his chilly disposition toward me for another minute. "What the hell is your problem?" I said, trying to keep my volume in check.

"My *problem*," he said with a sneer, "is that you're walking out in the middle of my daughter's visit. Way to make her feel welcome, Andi. Way to make her feel like she's a part of the family."

"Are you really that insensitive? I told you that something's wrong with my mother. I told you that she's reaching out to me. Doesn't *my* family mean anything to you? Besides," I pressed, and knew I was as good as throwing a lit match on a spill of gas, "I could've left without telling you and you probably wouldn't have even noticed until it was time for bed."

"Right. Like you're standing on the sidelines. Tutoring?"

"What, did I do something wrong? I thought you'd be happy to see that we're getting along."

"This isn't some competition for my attention, Andi."

"*Your* attention? You're the one who's competing for *her* attention!"

"She's not some ex-girlfriend; she's my *daughter*. I'm not cheating on you."

My thoughts immediately went to Andrew and the un-opened e-mail that I knew was lurking on my laptop.

"That's real classy, Dev. And way to manipulate me by bringing up my ex."

He looked insulted. "Who's bringing up your ex? I'm try-ing to reassure you, not manipulate you," he said. I took note of his lack of an apology.

I waited a beat before speaking again. "You're being in-credibly self-absorbed."

"Well, I learned from the best."

My jaw dropped. Dropped and hung open, as if stuck that way. I gaped at him, saw his cold eyes, and mentally scanned the house for a place to run to, since the guest room was taken. And what would Wylie think if she found me sleeping any-where other than my own bedroom? She already sensed the tension in the air and blamed herself for it.

"You're a real rat-bastard sometimes, you know that?" I said, and with that I snapped off the light, pulled the covers up to my chin, and turned my back to him. As I felt him settle in, I added for good measure, "Don't even touch me by accident."

In the morning my muscles were stiff and sore from David and I sleeping back-to-back the entire night and refusing to budge. I went downstairs following my shower and prepared a breakfast of pancakes and bacon, taking deep breaths and willing myself to put on my happiest face for Wylie. She entered the kitchen wearing pink pajama bottoms with puckered lipstick kisses on them and a purple thermal shirt. It was my first time seeing her without makeup. She was so much prettier without all that heavy liner and mascara, and looked twice as much like David. She hunched her shoulders and sat at the butcher-block table, tucking one of her legs under her.

"Morning," I said in feigned cheeriness. "Sleep OK?"

"I guess."

"Strange in unfamiliar surroundings?"

"Yeah, I guess so." She shuddered.

"Heat will come up soon, I promise. Want some hot cocoa or something?"

"Do you have any tea?"

"Coming right up." I filled the kettle with water and set it on the stove.

"Where's, um . . . where's David?" she asked.

"In the shower. He'll be down soon."

Wylie stared out the kitchen window at nothing. "Is it weird to be marrying one guy after being married to another?"

Why was she so preoccupied with my relationships with David and Sam?

"Weird for me, or weird in general?" I asked.

"Weird for you."

"Sometimes," I said. "It's not like I ever stopped being married to Sam. He and I would've still been together were it not for the accident."

"But you love David." She said this like a statement, but I knew she was asking a question.

"I love David very much," I answered, filling with guilt and regret over the previous night's fight.

"So what if you had met David while Sam was still alive?"

"Well, I knew David before Sam and I met. Back then we were friends." The term sounded disingenuous. "We got together after . . ." I trailed off.

"I mean, what if you and Sam were married, and you ran into David or whatever while you were still . . . would you have been attracted to him?"

"Oh." I flicked an ice-cream scoopful of pancake batter onto the griddle. "I don't know. Maybe. I doubt I would've acted on it, though."

"Why?"

"Because I was deeply in love with my husband."

"But you're in love with David now, right?"

It was as if she was trying to crack some code, find a secret hidden within me.

"Yes. It's different, though. David and Sam are very different. Sam was my best friend. We could tell each other anything, talk to each other for hours until our throats were sore. Being with him was easy. Not to say that it was like that all the time. And not to say that David isn't my friend as much as he's my—" I stopped short. Was it OK to use the word "lover" with a fifteen-year-old? "David's just . . . more alluring," I said after searching my thoughts. "He always has been. And it's not that it's hard to be with him; it's just that he and I have a different past, more complicated than what Sam and I had."

The kettle whistled, and I set a mug of hot water for her along with an array of teas from a box. She selected one and dunked it into the mug before letting it steep.

"Wow. I just thought of something. You have two husbands—or you're about to—and I have two dads. And one of them is the same guy."

Something about her statement sent a jolt of electricity through me. It was so blunt, so *true*.

"He's a good guy," I said in practically a whisper, fighting back tears that were pushing to the surface. *And I want him all to myself,* I thought, ashamed. Maybe David had been right the night before, and I had been somehow competing for his attention. Or maybe I got caught up in Wylie's hypotheticals about seeing David while Sam was alive and feared David would've come out the loser.

As if on cue, David entered the kitchen, and I couldn't help but wonder if he'd been secretly listening in on our conversation. I never heard him come down the stairs.

"Morning," he said with the same syrupy inflection as I had. He kissed my cheek, and I assumed it was for Wylie's sake. Then again, maybe he too felt guilty about what happened. He leaned over the griddle for a peek. "Banana buttermilk pancakes. What'd I tell you, Wylie? My fiancée can cook."

"Coffee's waiting for you," I announced, hoping it sounded more like something we'd say routinely to each other, a couple who were comfortable and happy. I hadn't lied to Wylie. I loved David, was in love with David, still loved him even when he acted like a rat-bastard. But at that moment, the sting of his words from the previous night hurt too much. Moreover, it occurred to me at that moment that banana buttermilk pancakes had always been Sam's favorite, and that familiar ache for him struck me without warning, only adding to the inner turmoil that swirled like a whirlpool, sucking me into its center.

David grabbed a mug from the cabinet and joined Wylie at the table. "Sleep OK?" he asked her.

"I guess," she said, and I couldn't help but shake my head and crack a grin, which she caught. We were tripping over ourselves from trying so hard.

115

"So, what do you want to do today? I promised your parents I'd get you home no later than seven tonight, but we've got plenty of time," said David.

"Why don't you go to the MFA," I suggested. To Wylie, I said, "David knows every inch of the Boston Museum of Fine Arts. Could pull off a heist."

"Someone's been watching a little too much *White Collar*," he said. I knew he meant it as a joke, but I couldn't help but hear a condescending edge on the words.

"Sure, I'd love to check it out," she replied.

He was practically glowing with delight. "I'll call your mother and make sure it's OK." He seemed to want to avoid the reality that Wylie already had a father, one who was there for her first day of school, her first bicycle ride, her first soccer game and slumber party and art exhibit. One who protected and disciplined her. "You have to check in with her too, remember?"

"Wish I could join you," I said.

And just like that, David's radiance clouded over as he got up to pick up the stack of pancakes I'd just removed from the griddle. "Yes, it's too bad."

So much for my guilt. Now I was ticked. I caught his glance and held it, returning it with a threat: *Watch it, pal.*

I turned off the griddle and put the bowl into the sink. "If you'll excuse me, I need to get ready."

"You're not going to have breakfast with us?" asked Wylie.

I shook my head. "I'll grab a bagel or something on the boat." This hadn't been my intention; I just couldn't face either one of them for another minute. Some part of me knew I was being irrational, that David had said "it's too bad" out of disappointment and not resentment. My intellectual side knew it wasn't a two-against-one situation. So why did it *feel* that way? What, exactly, had poked my sleeping insecurities awake, especially since Wylie was so willing to share things with me?

"She gets seasick sometimes," said David, as if that explained everything.

On the ferry, I sat in the cabin, wearing earbuds and listening to Depeche Mode on my iPad, mentally replaying recent events starting with Labor Day, and caught up in a whirlpool of hyperanalysis. I wanted David and Wylie to have some kind of relationship, but what, if anything, would I have to give up in order for that to happen? And if I didn't have to give up anything, then why did I feel like I did, and why was it so scary? I liked Wylie; couldn't I be some kind of friend to her, at the very least? Why did I sometimes act as if I were jealous of her, and would I have felt the same way had Sam discovered he had a daughter? And dammit, I hated when I missed Sam, because I feared it meant I didn't really love David after all, and when I realized how much I did love David then I feared it meant it was OK that Sam wasn't here. . . .

Ugh, make it stop!

There had to be an escape hatch from where we could all emerge unscathed.

Yet all the while I could sense an incessant knocking at a virtual door. And I knew what it was. Or rather, *who.*

Normally I didn't read on the ferry because it made me nauseous; but my curiosity refused to ignore Andrew's e-mail any longer.

Hey Andi,

Remember Pop's coffeehouse? The one we used to always joke about buying? Well, it's up for grabs. Turns out Brent never paid his taxes on the place. The Feds came in and repo'ed everything, right down to the beans. I was there when it happened. Two US marshals stormed in and ushered everyone out as two other guys started hauling the chairs right out from under our asses. Surreal. In all my life I never would've pegged Brent as anything so shady. He's so clean his shoes squeak when he walks. Or so I thought.

Anyway, we're all like sheep without a pasture now. I've been going to Corky's Café but it's just not the same. Too much Pearl Jam in there. And the muffins taste like they've been there since last fall. And Starbucks is too . . . well, Starbucks. Brent didn't own the building, so the space is available for lease.

What do you think—should I quit teaching and go into business? Given that I've played in just about every coffee shop in town, I know the lay of the land, right? How 'bout it—wanna go silent partner with me? (Kidding. Sort of.)

Anyway, hope you're doing well. I'd love to read your latest manuscript when you're ready for peer review.

Andrew

P.S. I think Brent is halfway to Vegas by
now.

I found myself enjoying his informality. It was something familiar, once shared between us when all was well. Like two people who were friends. Something about it felt uncomplicated. (Although "sort of" kidding? *Sort of?* What the hell did that mean?) But even I knew that ease was nothing more than a wolf in sheep's clothing. And a hungry wolf, at that. The *familiarity*—that's what attracted me. I always sucked when it came to facing the unknown.

I was about to draft a response to him when a chat box popped up in the lower right corner of my screen.

Andrew: Hi Andi.

The alert startled me, especially when it took me a few seconds to realize it was him.

I panicked. If I chose to respond, the second I hit Enter I'd be jettisoning myself into an even bigger minefield, and wouldn't be able to turn around. E-mailing was one thing. It offered me more control to choose words carefully, time between sending and receiving, and physical as well as emotional distance. Chatting, however, was spontaneous, immediate, uncensored.

The warning sirens were so loud in my head it was hard to believe no one else on the ferry could hear them. The war between my angels and demons commenced:

Don't do it! Not when you're feeling rejected by David and missing Sam.

But this is a guy who wants to talk to me. It isn't face-to-face communication. It's not like you can hear a voice. Besides, being on the water, between New England and Long Island, felt like neutral territory. *He's being friendly. That's all. And you could use a friend right now.*

Don't do it! You've got plenty of other friends.

Me: Hi, yourself.

Bloody hell.

Andrew: Hope you don't mind. I saw you were online and decided to say hello.
Me: Took me by surprise.
Andrew: Google owns us now.

I debated on whether to type an "lol" (I hadn't actually laughed) or a smiley emoticon (I had smiled, but the face seemed too friendly), but Andrew didn't wait for either.

Andrew: How are you?

You don't wanna know. Rather, you're not the one I should be telling.

Me: Fighting off seasickness.
Andrew: Where are you?
Me: On the Cross Sound Ferry to Orient Point. Going to see my mom.
Andrew: Good day for it.
Me: A little nippy outside. So I read your e-mail. To quote Shakespeare, that's fucked up.
Andrew: LOL. Yeah, I thought you'd get a

kick out of it.

Me: You weren't serious about going into business, were you?

Andrew: I was half-serious, like considering the possibility yet knowing all along that it was ludicrous.

Me: I hear it's real hard work. Not at all glamorous like TV and fiction portray it to be.

Andrew: You're probably right.

I couldn't think of anything else to type and stared at the screen, waiting for him to fill the void, which he did.

Andrew: Is your fiancé with you?

My stomach flipped, and I knew it wasn't due to the rocking of the boat.

I could lie to him. He wouldn't know. It would likely get me off the hook, as my guilt about prolonging this chat—and enjoying it—intensified with every passing second. Was I trying to punish David? Somehow level the playing field by having someone from my past coming into my life as well? Or maybe it was curiosity on my part. I had never really resolved things with Andrew, despite having forgiven him. In hindsight my forgiveness had seemed more like an obligatory gesture—a might-as-well resignation. But I'd been thinking that I owed Andrew something too. If not an apology, then an explanation. And he'd certainly been contrite.

Me: Just me. But I have to get going soon.

Andrew: Time to step out on the deck?

He remembered. There always came a point when I had to leave the cabin and spend the rest of the ninety-minute ride outside—didn't matter how snowy, windy, or rainy it was. During the winter months I brought an old quilt and wrapped myself in it, adding to the layers of thermal, wool and faux fur. The trip was too short for Dramamine, especially considering I had to drive before and after the boat ride. Sitting on the deck was the only remedy to my queasiness.

Me: You win the gold star. Plus I think my luck with this wireless hotspot is about run out.
Andrew: I'll let you go, then. Nice to chat with you. Talk to you soon.

Leave it to him to say that. Last thing I needed was to make this a regular habit. And yet, it took all my willpower not to type "I can hold out and chat for a little while longer." Because I wanted to. And I hated that I wanted to.

Me: Good-bye.

The sun shone brightly; the sky was blue and cloudless, the water calm. I sat on one of the benches outside the cabin—the less windy side (I checked)—and tightly wrapped the quilt around me, hugging my iPad in its case.

The reel of the last twenty-four hours replayed yet again as I stared at the landscape in the distance—a passing boat, a lighthouse, a stray seagull—and once more attempted to sort out my feelings like puzzle pieces. Wylie's question about whether I would've resumed a relationship with David, even solely as a friendship, haunted me. I couldn't see myself doing it. Not only because I knew Sam would never stand for it (and there's no way I would've kept it from him—or so I believed), but also because it would've been too big a box to open. It had been a struggle for David and me to navigate our way through and to each other after Sam's death. Too many feelings to sort through back then. Too much to renegotiate.

But here I was, attempting to go down this road with Andrew. Worse still, keeping it from David. I of all people knew what it was like when your fiancé kept a close friend of the opposite sex from you. Especially when that friend turned out to be more than a friend. That's how Andrew and Tanya had begun. Granted, Andrew and I weren't currently sleeping together—hell, we hadn't even yet *seen* each other. But we weren't just friends. We had been more. And I knew how I'd feel if the shoe were on the other foot, if David was suddenly in touch with an ex. In fact, he *was* in touch with an ex. More than an ex. *The mother of his child.* And she was going to be in his life from now on.

I had to stop this. Now. No more e-mails, no more chats. Andrew apologized. I forgave him. That was enough.

As the ferry sailed closer to Orient Point, I wondered what awaited me on the other side of the Sound. And I worried, for I somehow already knew I was going to return to find things had completely changed.

chapter twenty

I pulled into the gravel driveway at my mother's house around one o'clock. The lawn had been recently cared for, its grassy scent still lingering in the air, mixed with a woody, smoky scent so familiar to northeastern autumns. The leaves had been raked or blown to the curbs and streets, but so many strays found their way back to the lawn and driveway and crackled under my feet as I walked—a comforting sound, one I looked forward to. As a child I would look for the crispest, driest leaves that would make the best crunch when I stepped on them. When I had shared this detail with Sam, it became a game when we went for walks in the park.

Just as I'd flipped my keys around to the one that opened my mother's door, she beat me to it me by opening it herself.

"Were you waiting by the window for me?" I asked, stepping across the threshold, dragging an overnight suitcase and a shoulder bag with me. "Hi, Mom."

"You hungry?" she asked.

"Starving."

"Your brothers are picking up the pizza as we speak."

My mouth started watering at the very mention of pizza. It was one of the few things I still missed about living on Long Island. That, and the bagels.

I headed for the guest room with my bags, but Mom stopped me. "You're not in there, Andi."

"What do you mean?" I asked.

"Tony's staying in that room."

"Why is Tony staying over?" The East End was a good fifty miles from where Tony lived (it's called *Long* Island for a reason), but he never stayed the night unless the weather was bad or he had too much to drink, and both of those were once-in-a-blue-moon occurrences.

"I asked him to. Joey's staying over as well."

Mom had a three-bedroom house—modest by East End standards. She had impeccable taste and sense of design, and liked to keep things simple and in order. Manageable. She wasn't the type to throw dinner parties or have extended houseguests. But in the last few years we'd all been making more of an effort to do things as a family.

"So where am I staying?" I asked.

"You'll take the office with the futon. Joey offered to sleep on the sofa bed in the den."

"That's nice of him."

About fifteen minutes after I settled in, the front door swung open and my brothers entered, both in loud midsentence, until they saw me. I rushed to them, and each took a turn handing off the two stacked pizza boxes to each other and enveloping me in a bear hug while our mother looked on. As Tony released me, I caught her observing the three of us, a softened, sad smile on her face that I'd never seen before, like she was trying to freeze and preserve the moment, cling to it with white knuckles.

"How's life in *Baaaston*?" asked Tony, doing a horrid imitation of a New England accent. You'd think we hadn't seen each other in months rather than weeks.

"Chilly," I responded.

"Yanks are kickin' ass in the playoffs," said Joey.

"Sucks to be without Mariano though," I said.

"How's David?" asked Tony. "And what's up with that whole paternity thing?"

I shot my mother a displeased look. I hadn't mentioned anything about the situation with Wylie to my brothers—I'm not sure why, or what I was waiting for—but my mother had apparently taken the liberty to bring them up to speed.

I spoke as if the matter was as common as a new job or promotion. "He's got a daughter."

"No shit!" said Joey. "For real? DNA match and everything?"

"Wait till you see her," I said. "She totally has David's eyes. It's hard not to keep staring at her. For David too, I think."

"What's her name?" asked Joey.

"Wylie."

"Wylie?" said Tony, as if to imply, *What the hell kind of name is Wylie?*

"Yeah, Wylie. I like it," I replied, feeling inexplicably defensive. "So stop mocking."

"Who's mocking? I just asked—"

"Yeah, yeah," I interrupted.

"Enough," said my mother. "Boys, get the pizza into the kitchen." Forty and fifty-something, and she still called them "boys." "Andi, set the table."

"Can't I do dishes instead?" I whined.

"Fine. Joey, set the table."

"First I give her the futon, now I gotta do her chores too?" he complained.

"For God's sake, what is this—nineteen eighty-two? You're all acting like a bunch of children." I detected a hint of delight in her admonishment.

"I got Sammies," announced Tony, holding up a six-pack of Sam Adams. "Anyone want one?" Both Mom and I looked at him as if he were nuts. He knew I didn't drink, and our mother had always believed drinking beer wasn't "ladylike." "Hey, I'm just being polite." He took a bottle for himself and one for Joey, and hunted for an opener. It struck me at that moment how warm the house felt with all of us there together.

The conversation consisted of my filling everyone in on the situation with Wylie and fielding the many questions they had. There was nothing I could say beyond, "I don't know what's going to happen. He wants a relationship with her, and he's entitled to one. They both are."

"What's she like?" they asked.

"Your typical teenager, I guess. She's inquisitive, a little ballsy. . . ."

"Please," said Mom. "Pick another word."

I tried. "Feisty?" No, that wasn't it. "She speaks her mind, that's for sure. Anyway," I continued, "we're going through the awkward getting-to-know-you phase."

"Trust me, it takes a while. Tell David to be patient," said Joey. For the last six months he'd been in a serious relationship with a woman who had a nine-year-old daughter. So serious, in fact, that he was considering long-term scenarios, including the possibility of marriage, and he'd even mentioned the possibility of legally adopting the girl. Suddenly I felt ashamed for not being more supportive, not taking more of an interest and giving him a shoulder to lean on. David was right; I was more self-absorbed than I cared to admit.

"I had no idea," was all I could say, the pizza seemingly caught in my throat. He seemed to understand what I meant.

For dessert my mother presented a chocolate bundt cake drizzled with caramel glaze—a favorite of ours from when we were kids. Usually we got it for our birthdays, and while we all fawned over and joked about what we'd done to deserve it, my brothers and I exchanged furtive glances with one another, more worried than ever. After we cleaned every last crumb from our plates with our fingers, I cleared the dishes.

Mom looked at Joey and Tony. "You didn't bring your guitars by any chance, did you?"

They shook their heads. "No." There was a time when my brothers didn't go anywhere without their guitars. It would've been analogous to an asthmatic leaving the house without an inhaler.

She looked disappointed. "My fault for not thinking to ask you."

"We should leave one here in the house," suggested Tony. I was expecting her to refuse the offer, but she shocked me by suggesting he do just that from now on.

The four of us sat at the dining table; a pregnant pause had taken over, and we all knew it was time for my mother to speak. I almost waited for the clichéd tap on the glass with a utensil to signal attention.

"Well, I might as well get into it now," said Mom. "Last month I found a lump in my breast. The doctors biopsied it and turns out it's malignant. But that's not all. It's spread elsewhere."

I remember watching foreign films with Julian the Spanish teacher at NU. My Spanish was so rusty, and it took me so long to mentally translate that by the time I figured out what was said ten minutes ago, I missed the next ten minutes. The same thing was happening in the present moment as all functioning in my brain slowed to a halt in order to process those four sentences, starting with the key words: lump . . . biopsy . . . malignant . . . I was just processing *spread* when Joey's brain beat me to it. Sort of.

"What do you mean, *spread*?"

"It's cancer," she said matter-of-factly. "It spreads."

This can't be happening, this can't be happening, this can't be happening. . . .

"Why are you just getting around to telling us this?" said Tony. My mother's look communicated that she neither appreciated his question nor his tone, but she said nothing.

"Mom," I said, my voice cracking. "Are you OK?" I could hear myself say the words, like a little girl unable to fully comprehend the complexity or the severity of the situation. "I mean," I added, "are you in physical pain right now?"

"I'm tired," she complained.

"How—how long?" Joey stammered.

"What do you mean, 'how long'?" Tony shot at him. "Just because it's cancer doesn't mean it's automatically a death sentence."

"Hard to tell. Could be a year. Could be more or less. I start chemotherapy on Wednesday."

The word *chemotherapy* stabbed me like a needle, and I winced and cried out, covering my mouth with my hand. "Oh, God." I could barely process the rest of what she said before it.

"Wednesday!" Tony blurted. "You found out you have cancer *last month* and you *start* chemo on *Wednesday*? What the hell were you waiting for, an engraved invitation?" And with that, he stood up and headed for the front door. "I need some air."

"Tony," said Joey, "don't drive like this, man."

"I'm going for a walk," he said. "Don't come after me."

We all seemed to need a break at that moment. Joey got up and paced from room to room, while Mom went in the kitchen to run the dishwasher. But I remained frozen in place, invisibly tethered to the chair as her words pulled the knots tighter with every echo in my ears: *It's cancer. It spreads.*

Mom went from the kitchen to the living room. Joey went to look for Tony, and I finally moved to the wing-tipped chair opposite the sofa. "Mom, did you know about this when we met for lunch at Danford's that day?"

"I'd found the lump by then, yes."

"Why didn't you tell me? I'm not mad, I just—"

"What good would it have done? You had your own problem to deal with."

"*What good would it have done?* I could've *supported* you, for one thing! I could've dropped what I was doing and been there with you when you got the results of your biopsy. I could've—"

She interrupted me again. "You have a life of your own, Andi. You have a job and a relationship and a house to take care of, and now you've got this Wylie situation."

"You make it sound like there's no room for you."

"There *is* no room for me. There's not supposed to be."

"You really think that?"

"That's the way it's always been, Andi. You've fit me into the margins of your life. And that's fine. I can live with that. It's not like we ever subscribed to those mother-daughter luncheons and fashion shows and whatnots. My mother did the same thing with me."

Forty years of our frosty relationship played before my eyes, and all of it meaningless. And she was right: I'd blamed my mother for the way my life had turned out before I met David, or Sam. And after Sam's death, even though I'd worked so hard to make my relationship with her better, I still attached an asterisk to it. At that moment I regretted every minute of it—regretted not trying harder, not seeing that she'd passed down the sins of her own mother, who, when she died (also of cancer, I'd forgotten), probably hadn't been much older than my mother was now. I had been so young when she died. Too young. I was too young to understand cancer back then. Too young to understand death, to understand loss. Loss was something you stored away in a container and never re-opened, like nuclear waste. But you shut away a piece of your-self too. That was the way Mom handled it, and taught us all to do the same. It was why Joey never talked about his failed mar-riage, why both of my brothers performed themselves weary in nightclubs across the country for so many years until they were hollow. And it wasn't until my husband was killed that the loss had leaked before it could be contained—contaminat-ing everything it touched—and after all this time, no matter how much I'd cleaned and cleared it away, every now and then I still found a spot of it somewhere, hidden in a crack or crevice.

The facial muscles I'd been clenching to keep from crying gave out, and the first tears rolled down my cheeks. It wasn't my mother's diagnosis I was mourning as much as all that wasted time, all that stupidity and self absorption.

"That was beyond wrong, Mom." I was admonishing the both of us, and for the first time, I think she understood me without my needing to clarify or her getting defensive.

"I suppose so," was all she said.

About a half-hour later Joey returned, alone.

"Where's Tony?" asked Mom.

"He'll be back soon," was all he said. He sat at the other end of the sofa and seemed to be trying to speak. Maybe he was trying to think of what to say. Or maybe he was just as angry and frightened and confused as Tony and I were.

The three of us sat in dead silence. Even the usual squeaks and hums of the house had gone quiet. But that was on the outside. Inside each of us rattled screams, mobs, glass shattering into millions of shards.

It was about four o'clock and Tony was still MIA, and I was getting worried. Mom checked her watch.

"What can we do for you now?" Joey finally asked. I was so grateful he chose the word *we*; being the oldest, he knew to speak for us. And as if on cue, the front door opened and Tony strode in, seemingly collected. His eyes looked red and glassy, his face windburned.

Mom and I each exhaled a sigh of relief.

"I'm sorry for running out like that." He shook off a shiver as he spoke.

"It's OK," said Joey. "I just asked Mom what we can do for her." He sounded so diplomatic. All I managed was a sniffle that broke into a sob. Tony grabbed a tissue from the box on the end table and handed it to me without taking his gaze off our mother.

"Well, for starters, I'm going to need someone to drive me to and from my chemotherapy appointments," said Mom.

"Joey and I will switch off," said Tony.

"What about me?" I asked.

"What, you're gonna come down from Massachusetts every week?" he said.

"Why not?"

"It's a helluva commute, for one thing."

"It's not like I'm flying out of Guam or something."

"The ferry expenses alone are going to bankrupt you," said Joey.

"Money is not an obstacle," I insisted. I had never let on to my family about how well off David and I were. One more topic we avoided, especially since my brothers struggled financially as working musicians, and I felt guilty. I had once offered to help Tony buy a new car when his transmission went out. He flat-out refused, and I never brought it up again.

"We'll work something out with you, Andi," said Mom. "It doesn't have to be every week. I'm also getting my finances in order, appointing one of you as executor of my will—I've already written the will—and I also have another request. It's for you, Andi."

I sat up. "What is it?"

"Well, this is a lot to ask, but . . ." She paused as if to work up the nerve. "I want you and David to get married, before . . ." She trailed off.

I sucked in a breath and reflexively edged out my hand, palm down, the engagement ring catching the light and glistening. She didn't need to finish.

"Obviously that's something you need to talk about with him, but I hope you'll consider it."

"Of course," I said softly, as teardrops beaded down my face, one by one.

"That's enough for today," she said sternly. "We'll discuss more tomorrow." It occurred to me that normally I'd dismiss her tone as being bossy and shutting down as she always did, but in the blink of an eye everything had changed and it was as if we finally spoke the same language. She was drained—physically and emotionally. That's what she'd meant earlier when she said *I'm tired.* And not just from tonight, and the frenzy of the diagnosis, the prognosis, the overwhelming preparation and facing the unknown. She was tired from shutting so much of herself away all these years.

All four of us stood up, and without thinking, I made a beeline for my mother's arms and attached myself to her. She embraced me in a way she'd never done before, but released me quickly. Joey and Tony took turns afterward, and she did the same. But when she let go of Tony, I saw something I'd never seen on her before.

Tears.

chapter twenty-one

I awoke without an alarm clock the next morning. Rays of sunlight shone through the window, happily greeting me, oblivious to the heaviness inside. As if the day were a perky blonde telling us to buck up! and smiling sweetly. It didn't feel like a Monday, however Mondays were supposed to feel.

I had gone to bed without calling David—it had been too late, I'd rationalized, although that never stopped us before; the last time he traveled overseas without me, we defied the time difference and Skyped at all hours just to check in with each other. Since leaving him and Wylie yesterday morning (a year ago, seemingly), I'd done nothing more than fire off a text shortly after settling in to let him know I'd arrived safely. When I got out of the shower and towel-dried my hair, I checked my phone for incoming messages. Nothing. My chest tightened. Never before had I simultaneously ached to hear the sound of assurance in his voice or feel the protection of his arms and bubbled with resentment for his not calling to check in, not exhibiting the slightest bit of worry or concern, too preoccupied with his daughter and ticked off at me to care.

Judging by the circles under Joey and Tony's eyes when they emerged, they hadn't fared much better than I in terms of sleep. We all followed the delicious scents of breakfast into the sunroom (aptly named), where Mom had set out trays of bagels and lox, cream cheese, scrambled eggs and bacon, and a pot of coffee with a miniature carafe of cream next to delicate stacks of china plates and teacups and saucers and silverware and cloth napkins. Sunlight permeated the entire space, decorated in various shades of buttery yellows and lime greens and creamy whites, and I almost believed just sitting in here could melt away any ailment, as if the sunbeams could go straight through your skin and neutralize malignant cells, healing all the way to your soul. God, I was desperate to believe it.

Our moods couldn't help but be lifted, enough to make a few jokes, although we were all aware of the cancer in the room, plopping itself down and helping itself to our food and company like an uninvited, obnoxious guest.

"So what would you all like to do today?" Mom asked, almost sounding cheery. "I was thinking we could all take a ride into town. Or drive farther out to Montauk and spend the day at Gossman's Dock. Remember when Dad and I used to take you there as children? It's perfect now that we're in the off-season months. We'll practically have the entire place to ourselves."

"Are you feeling up to it?" I asked.

Her expression soured. "Now, listen. I don't want any of you pussyfooting around me, understand? If I wasn't feeling up to it, I wouldn't have suggested it. For God's sake, don't treat me like I've got one foot in the ground already."

Of course I couldn't help but feel once again as if I'd just been scolded, as if nothing I said or did was right. Tony, however, stifled a giggle. We all turned our attention to him.

"What," I said, annoyed.

"*Pussy*footing?" He pealed into laughter.

"What are you, twelve?" I said, but my own voice broke into a laugh, and it quickly spread to Joey.

Mom shook her head in exasperation. "You're all a bunch of degenerates." That only made us laugh even harder, and we dug into the feast before us. I couldn't remember a bagel ever tasting so good.

The four of us decided to forgo Montauk and stay local. We drove into town and walked along Main Street, perusing its boutiques and antique shops and cafés—a more upscale and affluent, less bohemian version of Amherst. Joey, Tony, and I played Punchbuggy while Mom seemingly stopped to say hello to everyone in town. For someone who never liked to host a dinner party, she sure was well-connected.

We hadn't spent a day like this since our trip to Rome.

I had reserved the latest ferry back to New London, and considered postponing my return for another day, but I knew my mother would see it as "pussyfooting" (I couldn't think of the word without conjuring Tony's mischievous smile) and scold me once again. A part of me couldn't help but wonder if the real reason I wanted to postpone going home was because I didn't want to face David and *his* new reality. Still, neither of us had called the other. As I took my bags out to the car, my brothers followed me out, with Mom lingering behind.

"So I'll be back here in two weeks for Mom's chemo," I reminded them.

"You sure this is going to be OK with your job? And what about David?" said Tony.

"Don't worry about it," I said. Then I pulled both of them to me for a group hug, and not just to warm me because the temperature had dipped in the last two hours. "I can't imagine going through this without you," I said, fighting to keep my composure, my voice muffled in their coats. "Please don't keep me out of this," I said. "I'll even move back here if I have to."

Joey let go abruptly and looked at me. "Seriously?"

"It's too soon to talk like that," said Tony. "Chill out on the ferry—literally—and go home and talk to David."

With that they headed back into the house. Mom was next. I looked at her arms crossed to shield herself from the cold. I never saw her look so fragile before. A wave of panic hit me that I might never see her like this again—hair intact, makeup applied, clothes stylishly put together. What image would stand in her place next time?

I held up my hand and made a V with my fingers. "Two weeks," I said, and smiled bravely.

"Two weeks," she echoed.

"If you need anything—*anything*—even just to talk, call me, OK?"

"OK."

The choice to hug Mom at that moment was a no-brainer, but I knew what she was thinking—she didn't want to be treated any differently. Our hugs in the past had always been obligatory. But hadn't *that* been the false gesture rather than the hug I *wanted* to give her now? The one she finally seemed willing to accept, and even reciprocate? Wasn't now the time for us to treat each other differently, like the mother and daughter we should've been? So cancer was the catalyst for that change. So we shouldn't have waited for it to come to this. Nevertheless, it had.

"Thank you for coming, Andrea." She said the words formally, as if she were thanking a business associate for meeting with her, but I could see what was behind them. "Today was a good day."

"Yes, it was. Thank you for telling all of us together, Mom. I really appreciate you doing that."

She hugged me, and it didn't feel like all the others. No, this was an *embrace*. Willing. Accepting. The little girl in me who had longed for her mother to hug her like that all these years wanted to cling.

"Thank you, Mommy," I heard myself say in a sob. It was the little girl's voice.

"I'll see you soon, dear," she said. Never in her life had she ever used a term like that for me. In fact, I'd never heard her call anyone "dear" except my father.

I sat on the deck for the entire duration of the ferry ride back to New London; that "dear" warmed me the whole time. I felt as if Sam and my father were sitting on each side of me. And yet, I also felt horribly alone.

chapter twenty-two

The house was dark except for the light in the stairwell and the bedroom. David was sitting on the bed, back against the headboard, reading. He looked up when I entered the room, luggage in hand, and he peered over his reading glasses at me.

"Dev," I said. And with that, the dam broke; I dropped the bags at my feet and erupted in tears. The strength to move had drained from me.

David hopped off the bed and rushed to console me. "What is it?"

I threw my arms around him, shoving aside the resentment I'd been harboring for the last twenty-four hours. "She has cancer," I cried. "My mother is going to die of cancer."

He sucked in a breath, followed by a remorseful groan. "Oh, Andi. Oh, *cara*, I am so sorry," he said as he stroked my hair and kissed my head. "I am so, so sorry." He pulled me even tighter to him. He was perhaps the only person who understood how I felt. The nature of David's relationship with his father had been similar to mine with my mother—he could do no right in his father's eyes; his father berated and even bullied him, disapproved of his interests and lifestyle. Only when his father got cancer did they make amends with each other—not that everything was suddenly all sewn up, but they'd finally reached a mutual understanding. They'd finally been able to *see* each other. And they'd come to realize that despite everything, they loved each other.

He was still Devin back then. Still the escort. In fact, the first time we ever slept together was the night of his father's funeral, when he'd been at his most vulnerable state, and I held him and rocked him and comforted him and we made love. It was the first time I'd made love, with him or anyone else. I'd had a lot of firsts with Devin.

"I'm sorry," he said yet again, softly, gently, and I knew it was for more than just my news. He'd been doing the same as I—sulking, being mad at me for not being there to support him, not seeing things his way. And maybe he was thinking of his own father at that moment. Thinking about the wasted years, feeling the pain of wanting so desperately to be loved and accepted by someone, and then losing him when he finally had been.

I don't know how long we stood in the middle of the room, me weeping and him holding me. I hadn't cried like that in a long time. Just as my knees were about to give out, David moved me to the bed and sat me down. He dabbed the tears from my face with his thumb. I gazed at his eyes—his magical, sienna eyes—and felt myself jumping into them, desperate to get lost inside. I could see every part of his wounded self: the lonely child, forgotten son, brokenhearted spirit. They were greeted by my own inner wounds. Next thing I knew I was kissing him, and we were pulling each other's clothes off and panting heavily, moving in rhythm to our breathing, my legs coiled around him, his arms cradling me, our moist lips moving across our skin, and our moaning, calling out, releasing, giving in, giving over, and collapsing into each other's arms.

"I love you," I whispered in the dark, succumbing to the heaviness of my eyelids, the exhaustion of my muscles.

"I love you too," he whispered back.

chapter twenty-three

"So tell me all about your day with Wylie," I said the following morning as I loaded up the blender with assorted fruit for a smoothie. We'd lingered in bed and then taken a shower together, and I finally felt ready to face reality again, determined to be supportive of David and put our fight behind us.

"You sure you want to talk about this?" he asked. "There's a lot to discuss regarding your mother."

"We'll get to it," I assured him. "First, Wylie. Did you have a good time? Did she?"

"It was slow going at first, but I think we finally got into a groove. She's a really good kid, Andi. She's spunky, smart, inquisitive. Reminds me of you in some ways."

I grinned in gratitude. "What else?"

"She's like me in the museum. You know, totally loses track of time, enters a painting and doesn't wanna come out. . . ."

I chuckled. "Yeah, I know."

"You'd think being a teenager she'd be bored or impatient, but not a bit. I'm turning her on to the Impressionists."

I couldn't help but feel a twinge of jealousy. Going to museums had always been something David and I did with each other, as far back as when he was an escort and we were spending time together despite our arrangement specifying that we weren't supposed to outside of our tutorials. And although I had developed an aesthetic appreciation, both for the art and David's passion for it, I'd never gotten to his level. That he could now fully share this with Wylie, a natural, jabbed at me.

David rambled on. "The drive back to Hartford was especially great. We talked about so much—growing up, school, friends . . . all the things I missed. The time just flew. She's thinking about becoming an art major," he said. "You have no idea what that means to me."

"I do, actually."

His face softened into a smile as he looked at me lovingly. "Yeah, you do. You're the only one who does. Anyway, we're going to try to work out a schedule where we can meet on weekends, alternate between who visits whom, and we'll Skype a couple of days a week too."

"That's good," I said, "but we'll need to coordinate *our* schedules too. I'll be driving to Long Island more frequently in the coming weeks. Joey, Tony, and I are going to take turns taking Mom to chemotherapy."

"What about your classes?"

"I'm meeting with Jeff today to discuss it. Mom's chemo is on Wednesdays, which, selfishly speaking, couldn't suck more regarding my Monday–Wednesday–Friday teaching schedule. I'll have to drive down on Tuesday, stay the Wednesday, then drive back up on Thursday and resume class on Friday. It'll be a roller coaster. To say nothing of the fact that if she has an adverse reaction, I can't leave her."

"Semester's almost half over. Maybe you can get someone to cover for you for the remainder and then take next semester off."

I cringed as my mind flashed to memories of when Sam died and I had to take emergency leaves of absence, first in the fall just after the accident, and again in the spring after I went back too soon and had a colossal meltdown in front of my students. The very thought sent shivers down my spine, and I shuddered.

"We'll see," I said. "I'll talk to Jeff and see what he thinks." As chair of the English Department at NU, my good friend Jeff Baxter had been super-supportive when Sam died. I knew he wouldn't want a repeat of my behavior from back then—I sure as hell didn't—but I also knew he'd want what was best not only for my students but for me.

"Don't forget about your promise to tutor Wylie," he reminded me. He sounded like a parent rather than a lover.

"Of course I haven't forgotten," I said.

As David and I were both getting ready to leave for our respective appointments, I said, "You know, we still haven't set up a schedule for our lessons. Remember, painting in exchange for pizzas?"

He looked at me apologetically. "Kinda got sidetracked, huh."

"Yeah."

"Still wanna do it?" he asked.

"I do."

He put his phone in his pocket and grabbed his keys. "OK. Tonight we'll sit down and plan everything out—Wylie, Genevieve, painting, and pizza."

"Oh, and there's one other thing," I said, remembering my mother's special request. "I'll bring it up later."

We walked to our cars; David opened my door for me and gave me a kiss good-bye before letting me slide inside.

"Hey, Dev, do you ever miss your escort days?"

The question came out of the blue, and surprised me just as much as it did him.

"I don't know," he said, scratching his head. "Not really. Maybe once in a blue moon. I can't explain it. Why?"

"I don't know. I guess I was just wondering if there was anything you miss about it. Maybe I was thinking of us—you know, the way we were back then."

"Do *you* miss it?" he asked.

I pondered the question. "I really don't know."

He kissed me again. "See you later?"

I nodded and kissed him back. "I'll likely be at Perch later if you're free," I said. "I haven't looked at my manuscript in ages." And with that I stepped into my car and strapped myself in. David closed the door for me and followed me out of the driveway and down the street in his own car.

⚬⟆⟆⟆⟆⚬

Jeff and I sat in the campus dining hall and caught up on small talk and department gossip before I eased into my news. But before I could, he beat me to the punch.

"So is that an engagement ring on your finger?" he asked.

"Oh," I said, reflexively holding up my hand. "It is, yeah."

He grinned. "Congratulations. Sorry, did I just steal your thunder? Is that what we're here for?"

"I wish it were, but no. There's something else. Work-related."

"What's up, kid?"

I took in a breath and spilled it out: "I got some bad news this weekend. My mother has cancer."

Saying it out loud only seemed to get harder.

"Shit, Andi. I'm so sorry."

I swallowed the impulse to start blubbering. "Thanks, Jeff. It came as a shock. Thing is, I want to help take care of her. Take her to chemo, and whatnot. Her appointments are on Wednesdays, which means—"

"Yeah, you've got a Monday–Wednesday–Friday rotation. Are you asking to be let off for the remainder of the academic year?"

"No, I was thinking more along the lines of going home once a month and just getting you or someone else to cover the Wednesdays."

"Won't you need the whole week off?"

"I don't see why, unless there are complications. In that case my brothers will be there."

"Andi . . ." Jeff started, and his skepticism completed his sentence for him.

"I know what you're going to say, Jeff, and this is nothing like what happened with Sam."

"Maybe not, but you're not going down there to babysit once a month. Do you have any idea what's ahead of you? I'm not just talking about the physical toll, but the emotional one. Cancer sucks the life force out of everyone who comes in contact with it."

"I know. David's father passed away about ten years ago." And Jeff's uncle, one he was close to, had died of cancer a couple of years ago, I remembered.

"And he's OK with what you're attempting to do?"

"He hasn't tried to talk me out of it."

"Is he at least going to be there with you when you go?"

I hadn't thought of this, and it bothered me that I hadn't. Why hadn't I even asked him? Or was it something that would come up when we talked later tonight?

147

"We haven't discussed it yet," I said. "There's a lot going on with David right now." I leaned in. "We haven't told anyone outside of our own families and a few close friends, but David has a teenage daughter."

Jeff had just taken a swig of soda as I spoke and coughed in response. "*What?*"

"We found out Labor Day weekend, day after the barbecue."

"Holy shit, kid. Talk about a full plate. . . . Is it . . . is he sure she's . . ."

"DNA test was positive. And if you saw her, Jeff, you'd know."

"Spittin' image?"

I nodded. "Especially the eyes."

He slowly shook his head in disbelief.

I pressed on. "So he's obviously trying to get to know her without totally railroading her parents, who've been less than enthused about all this."

"The girl's mother wasn't the one who told him? How'd he find out, then?"

"Wylie found him. His daughter. The Internet is a scary, scary place."

"Holy shit," he said again. I understood the lack of originality. The situation rendered me speechless sometimes too. It took us both a moment to figure out what to say next.

"So, about the schedule . . . ," I started.

"Look, Andi. You know I'd rob a bank for you if you asked me to. Getting coverage for you is no problem. I'm going to have to take it out of your pay, though. You know, to pay the sub a stipend."

"No problem," I said.

"But I worry about whether you really know what you're getting into. You misjudged things last time." He put a hand up to block me from speaking. "I know it's different; you're in a better place emotionally than you were back then, but it's not easier. And I'm going to take you off the schedule completely for next semester."

I didn't protest. I had foolishly believed I could handle my job responsibilities when Sam had been killed. But I also had twice as much responsibility at the time, and given that Sam had been a professor too, reminders of him lurked around every corner. Jeff was right—I had coping skills and a better support system in place now. For one thing, Maggie was physically present, as was Miranda. And I had David too. I wouldn't be going back to a cavernous bed night after night, a thousand needles of grief prickling me every second of the day. I'd have a chance to say a proper good-bye this time. I'd have something to come home to afterward. I'd have my husband.

And a daughter, maybe? Was it too soon to think like that? Was it right to assign myself such a role?

"I'm sorry I didn't tell you about our engagement sooner," I said. "Everything's just been so crazy."

"No sweat, kid. When's the wedding?"

I downed the rest of my water, wishing it were something stronger. "Your guess is as good as mine."

chapter twenty-four

I was oblivious to the chatter and light jazz music in Perch as I pored through my manuscript with a blue felt-tip pen, pausing only to move a strand of hair away from my face but never looking up, until I felt a shadow cast over me.

"This seat taken?"

I barely moved my head with more than a nod of permission when the tease of David's voice, accompanied by a sly smile, caught me in a double take.

He's wearing Versace.

Before I could speak, he said, "How lucky for me," and filled the chair as he extended his hand. "I'm Devin."

Then he winked.

It took me a nanosecond to realize what he doing—his wink revealed all—and I took his hand and shook it politely. "Andi Vanzant."

"So, Andi . . . you're either an editor, a teacher, or a writer," he said as he spied the manuscript. My outfit of dark jeans and flats and a burnt-orange cashmere sweater, with tortoise-shell-framed reading glasses, could've just as easily given me away.

"All three, actually," I replied, and couldn't help but enjoy the game. "But in this case, I'm an author working on my latest novel."

"What's it about?"

"Ahh, I never reveal my works in progress. Call me superstitious, but I think it impedes the creative process. After all, you don't take the cake out of the oven before it's fully baked, do you?"

"You don't tell anyone? Not even your husband?"

"What makes you think I'm married?"

David—no, *Devin*—leaned in. "Because there's no way a woman as beautiful as you is single. It's just not possible."

I laughed. "Really? *That's* the line you're going with? You can do better than that."

He laughed as well. "Guess that's what I get for trying to pick up a writer."

"And what do *you* do for a living?"

He paused to consider his response, squinting slightly. "Let's just say I'm in sales."

"Well, then, sell me something."

He raised his eyebrows, turned on by my dare, and I couldn't help but giggle. He scanned the table and set his sights on the beverage I'd barely touched.

"So what's this that you're not drinking?"

"Iced vanilla chai latte."

"Any reason why you're not drinking it?"

"Too engrossed in this," I said, patting the manuscript on my lap.

"In that case, I'm going to sell you that iced vanilla chai latte. In less than five minutes, you're going to want—no, *need*—to take a sip of that chai. You're going to crave it as if you've been thirsting for it your entire life, and it's going to be the best sip you've ever had. Your eyeballs will roll up into your head and you'll resist the urge to moan in ecstasy."

He was full-out Devin: alluring, provocative, impossibly gorgeous, electric smile, and those goddamn sienna eyes seducing me the entire time. Even the plastic cup was breaking out into a sweat. And wouldn't you know it, my mouth began to salivate.

"And how are you going to do that?" I asked.

"Hold out your hand."

I tentatively extended a hand, palm up, and he took it, practically caressed it, before lifting the cup and merging it with my palm, placing my fingers around it to ensure its hold. I wasn't watching the cup.

"Now take a sip."

"How can you be so sure it's the best chai I've ever tasted? It's been sitting here for at least twenty minutes. The odds are not in your favor, Devin."

He leaned in even closer this time, enough for me to smell his cologne mixed with pheromones, and I fought to keep my composure. Just like the first time we sat at a booth at Junior's in Brooklyn as he extolled the virtue of simple pleasures. Like vanilla chai lattes.

"Andi, I am so sure this will be the best chai you've ever tasted that I'm willing to give you a hundred dollars if you agree. No strings attached. One hundred smackers, right here, right now."

"And if it's not and I don't?"

"Then you go back to my place and have sex with me."

I laughed so loud that a couple of nearby patrons turned their heads. "Shouldn't that proposition be the other way around?"

"How do you figure that?"

"You want to get laid, don't you?"

"I wouldn't put it so callously, but OK."

"So, you just insisted that this is going to be the best damn thing I've tasted since Junior's cheesecake. If that were really the case, if that's what you're banking on, then wouldn't it make sense to make sex a condition on *that*?" Before he could answer, I added, "Which means you *know* it's not."

He looked at me coyly, saying nothing.

"I could lie to you—" I started.

"You could."

"—tell you it's the best, and you'll never know if I'm being honest."

He leaned in again. "But *you'll* know."

Damn. He had me. He knew he had me, not because of a persuasive argument or conclusive evidence, but because of his lips spread far and wide, the accent of crow's feet making him look sexier rather than older. His posture and body language, the way he penetrated my space, exuding confidence without arrogance. The current between us was so strong it could run the cappuccino machine. I felt as if everyone were voyeuristically watching us play out this charade. And I was so willing to play.

I brought the straw to my lips, refusing to divert my gaze from him for even a second, demonstratively puckered, positioning them just so, and sucked in the liquid.

Earlier I'd taken the first sip unconsciously, my attention already on the manuscript and pen already in hand. But now, fully mindful, I took in a mouthful, and although the melted ice had thinned the drink, the vanilla and cinnamon sweetness and whole milk caressed my tongue and glided down my throat.

It was good. It was damn good. Or maybe I was just so horny by then that a cup of crude oil would've tasted like a Creamsicle.

That was the magic of Devin. He could sell you anything. He could sell peace to a warmonger, sell capitalism to a communist, sell a closet to a claustrophobic.

He could sell sex to a stranger.

"Well?" he said. "What's the verdict? Am I out a hundred bucks?"

Without saying a word, I put the cup down and packed my manuscript into my briefcase. Cleared off the table and disposed of the chai. Then I picked up my coat and bag and headed for the door. He followed me out, and I caught his perplexed expression with my peripheral vision.

"Andi?" he asked.

I turned to him. "You don't look like a Devin."

He didn't respond, and I could tell he was trying to read where this was going, anticipate my next move like a chess player.

I drew in as close as I could without touching him, and tried to meet his face, hard to do given how tall he was and I wasn't wearing heels. Once upon a time this kind of ostentatious flirtation—role-playing or real—would've sent me into an abyss of anxiety, of feeling as if I were under attack and needing to protect myself. Would've meant putting all my defenses up, and shutting him down before he even had a chance to get started. Hell, he probably wouldn't have gotten as far as the chair. He would've known not to even approach me. And yet this same guy—this man for whom confidence was an instinct rather than a trait, who exuded sexuality like a superpower—had taught me to be receiving, to be unafraid and unashamed. To listen to my own instincts and let my sexuality out of its cage. To reciprocate and feel womanly as opposed to dirty. And I was eternally grateful to him for it.

How to play this?

Rising on my toes, I spoke into his ear, saying in my soft-est, most sultry voice: "That was the best vanilla chai I've ever had." I then stepped back and held out my hand, palm open. "Pay up."

He looked at me, agog, and took an extra second to re-spond, all that lust crackling between us like static electricity. If one of us touched the other at that moment, I swear we'd get a shock.

Finally, he spoke. *"You're lying."*

Checkmate.

I drew out the stare a bit longer before saying, "Where's your place?"

I honestly don't remember why we went to a nearby hotel and not the house, only that the moment we closed the door I practically ripped open his shirt the way soap opera vixens did to men in the throes of their calculated seduction, and I pulled his face to my open mouth and kissed him hard. He raised my arms over my head to remove my sweater and kept them there, preventing me from wrapping them around him as he pinned me against the wall and kissed every part of my upper body before he lifted me. I clenched my legs as he clutched my thighs, and we laughed out of pleasure and the delight of it all and kissed and panted as we moved around the room.

And that was just foreplay—the sex, God the *sex*! I don't think we'd ever had sex like that. I don't think Sam and I had ever had sex like that either. I'm not talking about positions (I mean, I doubt we'd bank any money on sex tapes, but we weren't exactly going missionary), but *intensity*. Passion. Fire. Or maybe we had and I'd forgotten; at the moment I was too busy concentrating on Devin, the guy who'd just solicited me in a coffee shop—or was he David now? It had been a long time since the lines were so blurry.

No. It was Devin. The siren of multiple orgasms that erupted from me confirmed it.

When we finally finished and lay beside each other, he turned on his side, facing me, tuckered out. "So was that really the best vanilla chai you've ever had?"

"Why Devin, you don't know? You're losing your touch," I said as I turned away from him, feigning rejection. He slid his hand under the sheets and caressed the inside of my thigh.

"Hardly," he breathed. And yet, he beckoned, "Tell me."

I climbed back on top of him. "Make me."

chapter twenty-five

I couldn't help but wonder if the impromptu appearance of Devin was a way for David and me to avoid the conversations we needed to have. Nevertheless, the days following our encounter passed without my bringing up my mother's request, and David and I returned to our routines.

Columbus Day weekend was around the corner, and David wanted Wylie to spend the weekend. "I can take her to all my galleries in Boston." He often referred to the galleries he did business with in the possessive. "You should see her work, Andi. She sent me a few photos and I tell ya, she's got talent. Send her to the right people and she'll be a star."

"David, are you sure you're not rushing things? I mean, she's fifteen. I'm sure she'd rather be at the mall with her friends this weekend."

He soured. "Way to kill my buzz."

"David, I wasn't—" I started, but he interrupted me.

"I'm still going to invite her."

He called her after dinner, and after ten minutes he handed the phone to me in the den, visibly disappointed. "She wants to talk to you."

Surprised, I took hold of it and spoke, "Hello?"

"Hi," said Wylie. "So I can't meet David this weekend because I'm going to my friend's Sweet Sixteen on Sunday. But I have a paper due next Wednesday for English and was wondering if you could help me with it. I thought maybe you could come on Saturday."

"Oh," I said, not expecting the request. "Just me? Or David too?"

"Well, I thought just you this time, and then I'd see David another time. I don't—please don't think that means I don't like him or anything."

"I didn't think that," I said, although I knew David might be thinking otherwise. "Thing is, this Saturday isn't the best day for me." I didn't need to look at the calendar to know why.

"Oh," she said, sounding just as disappointed as David looked. But something pressed on me. So this was what it felt like to let your kids down. I could never understand the guilt parents felt when they had to miss their kid's school play or recital or soccer game because of work or some other obligation. *What's the big deal?* I would think. *It's not as if there won't be another. Not as if you don't see the kid at all.* Wylie wasn't even my kid, and I felt as if I were kicking her in the shins.

However, I felt torn. If I agreed to tutor Wylie, then David would feel left out, and might even resent me. If I said no to Wylie, she might think I was rejecting her, and that could potentially affect her relationship with David; he would resent me for that too. And where did I fit into this? I hadn't yet decided how I was going to observe the day. I didn't think I wanted to be alone this year, but tutoring my husband-to-be's newly discovered teenage daughter hadn't come close to the agenda.

I caved. "Let me see what I can do. Maybe I can work it out," I said, intimating that I had specific plans to rearrange.

The lilt in her voice picked up. "That would be great. My mom wants you to come *here*, though, to our house."

I felt as if I'd dug myself into a hole, and Wylie just made it deeper. I swallowed hard. "That's fine. I'll let you know for sure tomorrow," I said.

"Thank you *so* much," she said, and with that I handed the phone back to David, who was watching me like a hawk the entire time, and he left the room to resume his conversation. Ten minutes later, he returned, and his expression made my muscles tense. I knew what was coming.

He sank onto the sofa, sitting beside me. "Wylie said she wants to see *you* this weekend. For tutoring."

"Yes," I said. "I'm sorry. Did she tell you it wasn't a reflection against you?"

"She said you're going on Saturday."

"I said *maybe*. You know what this Saturday is."

He paused for a moment, and I realized that he wasn't making the connection. I reminded him: "It's my anniversary. Both of them."

And then it registered. "I'm sorry, Andi. I forgot."

"It's OK," I said. Was it? Should I have been mad that he forgot? Or was it just one of those things about losing a loved one—the world goes on for everyone else? Neither good nor bad.

"I thought you wanted to be alone. Go away or something."

I had thought about going to visit my mother, actually.

"Do you want me to go away?" I asked. Of course, what I was really asking was if he wanted me to back off from Wylie. He knew that. And I think he realized he too was between the proverbial rock and hard place.

"Wylie obviously wants to see you. You shouldn't let her down," he said.

"Dev, I really think this is just about tutoring. She said she's not doing well in English."

David looked at me skeptically; he wasn't buying it any more than I was. "Andi. Please. If it were just about tutoring she'd get a friend or someone to help her. Not *you*."

The way he said *you* almost sounded like an insult. As if she were settling for me rather than making a special request.

"I can't imagine Janine being happy about it," I said.

"Maybe it was Janine's idea. Maybe she's checking up on you."

I sighed. "Dev, it's Sam's anniversary. And mine. Going to the Bakers'—into hostile territory—and tutoring your new-found daughter without you there is stressful under normal circumstances. And like I said before, this is all happening so fast."

As David processed this, he wore a conflicted expression. Finally, he took my hand. "It would mean a lot to me if you did it," he said.

"Really?" I asked.

"Yes."

I had to do it, I realized. David was more than my lover; he was my fiancé now. It meant I was committing to him on a higher level. And to make Wylie happy would make him happy. But his eyes gave him away. He didn't want *me* making her happy.

chapter twenty-six

Fourth anniversary of Sam's death

"Mrs. Vanzant? There's been an accident. . . ."

The words are burned into my brain—the tone, their inflection, every one of them a bullet to the heart. In the first few days following Sam's death, those words spoken by the police officer at my door resounded like a maniacal loop designed to kill me by way of insanity. And on every anniversary since, they have been the first words that wake me up, almost as if they've been programmed to do so, regardless of whether I know what day it is.

Four years. Four years since Sam went out for a bottle of sparkling cider, a meaningless detail of our anniversary dinner that he'd refused to ignore, and never came home.

Nine years since our wedding day. Nine years since I nearly skipped with glee down the aisle to greet him—he looked ridiculously handsome in his black tuxedo with white silk tie in a Windsor knot. And I, in a plain yet elegant Vera Wang gown, with my hair fixed in a French twist, sans veil. Sam was shaking so much he had nearly dropped the ring just as he was about to place it on my finger. ("Nerves?" I had whispered. "*You,*" he replied. "It's hard to stand still when I've just realized I'm going to be in love with you for the rest of my life.")

And we were in love with each other for the five years we were married. Rarely spent a day apart. Not that we were clingy or co-dependent; no, we were *friends*, best friends, the kind of friend you feel like your real self with, especially when you're *laughing* together. Sam and I were ageless when we were together. And showing him even the worst parts of me somehow made me feel safer rather than vulnerable. And I knew he felt the same with me.

This year I didn't want to dwell on the anniversary of Sam's death, but rather on the anniversary of our marriage. But somehow the two memories had fused into one: we got married, danced at the reception, and at the end of the day he got killed by a drunk driver. As if that was the way it had really happened.

I drove to Hartford to meet Wylie for our tutoring session, and spent the hour-long drive lost in the reverie of Sam Vanzant—his smiling eyes, blue as island waters; short, tapered hair; naturally athletic physique maintained by skiing and biking and the two of us playing Frisbee or catch on the quad at Edmund College, where he taught—he even occasionally was invited to a pickup basketball game with his students, and he never shied away from accepting. They especially loved when he joined them in the trash talk—only Sam could turn it into a teachable moment about rhetoric and language, and they happily listened and learned.

I also worried about David—despite his outward support, it was tearing him up that I was coming here without him, that Wylie specifically requested to see me and not him. I worried about how I would be welcomed by Janine and Peter. I still felt like an intruder, an invader, an occupier. Where would we work? It seemed rude to just waltz into their home and commandeer the kitchen or dining room table.

As I pulled up to the Bakers' house, once again I remembered the look on Peter's face when he dropped Wylie off at our home, as if his little girl had abandoned him. Or worse—she'd been stolen away. I could relate. I knew what it was like to have your heart ripped out at the hands of a stranger on your doorstep.

"Mrs. Vanzant? There's been an accident. . . ."

Maybe this was a mistake.

Wylie opened the door seconds after I knocked, and invited me in. Janine emerged, dressed in blue jeans and a close-fitting Giants hoodie. She wore the same amount of dark eyeliner and mascara as Wylie, and I tried to picture her without it. I wondered if she wore this much eye makeup when she first met David, when he was Devin. She was probably as pretty as Wylie without it, and I tried to see her as he would have. Tried to see what, specifically, attracted him. It wasn't hard.

"Hi, Mrs. Baker," I said, hoping my friendliness didn't sound forced. I extended my hand to her.

"Hello, Andi," she said. It was the first time she used my name. She shook my hand, which I interpreted as a positive sign.

"So . . . you're OK with my helping Wylie out with her English assignment?"

"Well, it's what she wants. I don't want you two leaving the house, however. You can work here," said Janine, pointing to their den.

Wylie led me into the room and emptied the contents of her backpack onto the table, located in the far corner, away from the television set. Before I could get started, she pointed to my chest. "Are those your wedding rings from your first marriage?"

Like a Pavlovian response, my hand went to the rings on the gold chain—I added them to the engagement ring for today—and clutched them, my palm over my heart. "Yes, they are."

"I don't remember seeing you wear them before."

"Today would've been our ninth wedding anniversary."

Wylie gasped. "Whoa. Seriously?"

"Yes." I went all in. "Unfortunately it's also the anniversary of his death. Four years ago," I reminded her.

She grew quiet and still.

I rapidly waved my hand in front of my face to keep from crying, and apologized. "I shouldn't have told you a thing like that. I'm sorry." In an attempt to regain my composure, I tried to divert the conversation back to business. "Where shall we start?"

She didn't respond. After a long pause, she said, "David knows, right? I mean about what today is? Your anniversary? Both of them?"

"Yes, he does."

"Is he OK? I mean . . ." she trailed off.

"He knows it's not an easy day for me, and he's very supportive. He's sad for me. But he knows I love him, if that's what you're thinking about. He's OK, Wylie. We both are. And I wanted to be here today."

I wasn't sure if I was being entirely truthful about that last part. She seemed more at ease, however. I sat up straight and started again, more professorial. "So, let's get to work."

"Here." She plopped a book in front of me: *Animal Farm*.

I picked it up and fanned through the pages, amused. "I haven't read this in ages."

"But you know it, right?"

"Pretty well, yes. It was one of the only books I liked in school. Reread it several times. That, and *The Outsiders*. God, I *loved* that one."

"We read that one already."

"Hard to believe schools are still assigning the same things we read," I said.

"I know, right? How long ago was that?"

I did the math in my head. "About thirty years." Holy crap.

Wylie seemed just as shocked as her eyeballs widened and rounded. "Seriously? Wow, you don't seem that old."

I laughed. "I'll take that as a compliment. So," I said, patting the book as if to signal the official start of our session. "What's your assignment?"

"We have to choose a theme and write about it, tying in the book. My teacher gave us a list to choose from, so I decided to go with 'the perils of conformity.' "

Wylie showed me the list and I made a disapproving face. "Ugh. These are the same kinds of themes I had to write about. You'd think they would have gotten more original over the years."

Again Wylie was happy to see me seemingly betray my profession. "They're the worst. And all they're doing is testing to make sure you read the book."

"I agree," I said. "So, did you?"

"Read the book? Yeah."

"And what did you think?"

She shrugged. "I don't know. What am I supposed to think? It was a bunch of animals who take over a farm. I mean, I get that it's symbolism and all that—we read *A Tale of Two Cities* before this, and let me tell you, that was super-boring—"

"Reread it when you get older," I interjected. "You'll have a whole new appreciation when you read it because you *want* to and not because you *have* to."

Wylie grinned. "See, that's why I wanted *you* to help me— you're so *honest* about these things. I like, totally believed you just now. Like, you suddenly made me want to read it again. And it was like torture getting me to read it the first time! Why can't teachers in school be this way?"

I've experienced the joy of getting through to students many times—nothing matched the high of a student telling you they "got" it, or seeing the look on their face that said it for them. Or, better yet, because of you they grew to *like* it, wanted to do more of it, be it writing or reading. Like getting an injection of *This is who I am*. But something about Wylie's approval was different—it swept through and sent ripples of validation to every part of me. No, not validation—something more, something I couldn't put my finger on. Almost as if a wound I never knew I had closed up and finally healed.

I couldn't help but return her grin. "Thanks. Most of them want to, believe me. They just can't."

"Why not?"

"That's a conversation for another day," I said rather than unleash my diatribe about the status of American public education. "OK, so here's what I want you to do: Write for ten minutes, nonstop, about *Animal Farm*—everything you know and don't know and think and feel and whatnot. You can write whatever you want—how much you loved it, hated it, didn't get it; you can even summarize it if you want. But you have to write for ten minutes *without stopping*."

"What if I suddenly freeze up and can't think of anything to write? That happens to me all the time."

"Then that's what you write about: *This stupid person is making me write for ten minutes about* Animal Farm *and I can't think of a single thing to say. . . .*"

Wylie laughed. "Yep, that sounds about right—except for the part about being stupid. You're totally not that."

Again I felt that wave wash over me.

"Ready? I'll even do it with you, if you want," I said, clicking my pen and opening my legal pad to a fresh page. She held her pen to the page, as if taking her mark on a racing track and waiting for the starter pistol. I made note of the time and waited for the second hand on my watch to hit twelve, then announced, "OK, start writing." It didn't even surprise me when, fifteen minutes later, I remembered to check my watch again and found Wylie locked in concentration, scribbling away, her pen not leaving the page. An image of Devin flashed before me: our first tutorial session; his freewriting about his relationship with reading and writing; my restraint from pouncing on him in a horny fit. . . . I took a sip of the bottled water I brought with me, flushed by the mere memory. It bothered me that I thought of Devin on this particular day. Sam and I had had plenty of our own writing rituals.

"Time's up," I said.

"*Already?*" said Wylie. "Geez, I feel like I just got going!"

I practically clapped my hands in triumph. "That's an excellent sign, Wylie."

"Now what do we do?"

"Now we read what we wrote."

She groaned. "But what if it's, like, really bad?"

"It's freewriting," I said. "It doesn't have to be even remotely good."

"Still, can you not read yours? I have a feeling your 'really bad' is still ten times better than my really good."

I smiled. "OK, deal." Wylie read her freewrite out loud as I closed my eyes and listened to the sound of her voice, trying to find traces of David. With my eyes closed, she could've been any fifteen-year-old girl. But once they opened and I looked at her, she was unmistakably David's daughter—the color of her hair (minus purple skunk stripe, which had faded in the last month), skin tone, even the shape of her nose, I noticed, and, of course, those piercing, electrifying, take-over-a-room eyes. I asked her to read it again and I focused more intently the second time, jotting down words and phrases, and afterward responded to what I called "the center of gravity"—specifically, what parts of the freewrite interested me, what interested her, and within the hour we found a way to write about *Animal Farm* and conformity that was more than a standard assignment, something of genuine interest to *her*. From there we sketched out more ideas and an outline. I loved the process of invention, loved how ideas appeared out of the ether, along with the words to go with it, and the excitement that came with it when you knew you were on to something good. The process wasn't always this easy; but when it worked, it was like falling in love.

By the time we finished, Wylie was giddy. "Ohmigod, I am actually psyched to write this paper! I like, wanna do it *right now!*"

Music to my ears.

"In that case, I'm going to let you do just that—and for now, just go with the momentum. The moment you lose it, stop writing. Don't worry about whether you're doing it the 'right' way or whether it's what you think your teacher wants. Just write it the way *you* want, and send it to me when you're done, OK?"

Wylie jumped out of her chair. "Thank you—thank you, thank you, thank you!" On the last thank-you, she practically bowled me over with a hug. And at that moment, I wanted to wrap my arms around her and pull her to me, cling tight, and not let go. Maybe it was the emotion of the occasion. I'd been wanting to cling to Sam all day. I could feel myself getting choked up. And just as I fully hugged her, I caught Janine at the entrance of the den, watching us, horrified by the sight. I couldn't even begin to imagine the betrayal she felt.

I diverted my attention away from Janine in that way strangers do when they've unintentionally made eye contact with each other, and let go of Wylie quickly. "You're welcome," I said politely, and began to pack my notepad and pens and reading glasses. "Maybe I should get going."

Wylie looked at the time on her cell phone. "What's the rush?"

I looked up and Janine was gone. "I don't know, I just thought . . ." I stalled, at a loss for what to say. "Was there something else you needed help with?"

"So, was everything OK when you saw your mom? You said it was important."

I was taken aback by this new line of questioning. I didn't want to tell her about my mother's illness, but I didn't want to shut her down either.

"Well . . ." I stalled again. "She needed to talk to us about some important family things."

"Did you have someone to talk to when you were my age? You know, because you said your mother didn't really get you."

I was astonished by how much she'd paid attention.

"Not really," I said. "I had books. I used to read a lot. And I'd make up stories."

"What kind of stories?"

"Well, for example, I had a crush on one of the guys who was in the movie version of *The Outsiders*."

"Ohmigod, we saw that movie after we read the book! The movie wasn't that good, but some of those guys were really cute!" said Wylie. "It's hard to believe they're like, my parents' age now and have kids and whatnot."

I deleted the image and smiled. "True. They were all pretty

boys. So anyway, I used to make up stories that one of them was my boyfriend, and he would listen and pay extra-special attention to me."

Wylie giggled. "Which one?"

"Sodapop Curtis." She outright laughed this time, and I rolled my eyes just like one of her teenage friends. "I know, silly, right? I also loved all of Judy Blume's books, and I used to pretend she was my mother. I imagined all these conversations we'd have."

"Did you ever show anyone the stories?"

"Never."

"Do you think that's why you're a writer?"

"I guess so," I said. "Isn't that why you paint? To tell stories?"

She pondered this. "I don't know. I just like it. Like, I feel like myself when I paint. Like it's something that comes easy to me. When I was little, I used to *love* to color. Painting feels more like a grown-up version of coloring."

I smiled. "I used to love to color too." The more she confided in me, the more I wanted to confide in her. And yet, the image of Janine in the doorway loomed, even if she didn't.

Wylie smiled back. "And it's not just painting. I like making things too." She switched gears without warning. "Is your relationship with your mother still complicated?"

I chose my words carefully. "It used to be."

Wylie tapped her pen on the table as we talked, and put it down for the first time. "I really like you, Andi. And I really like David too. He's, like, so well traveled and stuff."

"He really likes you too."

"And my sister thinks he's totally hot, which is like, totally gross to me."

I laughed. "You have to admit that he's handsome, though."

"He's probably someone you would've written one of those

secret stories about," she said. It was a perceptive, insightful observation.

"Better still," I said, "I got to live it." Was I referring to David, or Sam? I wondered. Maybe both.

Her eyes sparkled and turned dreamy. "What made you fall in love with David?"

Oh, Wylie. Not now. Not today. I just can't go there.

I traced little circles on the notebook paper in front of me, and couldn't get my voice to work. She either intuited my resistance, or rambled on out of impatience. "He's so different from my dad—I mean my stepdad. I'm trying to picture him and my mom together. You know, like, married. I mean, I get that he's good-looking and all that, but I'm wondering if there was something more to it for her."

And then I understood. She was trying to piece things together, trying to understand where she came from, how she'd come to be, was playing out the *what-if*s in her mind. Maybe by learning about me, she'd learn more about David, those little nuances that didn't require direct contact with him.

Or maybe she was acting out full-on teenage rebellion, choosing to align herself with the one person who could be the biggest threat to her mother. Not that I thought she was consciously aware of this, or deliberately using me.

A voice permeated the room. "This is English tutoring?" We both looked up, and I found Janine at the doorway again.

Wylie gasped in outrage. "God, Mom, have you been eavesdropping? We're talking about writing stories and stuff."

I hastily collected my things and said to Wylie, "I'd probably better get going. You're all set. Just send me your draft and I'll look at it. And next time I'll teach you all about revision."

"Thanks," she said. "Next time you can read your freewrite. Now I kinda wish you did."

I was touched by this, and ripped the page out of the note-book. "Here," I said, and handed it to her.

"Wylie, I'd like to speak to Andi alone. Say good-bye now."

Wylie shot her mother a threatening look. "Mom," she said through clenched teeth. But her mother's expression was more foreboding. Wylie looked at me apologetically, grabbed the freewrite and her notebook and *Animal Farm* and one of the straps of her backpack, and sang, "Seeya," to me before she bounded out of the room.

Janine took Wylie's place at the table without sitting down. "Don't think for a minute that I don't know what you're doing," she threatened, the volume of her voice turned down, lest Wylie had decided to linger and do some eavesdropping of her own, I guessed.

"Mrs. Baker, I—" I started, but Janine cut me off.

"Just because *he* wants a relationship with my daughter doesn't mean you get to weasel your way in too. Tell me, are you doing this whole little *Dead Poets Society* act to suck up to him, or to her?"

I was floored. "I'm just a writing instructor, Mrs. Baker. A coach. That's all."

"You can cut the 'Mrs. Baker' crap too. What, you think that formality somehow makes you better?"

"No, I don't. You never gave me permission to call you anything else."

She seemed momentarily flustered by this, but recovered quickly. "Nevertheless, you just taught your last lesson with my daughter. You have no right coming into *my* house and talking to her about things that are none of your business."

"With all due respect, your daughter confided in me. I wasn't prying, and I wasn't egging her on. I was listening, that's all. Sometimes the writing process makes students open up."

She looked at me in a manner that insinuated I was making things up, and she was intimidating as hell. But I knew exactly why her claws had come out.

"I wish she'd left well enough alone."

I surmised she was talking about the parental situation. "David had a right to know, Janine," I said. "So did Wylie."

She seemed just as offended by my using her first name as she had when I'd formally addressed her.

"Well, if you want David to have a relationship with her, then back off."

"You don't want me to tutor Wylie anymore?"

"Not just tutoring. Back off *completely*."

I couldn't believe what I was hearing. "Are you telling me I can't see Wylie at all? Can't have anything to do with her? Do you know how impossible that is?"

"You wanna test me?"

"What on earth did I say or do to you, Janine? I came here to tutor your daughter. That's all. And I appreciate your allowing me into your home."

She didn't budge. "What's it going to be?"

"Do you really think David's going to be OK with this ultimatum?"

"Please. You think he's going to stand by *you*? Blood is thicker, honey. Always was, and always will be."

"You can't stop David from seeing his daughter. You just can't."

"You're forgetting something. I can *out* him. I know who he used to be. How would his fancy art clients like to know he used to roll in bed with women for money?"

"How would Wylie like to know?" I countered. "Because if you open that door, you can't close it. Think of *her*."

"*I* am Wylie's mother. Not you. You're not even the step-mother. You have no standing here. You don't see her, you don't talk to her, you don't e-mail or text her, and you don't tutor her or read her English papers. Are we clear?"

I thought about David. His life had already been over-turned the minute he found out he had a daughter. I imagined the scandal of his art clients and friends finding out he used to be an escort, making false assumptions, his career and reputa-tion in ruins. I imagined the effect on Wylie. I imagined him being shut out of Wylie's life. He'd already missed her first steps and riding a bicycle and swim meets. I further imagined him missing her proms and high school and college gradua-tions and other milestones too. And I imagined him holding me responsible for all of it.

"Clear," I said.

When I got to my car, I took several deep breaths in an at-tempt to keep myself from crying. My hands shook as I gripped the steering wheel in an effort to steady them. Peter Baker was in the driveway washing Janine's car, his truck dripping in the autumn sun. He then dropped the hose and approached my car. A bout of anxiety rushed me, along with the irrational thought that he was about to yank me out of the car by my hair and beat the crap out of me. I locked my doors, but rolled the window down a crack.

"Everything OK?" said Peter.

Don't cry, don't cry, don't cry. . . . "Just fine," I lied. At least one tear escaped, and I quickly brushed it away.

"I overheard a little bit of your lesson before I came out here," he said. "You really made a connection with Wylie."

"Mr. Baker, I swear I didn't come here to steal her away or anything like that," I babbled, "I just—"

"Call me Peter," he said. "Look, I can tell my wife rattled you."

"She just cut me off from Wylie. Threatened to cut David off if I defied her. I understand . . . she's just protecting your daughter. But I don't know what I said or did to make her issue such an ultimatum. David might be a little overzealous, but he's just trying to make up for lost time, that's all."

Peter took a moment to consider this. "I don't think you and your husband arc bad people, and I don't think you're trying to take Wylie away. It's his right to know her, and vice versa."

I didn't bother correcting Peter regarding David being my husband.

"Just the same, Peter, I can't imagine how upsetting this must be for you and your wife."

He looked at me in a way that conveyed equal parts appreciation and sadness. I rolled the window almost all the way down.

"I'll see what I can do about your situation," he said. "I'd hate to see Wylie's schoolwork suffer because of this. I also wouldn't want to get into a legal battle if Janine tries to keep David away."

"I just want what's best for everyone involved," I said.

He seemed to deliberate on whether to speak his next thought. "You're a nice person," he said.

I made direct eye contact with him. "And you're a great dad," I replied.

I drove home in silence; didn't even listen to the playlist of Sam's and my favorite songs. When I got home, David asked me how it went.

"Fine," I said, my voice quavering. "I think she'll do well with her paper."

"You OK?" he asked.

There was no way I could tell him about Janine's ultimatum. If I told him and he came to my defense by defying her, she'd make his life miserable. Worse still was the possibility that he would take *her* side. I worried that Janine was right about blood being thicker. When given a choice between your kid and your girlfriend, you'd pick your kid, right? Even when we married, it wouldn't make a difference. I didn't share Wylie's DNA. And that was now a currency I would never, ever be able to afford.

"As OK as I can be," I said. "You know, the day."

I thought he'd take me into his arms, say something of comfort. Instead, he said, "Well, I'm sure Wylie appreciated your being there," and asked what I wanted for dinner.

Since when was he so insensitive? Or was I being overly sensitive?

Emotionally and physically exhausted, I went upstairs to the bedroom, logged into e-mails, and found one from Andrew.

Hey Andi-

I just wanted you to know that I know what today is, and that it's probably a difficult day for you. For what it's worth, I'm thinking of you. Hope you're well.

Andrew

I burst into tears. He was the only one.

chapter twenty-seven

"Don't you think that's a little creepy?" asked Maggie when I recounted the story of Devin's picking me up at Perch. I had already filled her in on the fiasco of Wylie's tutoring session and acknowledging Sam's anniversary. "I mean, he's basically pretending to be someone else. It's a way of acting out cheating on you without actually doing it. I would think you of all people would be bothered by that."

"I don't see it that way at all," I argued. "And even if it was, wouldn't you rather have your significant other play it out with you than actually cheat on you? Besides, he wasn't being someone else; he was being a former version of himself. He was being Devin."

"Yeah—an *escort*. A guy who used to sleep with other women—and before you tell me that he didn't technically have sex with them, may I remind you that you used to poke holes in that flimsy defense all the time."

"What's up with you, Mags? I thought you'd be totally into this. This was like, amazing sex we had."

"Amazing?" she imitated me.

"Yeah."

"Since when do you use the word 'amazing'? I thought you hated that word."

"OK, fine. Not amazing. *Thrilling*, I guess is the word. I mean, we had sex the night before, too, but it wasn't the same as *this*."

Maggie sat there, her mouth hanging open. "I hate you, you know. Just putting it out there."

"Hey, I'm just making up for a misspent youth, is all," I said.

"So why? Why be Devin after all these years? I pretty much thought that guy was dead and buried."

I confessed, "I think it was something I said. I don't know, I think everything that's been going on lately has stirred up some old stuff. First Wylie, now my mother . . ." I trailed off.

"What's up with your mother?" she asked.

"I was just getting to that." I straightened my posture and lowered my voice. "She has cancer."

She gasped and sat back in her seat. "*You tell me about the sex thing before you tell me your mother has cancer?*" she said loud enough to draw looks from both staff and patrons.

She slapped her hand to her mouth. Mortified, I shrank in my seat. "Yeah, so we're never coming back *here* again," I said.

"How bad is it?" she asked, her voice returned to normal decibel level.

I became solemn. "It's terminal."

"Oh, Andi. That sucks on so many levels."

"Tell me about it."

"What are you going to do?"

"What do you mean?" I asked.

"How long does she—what's the prognosis?"

"Not good. Anywhere from six to eighteen months."

She put her hand on her heart. "Oh, holy shit-fritters."

"Well said."

"So are you going to go back to Long Island?"

"Right smack in the middle of the week, at least once a month for the time being. Of course, this all comes as David's getting to know Wylie—without me, now." I was talking rapid-fire, changing subjects without warning or pause. "Oh, and I haven't even told David this one yet: My mother wants us to get married before, you know, before it's too late. She made a special request."

"Why haven't you told David yet?"

"Hel-lo . . . fabulous sexual encounter? He kind of distracted me with that one."

"Maybe that was his intention," she said.

"It worked." Of course, I'd had plenty of chances to bring it up since then, so what was my excuse?

"Or maybe he's going through some midlife thing."

I furrowed my brow. "Is he old enough to be going through a midlife thing?"

"Think about it, Andi: Teenage daughter shows up on his doorstep; mortality reminder shows up on his doorstep; you start bringing up Devin. . . ."

"Not to mention Andrew," I added, then caught myself and stiffened. *Shit, shit, shit!*

"What about Andrew? You didn't—you're not in touch with him again, are you?"

"I'll put a stop to it," I said in a feeble attempt to block the wrath that was about to follow.

"I can't believe you got in touch with him again. What's more, I can't believe you didn't tell me you got in touch with him again, which is a surefire sign that you know it's wrong."

"It was just a few e-mails, that's all."

More than a few, actually. But I could barely admit that to myself, much less to my best friend.

"Does David know you've been e-mailing him?"

I clamped my mouth shut.

"Oh, Andi, this is bad. This is, like, deal-breaker bad. Think about what you're doing here. It's bad enough you're not telling him about this ultimatum. But the last thing you want to do is keep secrets from your fiancé about your ex-fiancé. Especially when new fiancé is bonding with his long-lost daughter and old fiancé isn't tied to anyone. At least, I'm assuming he's not."

"He's not."

"You've got to tell him."

"Tell who what?"

"David. You've got to tell David that you've been in touch with Andrew."

"I don't think that's such a good idea."

"My God, it's like a bad reality show. Although that's redundant, isn't it."

I changed my tune. "You're right, Mags. I know you're right. I made a big mistake and almost fucked everything up and I'm better off telling David now than hiding it from him. I'll do it tonight, after I tell him about my mother's request."

"Good thinking. He'll be too *verklempt* over that to be mad at you for the other thing."

"Mags!"

"Hey, it was *your* idea!"

⌇⌇⌇⌇⌇

Later, when I got home, I found a text message on my phone from Wylie: Can we talk?

180

I thought about Janine's warning to stay away from Wylie. But I couldn't just leave her hanging.

I texted back: I'm sorry, but I can't.

About ten minutes later, my phone rang. I looked at the caller ID and saw that it was Wylie. I answered the phone. "Hello?"

"My mother says you're not going to tutor me anymore."

I didn't know what Janine disclosed, or if she offered any explanation; thus I had to tread lightly. "Yes, that's correct. I can't right now."

"Aren't you at least going to look at my paper?"

"I really want to, but I just can't. You're going to do great on that paper. I just know it." Tears came to my eyes.

"So, what, that's it?"

"I'm sorry," I choked out.

Wylie huffed. "Fine. Whatever. I gotta go."

"Take care," I said.

Take care? *Take care?* Ugh. I'd never want to see me again either.

After dinner, I retreated to my office with my laptop to catch up on some work while David went to the gym—I couldn't help but notice he'd been going more frequently. As I Googled books about coping with cancer, caring for family members, et cetera, Gmail alerted me to a new chat.

Andrew: Hey Andi. You there?

I groaned.

I could ignore it—I *should* ignore it. After all, I vowed to put a stop to this communication. Then again, this would be a good time to do so officially. Besides, I couldn't help but feel that somehow he would know I was here, deliberately ignoring him, and that he would be hurt. *Why the hell do you care?* A voice inside me asked.

Me: Hey Andrew. I can't talk for long.
Andrew: That's ok. Just wanted to see how you're doing.
Me: Busy. A lot going on right now.
Andrew: Anything you want to talk about?
Me: Not anything happy. I got some bad news regarding my mother's health.

What on earth was I doing?

Andrew: I'm really sorry to hear that.
Me: Plus the anniversary of Sam's death. Four years. Thank you for your message, by the way. I really appreciated it.
Andrew: You're welcome. I'm sorry I couldn't be of more comfort. Does it get any easier?
Me: Yes and no. It's not like it used to be, like the world is going to end all over again. But it's not exactly a happy day either. I still miss him. That never totally goes away.
Andrew: I'm just so sorry you had to go through something like that.

I was in the middle of typing a response when he beat me to it.

Andrew: This may be an inappropriate question,

but if somehow you knew what was going to happen ahead of time, would you have done anything
different?

Me: It's not healthy to ponder questions
like that. You can get caught in a vicious
undertow of if-onlys.

Andrew: I'm sorry.

Me: It's ok.

Enough. I had to put a stop to it. I ignored his next chat line
and typed my own.

Me: I'm sorry, Andrew, but I don't think we
should communicate with each other anymore.

Andrew: Have I upset you?

Me: No, it's not that. I don't mean for
now. I mean for good.

I waited at least a minute for Andrew to respond. A minute
was a long time under such circumstances.

Andrew: I understand.

Me: I'm sorry. It's nothing personal. In
fact, I've enjoyed our e-mails and chats, and
I appreciate your wanting to listen. It's
just that I've got a lot of family stuff
right now, and I don't think it's appropriate
for me to be talking to my ex-fiancé while
I'm currently engaged.

Andrew: It's ok. You don't have to apologize. And I'm glad you've enjoyed our e-mails
because I've really enjoyed them too.

I wasn't sure what to type next. "Well, seeya" seemed beyond curt. But what else was there for me to say without my getting into specifics, which I didn't want to do?

Andrew didn't wait for me.

Andrew In that case, I have one last favor.

I sucked in a breath.

Me: What is it?
Andrew: Can we get together once? I swear I'll never get in touch with you again; I just want to see you and talk to you, that's all. Just once. I'll even come to Northampton and meet anywhere you want.

Ohmigod, *Oh, my God!* My mind raced as I stared at the words in the little chat box, imagining him behind them, sitting at his keyboard, a cup of herbal tea beside him and Joni Mitchell playing in the background. I had the urge to get up and run laps around the block, jump into a lake, go twenty rounds with a punching bag, take your pick. I wished Maggie were here for consultation purposes. Then again, I already knew what she'd say—no, *scream*—at me.

Me: I can't.
Andrew: Will you at least think about it?

I stared at the screen, unable to move my fingers. This was a no-brainer. I had the upper hand, could close the door on Andrew Clark once and for all with a simple. N-O. So why did I feel like I was the one backed into a corner?

Me: OK.

My fingers trembled as I typed. Wrong two letters.

Andrew: Thanks. I really appreciate it.
Me: Don't get your hopes up.
Andrew: I understand. Good night.
Me: Good night.

I logged out and shut down my laptop. Then I looked around the room, as if expecting to find someone there.

"Well. Way to end it," I said out loud, as if speaking on behalf of the absent friends who would be telling me the same thing. Then, for good measure, I chided myself aloud with "Fuck."

I dreaded David's return from the gym. I was going to have to tell him everything. Tonight.

chapter twenty-eight

David is one of those guys who looks good sweaty. I don't mean dirty-sweaty; I mean when the ends of his hair are wet and his face is shiny but not dripping, and he's got dark, wet spots all along the front and sides of his sleeveless navy blue T-shirt clinging to him—way better than a tank top—and he walks while exhaling through his mouth interspersed with swigs from a water bottle, his sore muscles twitching as he does. Of course, it helps that David, pushing fifty years old, has a body that would make Adonis swear off beer and carbs and buy a treadmill.

He comes home this way, and were it not for the sweaty smell it would take all my restraint not to jump him the minute he walks through the door.

Tonight was no different, although I had been working off my nervous energy waiting for him—cleaning the kitchen, sorting the Tupperware, reorganizing the pantry—while I played out various versions of the conversation in my head. I was tempted to play dirty and use sex appeal to my advantage: put on a black lace teddy while he showered. But no, it was too shallow, too manipulative, and would cast even more light on my guilt. And no matter how much I rationalized my innocence, I knew I had probable cause for guilt.

I was, however, waiting in bed for him when he emerged from the bathroom with a towel wrapped around his waist. Hot damn.

"In bed already?" he asked.

"Just chillin' out," I replied. A book rested on my lap. "Reading."

He changed into pajama bottoms and climbed onto the bed. Holy God, he smelled incredible, a mix of musk and almond and ylang-ylang and that one-of-a-kind David scent. I tousled his damp hair with my fingers and took a whiff, practically purring afterward.

"How was your workout?" I asked.

"Good. I gotta get a massage, though. My joints are killing me."

"So listen, Dev, there's something I wanted to talk to you about."

I waited for his usual "uh-oh" reaction, whereby he braced himself, but instead he waited patiently. It occurred to me that we'd had so many serious things to discuss lately that he was probably expecting it to be related to my mother or work or Wylie.

"What is it?" he finally asked when I didn't speak.

I snapped out of it. "Oh. Well . . ." I placed the book on the end table next to me. "It's, um . . . it's my ex."

He seemed not to compute.

I forced myself to clarify. "It's Andrew."

Slowly his face registered the name and its association.

"Your ex-fiancé?" And then, with a bit of an edge to his tone, added, "The one who dumped you because you didn't—" he stopped himself. "The one who *cheated* on you?"

"Yes," I replied, trying to insert a tone of authority.

"What about him?" He sounded wary, suspicious.

"He e-mailed me a few weeks ago to see how I was doing—" I started, but David cut me off. His irises turned into embers.

"Nice that you're finally getting around to telling me this," he snapped. "What are you doing talking to the guy behind my back?"

My defenses shot up. "First of all, I don't need your permission to talk to anyone. Second of all, I'm not having some kind of clandestine affair with him. He e-mailed me a few weeks ago, I responded, we threw a few more back and forth, and tonight I said that I didn't want to communicate with him anymore."

"You *spoke* to him?"

"Gmail chat," I replied.

David practically growled. "God, Andi, do you know how this sounds?" The volume of his voice had steadily increased.

Not until I said it out loud.

"Not good," I answered. "That's why I'm telling you. I don't want to lose your trust."

"Why did you want to talk to this guy in the first place?"

"Because he's sorry for what he did all those years ago, and I wanted to patch things up as well."

"What do *you* have to patch up? You didn't do anything to him."

"Dev. You know what I was like back then. I was closed up pretty tight. I'm not saying I deserved his betrayal, but I could've done a lot of things better."

"You owe that guy nothing." He peered at me, and knew I was withholding information from him. "Anything else you wanna tell me?"

I sucked in a breath. "He asked to see me."

He shook his head, incredulous. "Of course. Of course he wants to see you. Just casual, right? Just as *friends*," he said.

I returned his sarcasm with some of my own. "Right. Because you know nothing about being just friends. You've never been in that kind of relationship before."

"Not with a woman who was engaged to someone else, no." He paused for a few beats. "You wanna see him, don't you."

The way he said it made me feel like a teenager getting involved with some dirtbag. "You make it sound like I agreed to go on a date with him. I just want to talk some things out over lunch. That's all. Nothing more. It's not a date. Not a reunion. It's . . ." *Don't you dare use the word "closure!"* "I think it could finally heal some old wounds."

"I don't see what seeing him face-to-face is going to do other than stir up a lot of shit."

This time I raised my voice. "There's already a lot of shit being stirred up. Look, I need this. I thought it was all behind me, but I need him to tell me he's sorry to my face. I need to look him in the eye and *see* that he's sorry, and I need to forgive him and move on. And I think that's what he wants and needs too. Can you try to understand that?"

"How do you know he's not just using that to manipulate you into seeing him so he can make a move on you?"

"Come on. He's not stupid. And neither am I."

David's eyes narrowed as he looked at me, dubious. And maybe for good reason. I'd thought back to all the e-mail exchanges and chats with Andrew, wondering if I led him on, or if he had indeed disguised his intentions. Things that would've been seemingly innocent statements, such as how hard David and I had worked to find our way back to each other following Sam's death and my "family issues," could be misconstrued by him.

But I refused to give David the satisfaction of possibly being right. Nor did I want to feel like a fool. "Gee, Dev, thanks for your high opinion of me," I said, hoping my hurt would cut into him even just a little bit.

He shook his head again and hopped off the bed. "I don't fucking believe this." He paced around the room.

"Why is it so hard for you to accept that some people change? They grow up over time, learn from their mistakes, become remorseful."

"*Some* people," he said.

"You sure as hell weren't the same person in Rome that I first met in New York. You were a better version of yourself. How can you be so sure Andrew's not a better version of himself? Doesn't he deserve the same consideration?"

"For chrissakes, he *cheated* on you! Are you forgetting that?"

"And you were doing every woman in Manhattan while stringing me along—are you forgetting *that*?" I yelled.

He practically flinched, as if the verbal arrow I'd just slung had struck him right in the chest.

He fumed. "How fucking dare you," he said, his voice an octave lower, menacing, frightening, even. "How dare you use my fucking past—*our* fucking past—against me like that and put me on the same level as him. I was not sleeping with those women and engaged to someone else at the same time. Hell, I wasn't sleeping with any of them, and you and I weren't even *dating*."

"Right. Because it was against the rules," I mocked. "David, if you can't trust me, then you'd better tell me now; otherwise marriage is out of the question."

He stood there, dumfounded by the line in the sand I'd just drawn. I was desperate to read his mind, to know what he was thinking, afraid he would say, *You're right, Andi.*

David opened the door and stormed out of the bedroom without saying a word.

My heart raced as I sat for a few minutes, trying to catch my breath. I went to the bathroom and splashed cold water on my face. The scent of his aftershave lingered. After taking a few deep breaths, I calmed down and left the bedroom to look for him, and found him in the den with the television on, obliviously channel surfing.

He was seated at the end of the couch. I sat closer to the middle, one leg tucked under, and gradually inched toward him.

"I'm sorry I didn't tell you about the e-mails," I said. "It was wrong of me to keep that from you. You have every right to be angry about that."

He didn't answer. Just kept channel surfing, refusing to look at me.

"Say the word, and I'll never see or speak to him again. I'll even show you the e-mails, if you want."

He flicked off the TV and turned to me.

"I don't want to. You know why?" He didn't wait for me to answer. "Because then you'll resent the hell out of me. And you'll want to see him even more. And you'll go behind my back again. I'm not going to be some control freak who hacks into your e-mail and checks your cell phone when you're in the other room, Andi. I'm not going to be that asshole."

"You are so wrong, David." I added a beat between the words to emphasize them the second time. "So. Wrong. If there were a scale for wrong, you would've broken it. I would *never* resent you. And I would never go behind your back to see him."

David put his hand to his forehand and pinched the space at the top of his nose, between his brows. I'd seen him do it before, as a way to keep himself from crying.

"You already have," he said, his voice breaking.

My God. He was right.

"Andi, I don't want you to see him," he said, softer this time. Wounded. "But not because *I* don't want you to. I don't want *you* to want to see him."

The words punched me in the gut. I didn't want to want to see him, either. But the feeling wasn't going away. Why? Why did I have to feel anything?

Filled with guilt and shame and remorse, I started to cry. "I'm sorry, David," I said as I jumped up from the couch and ran upstairs, back to the bedroom. As I lay in darkness, drowning in the confusion—what did I *really* want with this meeting?—the touch of David's hand on my back was like an anchor pulling me back to shore. He tenderly rubbed the spot before lying down and spooning me, neither of us speaking, waiting for my tears to subside.

"It's too much, Andi," he finally said. "It's Wylie, and your mother, and now this? How are we supposed to manage it all?"

"By getting through it together."

The moment I said the words, it was as if a switch had turned off. I didn't want to see Andrew, didn't need to. Closure had happened a long time ago, the moment Sam came into my life. And that wouldn't have happened were it not for Devin the Escort cutting the chains that bound me for so long with just one breath of acceptance for who I was, for *seeing* me in the first place. No, it was *David* who had that x-ray vision. But Devin was the one who was able to sell me on it, to get me to see me too.

I was ready to tell him that I was going to inform Andrew that I would not be seeing him, chatting with him, e-mailing him, sending smoke signals, nothing; and I knew David would believe me. The resolute tone of my voice would be enough. But just as I opened my mouth, David spoke first.

"In that case, I should tell you that I've been keeping something from you too."

chapter twenty-nine

As I lay beside David, every part of me, right down to my breath, turned to stone, a deer intuiting the barrel of a gun in range.

"Whaaat?" I drew out, sounding like a high school girl.

David continued. "I met with Janine. Twice."

And that cracked me out of my frozen pose. I flinched and pulled away from him. "*What?*"

"Remember when you went to meet your mother for lunch? Well, Janine and I met for lunch too. Just the two of us. The second time, I drove to and from Hartford on one of your teaching days."

I've never had a sumo wrestler sit on me, but I imagined it felt something like the weight of his confession on my chest and stomach.

"Why—why did you see her without me? More to the point, why did you see her and *not tell me* about it?"

"Because I had to establish a trust with Janine. She already felt you and I were ganging up on her. I wanted to show her that when it comes to Wylie, I'm all in."

"That doesn't explain why you didn't tell me."

"There's something else. She called me the day after your tutoring session."

I sat up and snapped on the light, squeezing my eyes shut in reaction to the brightness. "What did she say?"

"She said she doesn't want you to tutor Wylie anymore."

"And that's all she said?"

He hesitated. "She also said she doesn't want you spending time with Wylie alone, without me. Nor does she want you to have any contact via e-mail and stuff."

This was Peter's getting through to her? This was working something out? Granted, it was better than the previous ultimatum, but still . . . "Did she tell you why?"

"She said you and Wylie were talking about her behind her back, bad-mouthing her and comparing me to Peter, showing him up. Said you pushed Wylie too hard during the tutoring session. I said that didn't sound like you, but she was pretty obstinate."

I smoldered. "And what did *you* say?"

"I said I'd honor her request. Look, Andi, it's just temporary, while Wylie and I are getting to know each other. Janine will come around. But for now it's best to give her what she wants."

Sonofabitch. Janine was right. Blood is thicker.

"And you thought the best way to do that was to go behind your fiancée's back, not give her—*me*—the benefit of the doubt? Geez, Dev, you didn't even ask me for my side of the story. Wylie and I were not talking about Janine behind her back, or whatever she accused me of doing—at least not in some vicious way. Wylie was just confiding in me about stuff that teenagers confide to women other than their mothers. And, I don't know, Janine lost it. I don't believe this," I said after a beat. "You sat there persecuting me the whole time knowing that you were just as guilty. You hypocrite."

"Andi, it's not the same."

I laughed angrily. "Oh, I have to hear this one. Go on. Explain to me how it's not the same."

"Because Janine and I have a child together. We needed to talk about what's best for our child, and we needed to work out our own differences in order to do that."

"You needed *closure*," I offered.

"No, we needed a mutual understanding and a new relationship, for Wylie's sake. I'm not saying we're all kosher now, but we found common ground. And we needed to find it without any spousal interference."

"So, because Andrew and I don't have a child together, I'm not allowed that."

"I didn't say that."

"Because Andrew cheated on me. Janine only concealed your daughter from you for fifteen years. Of course he should be crucified and she gets to find *common ground* with you."

"Stop it," he said.

"You could've told me! You could've said, 'Andi, I'm going to meet with Janine to talk over some things. This is something I need to do without you.' I would've understood and supported you."

"You're right. I should've told you. But Janine asked me not to."

"So of course you listened to the woman who kept the mother of all secrets—forgive the pun."

"Watch it," he said through clenched teeth. "She's the mother of my child."

I dropped my jaw. "She *lied to you* for fifteen years!"

"You reminded me of that several times, thank you."

"It doesn't seem to be sinking in."

"You think I'm not angry about that? I'm furious with her, Andi, and I told her so! But what good is it to hold a grudge against her now, when I've got my daughter to think about? I want a relationship with her, and if that means forgiving her mother and making a fresh start, so be it."

"And you think Andrew doesn't deserve the same courtesy from me just because he didn't knock me up?"

"Your being flip isn't doing anything other than pissing me off something fierce," he said, "so knock it off."

I grabbed my pillow and headed out the door.

"Where are you going?" he called after me.

I charged to the guest bedroom and then ground to a halt the moment I slapped on the light and entered, feeling choked by invisible hands. This was no longer the guest bedroom; it was *her* room now. It was the smell of it that choked me, I realized. The smell of the room had changed.

I did an about-face and stormed down the hallway toward the study when David blocked me.

"Andi, let's talk about this."

Refusing to look at him, I pushed past him like a passenger on a New York subway. "Out of my way."

"Come on." He followed me into the study. I chucked the pillow onto the end of the leather sofa and grabbed the fleece throw that rested on the arm, whirling and wrapping it around me like a cape.

"You're sleeping in *here* tonight?" he asked.

"No, assclown. I'm meditating."

From my peripheral vision I saw him clench his fists and clamp his mouth shut. He looked ready to tell me to fuck off, and I knew I deserved it for that last jab.

"Fine," he fumed, and he left the door open as he exited. "Good night, Andi," thundered from the hallway.

Cocooned in the throw, I curled up in a fetal position, closed my eyes, and cried softly. Not only had the switch flipped back on, but I wanted to see Andrew even more than before, and it made me nauseous.

Hours later, still unable to sleep, I went downstairs, took my iPad out of its case, and typed an e-mail:

```
Andrew,
    I thought about it. If you still want to
meet, I'm OK with it.
                                        Andi
```

chapter thirty

While we sat in a waiting room of the Cancer Center in Stony Brook, my mother fanned through a *Good Housekeeping* magazine as I read and commented on a student paper, the stack beneath it sitting comfortably in my lap. At one point I could feel her watching me, and I diverted my attention. She wore an expression of fascination mixed with something like remorse or regret.

"What is it?" I asked.

"I've never seen what you do. Your job, I mean."

As the revelation sank in for both of us, I saw her eyes misting over; but before either of us could continue, a nurse stepped out and called my mother's name. Mom cleared her throat and dabbed her eyes and stood up and pressed out her pantsuit with her hands. I gathered my things and followed them both. This was Mom's third treatment, and she already knew the way.

The walls of the room were painted bright yellow and adorned with framed 8" x 10" photographs of hibiscus flowers, but the sunny disposition didn't outshine the ubiquitous antiseptic smell or detract us from the reason we were there. "You can sit here." The nurse directed me to a chair beside the station where Mom sat while an assistant hooked up an IV to her. Mom looked impatient, but I could see she was just trying to mentally distract herself from the pinch of the needle insertion, the dread of the side effects (so far the nausea had been at a minimum, but it was the unpredictability she couldn't stand), the whole goddamned thing. Once she was hooked up, the nurse and the assistant left us alone with an assurance that they'd check back in a few minutes.

"They seem to be nice enough here," I said, trying to make small talk to further distract her (and myself).

"At least they're not patronizing."

My brain searched for something else to say, but what kind of conversation do people make when they're getting chemotherapy? I should've asked Joey and Tony what they talked about.

As if reading my mind, Mom stamped out the silence. She pointed to my briefcase with a nod. "Tell me about what you were reading."

"It's part two of a three-part memoir. The assignment is to take three different life events, seemingly unrelated, find the common link, and then write about them in a three-part series."

She processed this. "Was the assignment your idea?"

"It was. The one I was reading in the waiting room was about the day the student decided to come out."

"Come out?"

"He's gay."

She made the connection. "Oh." Mom remained focused on the briefcase, as if she could see through it and read its contents. "What do you look for when you read them?" she asked.

"I often don't know until I see it. Generally speaking, I'm observing how well the elements of memoir are expressed—a narrative voice, character development, use of sensory description and scene-setting. . . ."

"Character development? Aren't memoirs nonfiction?"

"Yes, but even real people are characters. You want the reader to be as invested in them as they would be in any fictional character."

I let her ruminate on this.

"I yelled at you once for writing about all of us," she said, as if it were news to me.

"More than once," I said, "and you refused to read anything I wrote after that, regardless of what it was." I instantly regretted saying it, realizing she'd think I was being judgmental rather than pointing out a fact. But before she could respond I added, "I don't blame you for getting angry. Not everything I wrote was pleasant. In hindsight, I think my real purpose for writing those memoirs wasn't about my telling a truth as much as it was about power. It was the only control I ever felt. In fact, I don't even like to read most of what I wrote anymore. It all rings very inauthentic to me now."

She seemed taken aback by this admission, as if she'd never considered it before.

"It's a very powerful tool, isn't it," she said. "Writing, I mean."

"Yes, it is."

"When was the last time you wrote something nonfiction?"

"Just an occasional scholarly essay with Maggie," I said. "I've been enjoying writing fiction too much."

"Why?"

"Strange as it may seem, it feels more honest to me, even though I'm making up the stories."

The nurse interrupted us to check on Mom, ask if she was OK, inspect her IV. She left, and Mom closed her eyes for a few seconds.

I echoed the nurse. "You OK? Is there anything I can do?"

"What events would you choose?" she continued.

"Excuse me?"

"If you were doing your own assignment. What three events would you write about?"

My students had asked me the same thing in the middle of a brainstorming session. I told them I had no idea, but I had thought about it ever since.

"Do you remember the day I fell off my bicycle? I was racing down the hill in front of the house, hit a patch of sand, swerved, and just missed a car."

"Got the wind knocked out of you pretty good," she said. I was surprised she remembered.

"You just so happened to be looking out the window when it happened. Raced out to help me."

She nodded, and I could tell that in her mind's eye she was there, in the street and by my side, all over again. "Scared me to death."

"That's one. The second is a day when I worked at Macy's. A guy had shoplifted, and I'd let him walk right out."

"Why?" she asked.

The question seemed odd. I didn't respond. "The third was a date with Devin."

"Who?"

My eyes widened when I realized what I'd just said. Then I overcompensated. "David. David and I had had a date a long time ago, and . . ."

"I could've sworn you said Devin."

And then suddenly, inexplicably, every fiber of my being told me to come clean. And suddenly, inexplicably, I heeded it.

"I did."

"Who's Devin?"

"David was."

"What do you mean?" she asked.

"When I first met David he didn't go by *David*. He went by *Devin*."

"Why?"

"He . . ." Oh God, how was I going to get myself out of this? Or worse, how was I going to get through it? "Maybe I should talk to David first. It's a bit personal."

"Was he into something illegal?"

"No, it wasn't illegal, not exactly."

"*Not exactly?*"

"I suppose you can say it was morally questionable, though."

"Geez, Andi, what was he doing, running an escort service or something?"

Of all the dumb fucking luck!

"Wow. That was an incredible guess." I shouldn't have said anything at all. But I was too baffled to think straight. Like watching someone slip on a banana peel in slow motion and not doing anything to stop it or help.

"You mean I was *right*?"

I sheepishly nodded. "An escort service. And he was one of the escorts."

Mom looked as flummoxed as I felt. "When?"

"Long time ago. When I moved back to Long Island after Andrew and I broke up."

"Where did you meet him?"

"Cocktail party."

"Did he solicit you?" she asked. The way she said *solicit* sounded so sordid.

"No!" I recoiled.

"Oh God, you didn't . . . did you solicit *him*?"

"Not at first."

Mom dropped her jaw in horror. "Andrea!" she said. A patient sitting nearby turned her head in our direction.

"It wasn't like that," I backpedaled, lowering my voice. "We met casually, through mutual acquaintances. I got in touch with him, and we got to . . . to know each other. We became friends."

"So you never . . ."

"No," I said sternly. "Not until after Sam died," I lied.

Mom exhaled a sigh of relief. I, on the other hand, felt like the wind had been knocked out of me again.

"You should have," she said after a few minutes had passed.

"Should have what?"

"Solicited him. Probably would've loosened you up."

I burst into astonished laughter. "Are you serious? This coming from one of the most sexually repressed parents on the planet?"

"I was never *repressed*," she said in a staunch tone. "I just didn't believe that was proper dinner talk."

"You didn't believe it was proper anything," I corrected. "You all acted like I was supposed to remain a virgin my entire life. I'm surprised you didn't send me to some convent!"

"You're exaggerating just a little, don't you think?" she asked.

"Are you kidding? I'm being subtle!"

She mulled over this before she shot her next question.

"So when did you lose your virginity?"

I sprang up and held out my hand as if to block her. "Whoa. OK. Mom, if you're making up for lost time, this is totally weirding me out."

In perfect timing, the nurse returned to the room. Mom's treatment was done. Hospital protocol required patients to be wheeled out to the lobby. I left her there and retrieved the car, replaying the last part of our conversation, squinching my face as if I'd just sucked on a lemon and muttering, "Ugh."

Mom stepped out of the chair and into the car slowly, and leaned back against the headrest, closing her eyes. Neither of us said a word for the first forty-five minutes of the drive. She opened the window, a sign that she was feeling nauseous.

"You want me to pull over?" I asked, a wave of fear crashing over me.

"Not yet," she said. "I need the windows open, though. I'm sorry if you're cold."

"Please don't apologize," I said.

I slowed to just under the speed limit, flipping off impatient drivers who zoomed around me and honked their horns. Gotta love New York. I didn't know whether to talk to my mother or leave her be.

When we pulled up to the house, I could tell she was miserable. I ran to the other side of the car, opened the door for her, helped her into the house, and finally to bed. She kept an empty waste pail next to it; the sight of it sobered me.

"Have you ever used that?" I asked.

She shook her head. "Not yet." Somehow I knew its christening was coming. "Leave me alone, please," she said. Her tone wasn't angry or impatient. More like a plea.

I left the door ajar, retreated to the kitchen, and heated some broth just in case. I made myself a peanut butter and jelly sandwich and took two bites before pushing it away after hearing the sounds coming from my mother's bedroom. Those sounds would haunt me for the rest of my life.

∽ᴑᴑᴑᴑᴍ∼

Hours later, when the house had gone dark, I tentatively opened the door and peeked in, frightened of what I might find.

"Mom?" I called out softly. A night-light was plugged into a nearby socket, and I switched it on. When I entered the room, the stench of vomit pierced my nostrils, and I covered my nose and mouth with my hand. I took the pail, threw it in the tub, and twisted the faucet on, trying not to look at any of it. I then stifled a gag and splashed some water in the sink on my face before shoving a cupful into my mouth and spitting it out. I turned off the tub faucet and left the bathroom, closing the door behind me.

This is what it's going to be like from now on, I thought. *And it's only going to get worse.*

I crossed her room and opened the window a crack. Then I returned to her side of the bed. "Mom?" This time she stirred, and her eyes fluttered open.

"What time is it?" she murmured.

"About eight thirty," I answered.

"What day is it?"

"It's still Wednesday."

She closed her eyes again.

"I made some broth. Can you—do you want me to heat it up?"

"No," she said over me, her voice exerting more force.

"OK. Do you mind if I sit here for a little bit?"

She nodded weakly. "Please."

I pulled up a chair to where the pail had been.

"Do you want me to read to you or anything like that?" I asked.

She shook her head. I sat in silence and listened to the whistle of the wind through the window.

"Andi?"

I leaned in. "Yes?"

She opened her eyes. "What was the connective theme? Of your events?"

It took me a second to realize she was referring to my writing assignment and our conversation in the chemo room.

"Safety," I answered.

She closed them again in satisfaction.

"You used to sing with your brothers," she said after a moment.

Emotion took my throat into a vise grip. She had never brought the subject up, never recalled the memory, out of nostalgia or fact or for any other reason. No one did. Not even me. "That was a long, long time ago," I finally managed to say just above a whisper, a tear slipping down my cheek, followed by another, like a parade.

"You had a lovely singing voice," she said. "Did you know that?"

I shook my head, although she couldn't see. "No." I forced the word out. "No one ever told me." *No one* meaning her or Dad. "I mean, Joey and Tony said it was good, but, well, I guess I never believed them."

"Sing to me, please," she beckoned, her own voice frail.

I choked on a sob. "I don't know what to sing." *And I don't know if I can.*

"Anything," she said.

My mind went blank as every lyric to every song I'd ever known disappeared like deleted computer files. And then one surfaced, as if summoned: And then one surfaced, as if summoned: "Two of Us." The Beatles song Tony and I sang at a brother-sister talent show when I was still in grade school, and we took home first prize. The song that had been Sam's and my wedding song.

I don't know how I managed to sing the first verse. Every note had come out rusty, the key broken. I sobbed it more than sang it. But when I finished and couldn't bring myself to open my mouth for another verse, Mom said quietly, "That was very nice, Andi. Thank you."

She went to sleep. I sat in the chair for hours and cried until I was so tired I circled to the other side of Mom's bed, crawled in, and closed my eyes.

chapter thirty-one

After a battle with Mom about my wanting to stay an extra day and her practically throwing me out (the rest had done her good, although she was still weak), I took the last ferry out of Orient Point that evening and didn't arrive in Northampton until late. Even though we both apologized, David and I had spoken little since the fight that sent me to spend the night in the study, and I'd been too preoccupied with Mom to properly patch things up.

When I pulled up to the house, the outside light flicked on and David emerged from the front door. I killed the ignition and he opened my car door for me like a valet or a chauffeur, popped the trunk, and retrieved my overnight bag. Once inside the house, I dropped my briefcase and shoulder bag, as if surrendering in defeat, and fell into his arms, where he caught me and held on tight.

"Why didn't you tell me?" I asked him after he practically carried me upstairs to bed.

"Tell you what?" he asked.

"You never told me what it was like when your dad had cancer. The treatments, the side effects . . ."

"That's because I didn't know. At least not firsthand. He never let my sisters or me see him that way. Only my mother. I was so mad at him for that, thought it was unfair for her to shoulder that burden all by herself. But she insisted that he was trying to spare all of us, that she would've done the same in his place."

"It was awful, Dev. After the treatment, I mean. She was sick as a dog."

"I'm so sorry, *cara*."

"I remember telling you once that you were lucky because you had the chance to say good-bye to your dad and tell him that you loved him, and I didn't have that with Sam. But at least he was killed on impact. He didn't suffer. I didn't have to watch him deteriorate. I know that last part sounds selfish, but—"

"No, I understand," David finished for me. "He probably wouldn't have wanted you to see him suffer, either. No one wants to put their loved ones through that."

I sighed in an effort to exhale my mental exhaustion. "Can we talk about something else, please? Any good news to report?"

"I'm going to visit Wylie this weekend. She asked if you were coming, and I told her about how you're preoccupied with your mom."

"You told her about my mother having cancer?"

"Why wouldn't I? Andi, she's family now. I think she was a little disappointed that you didn't tell her yourself."

"Didn't it occur to you that my mother might not want the entire world knowing?"

"What, you think Wylie's going to post it on Facebook?"

"What *has* she been posting on Facebook? About you, I mean. Did her friends know her father wasn't really her father in the first place?"

"I haven't asked her about it."

For some reason I didn't believe him. Although, come to think of it, I hadn't asked her either. Why?

"Well, maybe you should. After all, that's your life she's making public as much as hers. And mine. Ours."

"So?"

"So . . . so you never know who she knows. She might know someone who knows someone who knew you back when you were an escort. In fact, that you've managed to keep your former life out of your clients' sight this long is pretty remarkable, don't you think?"

"She's a teenager, Andi. I doubt she knows anyone who—"

"It's a small world, Dev."

"OK," he said, "I'll make sure she's being discreet." He turned out the light and kissed me gently on my forehead, pulling a strand of hair away from my eyes.

Once in bed, I lay still and replayed the conversation, wondering why I was so defensive. It came to me moments later.

"David?" I called.

"Yes?"

"Did you not want me to come with you?"

"I just figured you'd be busy catching up with your classes and whatnot."

I didn't believe him. Could hear the lie in his voice. Or, if not the lie, the omission.

"You could have at least asked me," I said. "I would have liked to have come with you."

The room was dark and silent.

"Janine doesn't want me at the house, right?" I said. "Even with you there."

He didn't respond right away. "She'll come around."

So that was that. David's telling Wylie about my mother was a convenient cover, an excuse for me to be out of her life. And I had no choice but to give in to what David and Janine, and perhaps even Peter, wanted.

I fell asleep, and dreamed that I was serenading Sam in his wrecked Mustang, singing "Two of Us," as if it were the only way to bring him back to life. I even remember thinking how stupid I'd been for not trying it years ago.

chapter thirty-two

I overslept the next morning, but still made it to class on time. I had considered canceling, but given that I was already getting someone else to cover for me once a week, I didn't want to give students the impression that I didn't care. I dragged myself from hallway to hallway, room to room, keeping lessons brief and ending workshops early. Jeff was right yet again—I didn't know what I had gotten myself into. But the semester would be ending in less than two months, with Thanksgiving break smack in the middle. Surely I could hold out for two months, couldn't I? I wouldn't be going to Long Island again until Thanksgiving, and then I'd wait until the semester was over and stay there straight through Christmas break. David and I discussed it.

As I walked across the parking lot, classes completed, my cell phone rang. Normally I turned it off during the school day, but because of the situation with my mother I now kept it on at all times. And sure enough, it was her.

"Hi, Mom," I said. "What's up?"

"Andi?"

I stiffened the moment I heard the alarm in her voice.

"Mom, what is it?"

She cried. "My hair is falling out! I knew it was going to happen, I just didn't expect it to . . . I can't go anywhere like this, Andi! I don't know what to do or who to call!"

I did an about-face and raced back to my office the moment she spoke, closed and locked the door, and went to my desk, as if sitting there would allow me to think more clearly.

"Is there someone at the Cancer Center who can help you?"

"I have to buy a wig. How am I going to buy a wig looking like this?"

"Where are Joey and Tony?"

"Are you listening to me?" she yelled, panicked. "I can't let *anyone* see me like this! Especially not your brothers. Please, Andrea, I need *you*."

"Mom, even if I were able to get standby on the ferry, by the time I got to Long Island the stores would be closing. Plus it'll be rush hour. . . . I just can't." Despite my compassionate tone, I felt like I'd just slammed a door in her face. I closed my eyes and took a deep breath so as not to be swept up in her panic. I knew what she was asking. This was my mother, Genevieve Cutrone, who never left the house without a full face of makeup, even in the first days after my father died. Come to think of it, I don't think I've ever seen her wear a pair of blue jeans.

"I'm going to leave first thing in the morning, I promise. In the meantime, call the Cancer Center and ask them what to do. It's going to be OK, Mom."

"We should've done this weeks ago," she scolded. "We should've been prepared."

"Yes, you're right," I said. "I should've thought of it."

She cried. "I didn't want to think about it. I didn't want to admit that this is really happening."

I willed to keep my composure. "No one does, Mom. You're human."

She didn't answer.

"Call the Cancer Center," I said again, trying to be direct but nurturing. "OK?"

She finally got herself together. "OK. I'm sorry, dear."

Her tenderness toward me in the midst of her upset touched me, and my eyes welled up. "It's OK. I'll be there tomorrow and we'll go wig shopping first thing. Scratch that—we'll go get *bagels* first; then we'll go shopping."

She managed a tiny laugh, and I smiled in spite of myself. "I'll be there soon."

"Thank you," she said, and we hung up.

When I got home I explained the situation to David before calling Joey and Tony afterward.

"Too bad the ferry isn't on the way to Hartford. I would've dropped you off instead of you driving—although come to think of it, you would then need someone to pick you up at Orient Point."

"You're still going to see Wylie?" I asked, flabbergasted.

"Why wouldn't I?"

"I'm having a bit of a crisis here, in case you haven't noticed."

"Andi, you just told me your mother won't let your brothers see her. What makes you think she'll want me around?"

"I need some support too, you know."

"So, what, you want me to just sit around on the Island? Or here, for that matter?"

"Would it kill you to do that for me?"

"Wylie's going to think I don't care."

I lost it. "Well, you know what? Too bad. She's going to have to learn that the world doesn't revolve around her, just like every other fifteen-year-old. Frankly, I expected you to be more supportive. I seem to recall you canceling appointments left and right when your father was sick."

"I wouldn't have canceled on my daughter."

"You don't know that," I argued. "You don't know what you would've done. Besides," I said, "It's not like she needs you. She already has a father. And a mother. She doesn't *need* us, Dev. We're not her family. We're . . . we're *home wreckers!*"

David's face turned hot tamale red with anger; invisible smoke shot out of his ears like a pressure cooker.

"This time *I'm* going to sleep in the study." And with that he slammed the bedroom door behind him.

⁓෴෴⁓

I arose early the next morning without an alarm and drove to New London without saying good-bye to David. While waiting for the ferry I chatted with Andrew via Gmail chat—we kept the conversation casual, but I found myself wanting to tell him about the fight with David. Why did I want to tell *him* and not Maggie or Miranda? Worse still, when had *David* stopped being my confidant? Why didn't I follow him into the study last night, lock the door, and refuse to leave until we worked things out? That was more our style.

Maybe because David had stopped confiding in me. Wylie was his priority now. And maybe even Janine. I had the urge to call Peter Baker and ask him how his marriage was holding up, if he'd spent any nights on the couch lately. At least he and I could commiserate.

Before I boarded the ferry, Andrew and I arranged a day to meet.

Me: Just so you know, I'm going to tell David about it. I don't want him (or you) to think this is some kind of date between you and me.

I wondered if that caveat was for Andrew's sake or for mine.

Andrew: I'm sure that's a wise thing to do. And I don't think it's a date.

When I got to Mom's house, I entered using my key and found her bundled in her fleece robe and asleep on the couch, a scarf ineptly wrapped around her head. Tears came to my eyes. I covered her with a blanket, went to my room, and dropped off for a nap.

chapter thirty-three

November

"You can't keep doing this," said Maggie. "You've lost weight. You're pale. You've got dark circles under your eyes. I haven't seen you this ragged since Sam died."

"Gee, thanks, Mags."

"Take a look in the mirror."

Thing is, I knew she was right. We were sitting on one of the couches at Perch (rather, she was sitting; I was slouching) after classes. I'd just recounted the story about the Great Wig Emergency. Despite her being so frantically upset when she called, the next day Mom awakened with the tenacity of someone on a mission. The counselor at the Cancer Center recommended a store, and when we arrived I couldn't help but feel like a mother and daughter playing dress-up. I tried on just as many wigs as she did, and the sales assistants were top-notch (unfortunately, they had assisted many customers who were cancer patients—too many). Together we struck poses in the mirror, rating each other's picks on a scale of one to ten—the retro Cyndi Lauper got a five on me, while the Senator Hillary Clinton got a seven on Mom. I even convinced her to try on a neon pink bob that made her look like a trendy Hamptonite. She fixed each one over the scarf she wore around her head—she wouldn't let anyone see her without it, not even me. And maybe it had been a good thing that she did, because I probably would've stared at her, not in a gawking way but one that drew me into her vulnerability, her personhood, her inner woman that I had been too self-absorbed to care about but now couldn't get enough of. Every glimpse drew me closer to her, and I wanted to stay there.

Best of all, we *laughed*. My mother actually laughed and smiled and even encouraged me to buy one as well. I recalled an old *All in the Family* episode when Gloria buys a brunette wig, but accuses Mike of secretly wanting to sleep with another woman because he's so turned on by the wig that he wants her to wear it during sex. The scene further prompted me to recall David's and my recent encounter when he was Devin. Which was what had prompted me to buy a wig of my own—the same style as the neon pink one, only in neon blue. Mom wound up buying three wigs, all silver and similar to her traditional hairstyle.

Maggie, however, seemed more fixated with the other part of the story, which was David's weekend in Hartford with Wylie.

"You mean he went anyway, given what just happened?" Maggie asked.

I shrugged a yes. "What else was he going to do, sit around and twiddle his thumbs at home?"

"Um, hello? He could've come to Long Island instead and supported you and your mother."

"My mother wouldn't even let my brothers see her without hair—no way she was going to let David within ten feet of her." I wasn't sure why I was suddenly defending David to Maggie when I had judged him for the very same things. I crashed to the side of the couch and lay there for a moment. "I'm burning out fast. The booster rockets aren't firing. Impact is going to be at a crushing velocity—"

"Enough with the NASA metaphors!" she said. "We get it, you're a mess."

"There's more."

"*More?*"

"I'm meeting Andrew," I blurted, then winced and braced myself as if she were about to hit me.

She dropped her jaw and kept it there for a full five seconds. "Are you *crazy*? Did you wake up one morning and drink a bottle of crazy juice?"

"Isn't that what Red Bull is?"

Maggie gave me an ominous look. "Andi. You and David aren't even married yet, and already you're putting your marriage on the line."

"It was on the line the moment he found out he had a daughter," I argued.

"No. Don't make Wylie your get-out-of-jail-free card. I'm not saying it's not a situation wrought with complications, but it's something you can get through *together*. And it seems to me you *were* getting through it together, until Andrew came into the picture." Maggie stopped and put her hand to her chest. "Oh God, this is my fault. I never should've told you he was looking for you. I never should've opened my big fat mouth to him in the first place. . . ."

I put my hand on Maggie's. "Whoa. Mags. Stop. You didn't do anything wrong. Andrew would've gotten in touch with me one way or another." I pressed on. "It's not Andrew's fault either. And it's not mine, or David's, or anyone else's. Things are just . . . messed up. And Andrew's been a friend. It's just a lunch—a lunch between *friends*," I emphasized.

Maggie remained unconvinced. "Please tell me you at least told David you're meeting him."

I nodded. I told him when we each got back from our

respective weekends. My intent was to wear the wig, play out another little game with Devin, and have much-needed makeup sex. But David was in no mood, and I wound up blurting out the news about Andrew.

"And?" said Maggie.

"And let's just say makeup sex has been postponed."

"Can you blame him?"

"Hey, he's no saint in all this." I sighed heavily. "Let's talk about something else, please. Still no plans for Thanksgiving?"

"I'm following Jeff and Patsy's lead and getting the hell out of here. Going skiing in Vermont."

Jeff Baxter and his wife Patsy had shocked everyone when they announced they were taking a cruise Thanksgiving week. At the present moment I was considering stowing away in one of their suitcases. Maggie had lost her parents years ago, and she was an only child. Usually she spent holidays with cousins or friends or whomever she was involved with at the time, but lately the prospect of being by herself, of not feeling as if she'd been dropped off on someone's doorstep or being taken in out of pity, appealed to her, and I empathized.

"How about you?" she asked.

David and I usually switched off the holidays between my family and his, but we agreed that we were going to be with my family this year. In fact, Joey and Tony and I already agreed to take charge of cooking dinner, and we'd stay either at Mom's house or in town for Thanksgiving. Mom complained profusely about not being the one to cook—she'd had that duty for the better part of twenty-five years—but I knew she was also grateful to have all three of her children there. Joey was planning to bring his girlfriend and her daughter, Lisa, for dessert.

"What about Wylie?" asked Maggie.

"What about her?" I replied.

"She's not joining you?"

"A little soon for that, don't you think?"

"David is obviously working very hard to have a relationship with her. Why wouldn't he want her there?"

"Wanting her there and inviting her are two different things," I said. "Besides, would you invite a kid you've only known for two minutes to *my mother*'s house, even when she's at the peak of health?"

Maggie considered this. "You've got a point."

I instantly felt guilty for the remark. "I shouldn't say things like that anymore. She's changed a lot these last couple of months." God, was that all it had been? Seemed much longer. "The last few years, really."

"You can be angry at someone who has cancer," said Maggie, no doubt thinking about her boyfriend James, who had lost his life to Leukemia about fifteen years ago. "I mean, you don't want to stay angry at them, but it's OK to be that way every now and again."

I knew what she was trying to tell me. But I couldn't help but see the bigger picture. In the past, when I took such potshots at my mother, I justified them as payback for all the grief she'd given me throughout my life. But in the present moment, I finally saw it for what it really was: petty resentment. It was time to stop. Time to let her off the hook once and for all. It was time to *start over*. Time for me to be a better person. After all, hadn't I credited Andrew with that? And David? And her? They deserved the same from me, and more. Much, much more.

⁓∞⫘∞⁓

That night I suggested to David that we go to a movie—we hadn't done anything "datelike" in ages. He agreed, but with little enthusiasm. We were quiet to and from the theater, and although we held hands during most of the movie, the tension between us was palpable.

When we came home, before David could turn on the lights inside the house I pulled him to me in the dark and wrapped my arms around him. We held each other, the only sound being our breath. I shut everything out for that moment and focused on the feeling of our embrace: Safe. Solid. Real. I wanted to be present and committed to it.

He found my lips with his fingertips and kissed me.

"*Mia cara*," he practically whispered. "I miss you."

I hadn't expected him to say that, and I wasn't even one hundred percent sure what he meant. Was he missing my physical presence because of my trips to Long Island? Was he missing my company? My trust? All of the above? Was I missing him too? I was certainly missing the way things used to be, when it was just the two of us and no one else pulling us in different directions. Or maybe for the first time we were letting ourselves be pulled.

I embraced him again. "I miss *us*," I said. With every inhale, I longed to breathe in David's love, his firm grasp, his familiar fragrance.

"Do you really have to go?" he asked. He sounded on the verge of tears. It took me less than a second to realize that he was talking about my lunch meeting with Andrew the next day.

"I'll be back," I promised.

He held me even tighter.

"Where are we?" he asked.

I didn't understand the context of the question. But asking him to elaborate would only pull us farther apart; after all, shouldn't I know what he meant? Was my inability to read his mind one more warning sign that we were in trouble? And how many more signs would I need before I finally heeded them?

"We're home," I replied.

He didn't say anything else. I had no idea whether I'd gotten it right.

chapter thirty-four

Trying to decide what to wear for my meeting with Andrew was like trying to decide what to wear for a blind date. On one hand, I didn't want to get all dolled up—I didn't want to care at all, wanted to dress the way I would if I were meeting Jeff or Maggie or Miranda for a burger.

But I *wasn't* meeting Jeff or Maggie or Miranda. I was meeting a man whom I had once been in love with a lifetime ago, who had once been in love with me. And I couldn't help but want an eat-your-heart-out moment—for him to feel a pang of regret for having dumped me for Tanya. Hence, I showed up to Bertucci's in Harvard Square (an approximate midpoint from where we each lived) dressed in boot-cut blue jeans (which were loose on me—Maggie was right about my having dropped weight since Labor Day weekend), a red cashmere sweater (Andrew used to say I looked good in red), and suede boots with a heel high enough to give me some confidence in the vertically challenged department, but not so high that they felt as if I were walking on stilts. I managed to fix my hair into some semblance of a style, and I did the best I could to conceal the dark circles with makeup.

Andrew was already waiting at the table for me. He looked different. His hair had gone considerably gray—the kind of gray that made a man look intelligent and distinguished rather than old—and was clean-shaven, as Maggie had reported, a change from the last time I'd run into him. Although he'd always been thin and a runner, he now looked as if he'd been weight training. He was dressed in blue jeans and a black cotton button-down shirt—he must have remembered that I always thought he looked good in black. Today Andrew looked stylishly handsome. He looked . . . humble.

He broke into a wide grin when he saw me and stood up as I strode over to him. And then he opened his arms. *Oh God, he wants to hug me.* My body tensed up as I allowed him to fold me in, and damn it for feeling nice. The scent of him took me back to another lifetime.

"You look wonderful," he said, still grinning ear to ear.

"For someone who hasn't slept in six weeks, sure," I said as if making a friendly joke, but was secretly grateful for his assessment. "You, on the other hand, look like you've been taking care of yourself."

"Stop," he said. "I mean it. You're so pretty." I blushed. We sat at the table, and he stared at me for a few seconds, almost as if trying to place me. "God, Andi. It's like you're a completely different person."

"I am a completely different person."

"Even the way you walk. It's—I don't know, it's like looking at someone who's both familiar and foreign at the same time."

"Yeah, I know what you mean," I said.

We barely had a moment to get the small talk out of the way when a server came to collect our drink orders.

"Ginger ale for you, right?" said Andrew.

"Actually, just water is fine."

He ordered a Diet Coke for himself and we opened our menus. I didn't think I'd be able to swallow anything, my stomach was so tightly knotted.

"Should we just split a pizza?" he asked.

"Fine by me," I replied. He placed the order when the server returned with our drinks, handed the menus over, and then returned his attention to me. I could hardly sustain eye contact with him for more than a second. Every time I did, he erupted into a smile, which then pulled one out of me.

"So . . . ," he started. "First off: your books." And as if that were the starter's pistol, we were off and running. We moved from the topic of my writing to his to others', caught up on teaching, retold funny stories about our former colleagues, and I could feel the knots loosening as I laughed. When our pizza arrived and Andrew plated a slice for me, he asked me questions about my mother, and I talked past it until I finally had to change the subject, which I decided was sports, followed by politics, followed by music, followed by movies. Occasionally I inserted David's name into the conversation as part of a story or a remark, and not deliberately, but Andrew asked me nothing directly about him, and I didn't go near Andrew's love life.

Some part of me was standing outside of myself and observing all of this—observing *me*—and taking note of how comfortable I was with Andrew, how quickly we'd found a groove and stayed there, how easy it could be for either one of us to reach out and pat the other on the arm, make some kind of physical contact, and think nothing of it. I wondered, had the last few weeks of e-mail communication allowed us to be so open and casual with each other, or the fact that we had once been intimate with each other? Or was it that I'd grown into an emotionally available woman as opposed to the chick who'd refused to hatch back then?

Or maybe it was all of the above.

Whatever it was, I liked it. And so did Andrew, I could tell.

But we'd not yet talked about what we came to talk about. Or maybe this was precisely what we'd come to talk about: Maybe we'd come to tell old and new stories, to find out what had become of the good ol' days, to make each other laugh.

I hadn't even realized that an hour had passed since we'd paid our check. Didn't even look at my watch once. Neither did he. Not until I looked around and noticed that, in addition to another couple (another *couple*?), we were the only ones there.

"I should probably head home," I said. "David is waiting for me."

Neither of us moved.

"You know, my fiancé isn't too thrilled with my being here," I said. "I almost canceled half-a-dozen times."

"Why didn't you?" he asked.

"Because . . ." I couldn't finish the sentence. *Because I wanted to see you* sounded way more charged than I meant. Maybe I didn't want him to get the wrong impression. Or maybe I was afraid it meant exactly what I didn't want him to think it meant.

"I'm glad you didn't cancel," he said. "I've missed you."

"Are you sure?" I asked.

"What do you mean?"

"Well, I'm not the person I was when you and I were together. So who, or what, are you really missing? I can't believe it's the old me. I hope it's not."

He looked pensive. "That's a good question." He mulled it over. "Maybe you're right. Maybe it's not you—the old you. Maybe I'm just missing *this*—the way we've been with each other today. Even in the e-mails. I feel like I'm not even trying—and I don't mean that—"

"I know what you mean," I finished for him. "And I'm glad we're at a place where we can be this way with each other. I like being able to look at you without wanting to bean you with a frying pan."

He laughed. "I like that too."

"Seriously," I said. "I like that it doesn't hurt anymore. Maybe because everything worked out exactly the way it was supposed to. There was no way we would've been happy, Andrew. Even if you hadn't cheated on me with Tanya."

He winced with regret. "I want us to be friends," he practically begged, a mixture of sadness and longing in the words as well as his eyes. "Can we be friends?"

"What does being friends mean to you? What does it look like?"

"This," he said. "E-mailing. Talking on the phone. Meeting for lunch every now and then."

The images of our proposed friendship flashed before me, and it all looked good. In those split seconds I tried to convince myself that such a friendship wouldn't be any different from my friendship with Jeff or, in earlier days, Julian the Spanish teacher. But I knew better. And then I thought of David. All during the drive to the restaurant, I worried that maybe this was the final straw and David was packing his things despite his desperate attempt to get past the hurt and the fights. He even wished me a good day this morning.

Andrew was my past. David was my present and my future. He was my husband-to-be. A friendship with Andrew— hell, any further communication between us—would be a permanent wedge between David and me. And that thought was too much to bear.

"If only we could, Andrew. But it's just not possible."

"Why not?"

"Because there would always be an asterisk attached. You were once my lover—perhaps not literally in the physical sense of the word, but you and I were intimate with each other, as intimate as I could be at the time. That will never change, and is never far from my awareness. *That*'s the easy part you're feeling right now, what I've been feeling all day. But the thing is, I can't in good conscience sustain that with you and at the same time be with the man who is going to be my husband. It's just not fair to him. Especially since you're . . . *unattached* right now."

"But if he knows we're friends, if we're being completely transparent . . ."

I shook my head. "No. You have no idea what's been going on lately. There's a lot of family stuff that I haven't told you about because it's just too personal and I can't bring myself to go there with you."

"Why? If we both feel so comfortable, then why not?"

"Because it would be too easy to. Because a part of me *wants* to, and that's dangerous."

His failed attempt to hide the glimmer in his eye only confirmed the danger signal sounding in my head like a submarine red alert. Dammit, I knew I shouldn't have disclosed that much.

"Are you and David having problems?" he asked.

I didn't answer.

"Because of me?" he prodded.

"David and I are fine," I lied. "Better than fine. We're getting married."

He looked disappointed, but resigned. "I understand."

"I'm super-grateful we did this—it healed a lot of old wounds for me. But—"

"I got it," he said. "I really appreciate that you agreed to see me in the first place, especially with everything that's been going on."

"I'm sorry, Andrew."

"There's no need to apologize. It's OK. We're OK." He paused for a beat. "C'mon, let's get going. I'll walk you to your car."

We exited the restaurant, commenting on the foreshadowing of winter and Christmas, and when we reached my car, Andrew held his arms open for me one last time. I stepped into them, and as he closed them tightly around me, I took hold, simultaneously grabbing onto and letting go of the Andrew Clark Years, beginning with when we first met to the present, all zooming past me at light speed. His embrace was so warm, so reminiscent of the good our relationship had once been, the good I believed it to be now, and I needed to run away, lest it suck me in completely.

Just as I let go, I caught our reflection in the car window—seeing us side by side with his arm still around me, the way we had once been, was surreal.

"I have one more request, Andi."

I groaned. "No. Please, Andrew."

He took hold of my arm before I could escape into my car. "Please. Just come see me play this Saturday night. I'm playing at a club in Amherst, near you."

"Why so out of the way for you?"

"I've been thinking about relocating for some time now. Amherst is such a great college town. I'm sure it wouldn't be hard to get a teaching position, if only part-time, and the music scene can't be all that bad either. Better than where I am now."

"You never said a word about it," I said.

"I was afraid you would think I was doing it because of you. But I'm not, I swear. It just seems like a great place to live, and you certainly love it there. So I figured I'd test the waters a little, check out the music scene. But I need to get some warm bodies in the club for the gig to pay off. You know the deal."

I did. Some club owners paid bands, especially those new to them, a percentage of the cover charge. Or booze sales. Or just a flat fee. It was crucial to get people to show up, especially if you wanted to return to that venue.

I shot him a suspicious look. "Andrew. You're asking a lot of me."

"Please? I need some friendly faces! Come see me on Saturday and I'll never contact you again."

"That's what you said about today."

"This time I mean it for good. You can even bring David if you want. In fact, I insist you bring David. After everything you've told me, I'd love to meet him."

An image of a bar brawl popped up before my mind's eye, instigated by David walking onstage and smashing Andrew's acoustic guitar, like Pete Townshend from the Who. Then again, if Andrew had ulterior motives, he wouldn't be so insistent about my bringing David, would he? Besides, I knew how tough it was for musicians to fill a room when they were new to the scene. And because of my brothers, I couldn't turn my back on a musician.

I'd made my position clear. And David's presence would seal the deal. Maybe this wasn't such an unreasonable request.

"I'll think about it," I said, and before he could say or do anything else I jumped into my car and closed the door. I heard him call, "Drive safe," but all I could muster was a polite wave as I started the car and pulled away as quickly as I could.

I ached for Sam. I ached for Devin. I ached for my mother and brothers. I ached for this feeling to go away.

chapter thirty-five

The sun had just set when I entered the house and called out for David. We met up in the kitchen as I perused the mail.

"You're home later than I expected," he said, his voice stony. Not even a kiss hello.

"Traffic," I said.

"How was it?" he asked.

"Good. I mean, it was fine." I knew he was waiting for me to elaborate, but I couldn't get the words out.

"Hungry?" he asked.

"Not really. I'll just have a yogurt or something."

"Fine," he surrendered, and left the room. I felt like dirt.

Later that evening, David entered the study, where I was sitting at the desk and staring at my laptop screen after responding to student e-mails. I put in a call to Maggie, but had gotten her voice mail and no callback thus far.

David stood behind me and massaged my shoulders. A thought that he was preparing to choke me and dispose of my body in the Charles River popped into my head. Can't say I'd blame him.

I took hold of each hand and caressed them with my thumbs. "I'm sorry," I said, still staring at the laptop. "For everything." Tears slid down my cheeks.

"It's OK." He bent over and buried his face into my shoulder and neck for a moment, inhaled and exhaled deeply. His warm breath made my skin tingle. "Come sit with me," he beckoned. I stood up and followed him to the couch, where he pulled me close to him and put his arm around me. We sat there, eyes closed, still and silent save the sound and sensation of our breathing.

He finally spoke, his voice soft and calm. Soothing, even. "If you don't want to talk about it, I understand. I'm trying really hard to be supportive of you."

"But . . . ," I said, drawing out the word.

"But I'm going out of my mind."

I felt weary, as if I'd been awake for months on end. "I really want to tell you," I said, "but I'm just not sure how to put it all into words."

"Did you like seeing him?"

"Yes, I did. But not the way you think. It was nice to see him and not feel the hurt and rejection that used to consume me. And I suppose it was equally nice to see him look at me in a way he never has before. Like he noticed me for the first time."

"You have that effect on people," he said. "Men in particular," he ended with a soft chuckle.

"He's a better person, Dev. If nothing else, it was nice to see and share that."

"I'm glad. For your sake, anyway. So what's got you so troubled? I can see it on your face."

I took in a breath. "He's playing a gig in Amherst this Saturday and invited both of us to go."

I faced David so I could gauge his emotional reaction. He shook his head in disgust. "You still think this guy just wants to be your friend?"

"Look, if he had ulterior motives, then why would he invite you to come along? In fact, he *insisted* you come. And I told him that this would be the last time, and we're not going to see or communicate with each other anymore. A friendship with Andrew Clark isn't worth very much if it tears you and me apart. He was OK with that. Understanding, even. He just asked for this one last favor. And I believe him when he says this is the last one."

David guffawed and muttered, "Well that's very nice of him." He paused for a beat. "You wanna go."

"Not without you, I don't."

"Why do you want to go with me?"

"Because I want to prove to you that there's nothing beyond a friendship." Was it possible I wanted to prove it to myself too?

"I don't believe you, Andi. What's more, I don't believe *him*."

"David, if you can't trust me . . . ," I started, but didn't finish my sentence. Too many ultimatums had been handed out already. "So you're not coming with me?"

"I'll pass, thanks. But you do what you want." He stood up and left the room. I followed him down the hall to the bedroom.

"Dev," I started. "Please. Let's talk about this. We don't talk anymore."

He whipped around. "Talk about what? You made your choice."

I gave him a cold stare. "And you made yours."

chapter thirty-six

I went to Jeff Baxter's office, poked my head in without knocking first, and announced, "I hate you for being right," before walking back down the hall to my own office. Moments later, Jeff found me, my head down on my desk, exhausted.

"Go ahead and say it," I said, my voice muffled by my face buried in my hands.

"I don't have to say it, kid," said Jeff. He took the seat next to my desk.

I picked my head up. "OK, then I'll say it. I was a fool to think I could handle this."

"Handle what?"

"My mother's chemo treatments are no picnic. And every day is a reminder of how much time we wasted and how little time we have left. Then there's Wylie, David's daughter. Her mother won't let me see her; says that if I do she'll make David's life hell. Meanwhile, David's getting to know her without me. Between that, my mother, classes, the holidays—" I stopped short of mentioning Andrew. I was so worn out just listing everything that I put my head down again.

"Can I get you anything? Water? Tea? Time machine?"

I couldn't help but chuckle as I picked up my head again and slouched in my seat. "I don't know, Jeff. When Sam was killed, it felt as if my entire world blew into smithereens. Now it feels like it's being chipped away piece by piece."

"You think one is better than the other?"

"I suppose there are pros and cons to both, although I can't believe they're on equal footing."

"Can I put something out there, as a friend?" asked Jeff.

"Shoot," I commanded.

"You really hate change, don't you."

I chuckled again. "My therapist pointed that out to me a couple of years ago, yes," I said. "I thought I had learned to adjust to it, even like it. But there's just so much of it happening all at once."

"When you hit a patch of ice and you start to skid, the instinct is to resist the skid, right? But the best thing to do is to turn *into* the skid. Doesn't mean you'll avoid slamming into something else, or someone slamming into you, but you'll likely do a lot less damage."

"You're telling me to turn into the skid?" I said.

"All the way, baby."

"Baby? Are you regressing?"

"It sounded more macho. For what it's worth, kid, I think you've got to give yourself more credit. As far as coping goes, you've come a long way since losing Sam. Don't forget that."

"Then why do I still feel so inept?"

"Because let's face it: You're the A-Rod of stress. You get everyone around you to believe that you're a pillar of strength, but then you choke in the clutch."

A boisterous belly laugh escaped me. One of those maniacal, feels-so-good-to-let-it-out laughs, the kind that has you in tears, until you realize that the tears aren't from the funny. My head wound up on Jeff's shoulder as he took me in his arms and patted my back. "Geezus, I had no idea you were such an A-Rod fan," he quipped. I laughed and cried again.

"You suck," I said. "And I love you for it."

I let go of Jeff and tried to dry off his shoulder by blotting it with my hand. He picked up the box of tissues on my desk—nearly empty—and handed it to me. I yanked one out and dabbed my eyes dry, looking at the dark rings of mascara imprints. "You know, Michael J. Fox called his Parkinson's diagnosis 'the gift that keeps on taking.' That's ironically optimistic, don't you think?"

He nodded. "And sadly accurate."

⚬⟋⟋⟍⟍⚬

"Seriously? You want *me* to go with you?" asked Maggie when I approached her about Andrew's gig.

"Well, I can't go by myself, can I? And David refuses to go."

"That should tell you something."

"It tells me he's being a stubborn jerk."

"Right," she said. "*He's* being a stubborn jerk. And you're just going because it's Support a Starving Musician Day or whatever you're rationalizing."

"Mags," I protested.

"Tell me why you insist on going if David doesn't want to."

"Because I'm mad at him, OK? Because I've stayed out of the way where Wylie is concerned just so he can have a relationship with her, and he doesn't even seem to care. And fine, I'll admit it—because Andrew's been a friend to me these last couple of months."

"So have I," she said.

"I don't remember you having this much animosity toward him."

"Let's just say I liked him better when the two of you were far apart."

I sighed. "Look, I'm pretty sure David knows that when it comes to Andrew, you're on *David's* side, not mine. Thus, if you go with me, then he'll know he won't have anything to worry about."

"Or you could not go at all and he'll have nothing to worry about."

I dug in my heels. "It's the principle of the thing now, Mags. It's a test. If David can't trust me, then what chance will our marriage have?"

The venue was on Main Street, where NU faculty occasionally mixed with UMass faculty; I'd been there before. The place regularly hosted open-mic nights and jazz nights and acoustic sets, the talent typically college age. Whereas I had put effort into my attire for our lunch meeting, this time I dressed down in Sam's old Edmund College hoodie, faded blue jeans, and hiking shoes. Maggie, however, towered in dark boot-cut jeans and a peasant blouse. She lightened her hair and swapped out her glasses for contacts.

Andrew was setting up his gear, dressed not much differently from the other day, when he saw us and waved before ambling over to us, looking happy to see us. Excited, even. "Hey, I'm so glad you could make it!" He didn't hug me this time. "Where's David?"

"He wanted to come, but couldn't make it. Wasn't feeling well," I lied, as Maggie eyed him coolly.

"That's too bad," he said. I couldn't read his expression, whether he was genuinely disappointed or secretly pleased. "I was really hoping to meet him." He finally greeted Maggie. "Hey, Mags."

She looked as if she was about to deck him. "Hey."

"Set's gonna start in a few," said Andrew. "You want something to drink?"

"We're fine," I said. "In fact, we'll probably watch from the bar."

He smiled amiably. "Sounds good. The acoustics in here are pretty decent, so you'll be fine no matter where you sit. Well, I gotta get back to setting up. Hope you enjoy the show."

"Have a good gig," I said. It was something I used to say to my brothers all the time, and Andrew when we were dating. He appreciated the nostalgia with an extra-wide smile.

I turned to Maggie. "Did you hear him? He was disappointed David didn't show. Does that sound like a guy who wants to be more than a friend?"

She gave me a look that said she wasn't convinced. We claimed a high table near the bar and climbed onto the seats. She ordered some fruit-tini thing, and I ordered a virgin Bloody Mary. About ten minutes later, a guy who could pass for one of my college students introduced Andrew, who was greeted by scattered, polite applause. He took a quick bow of acknowledgment and tuned his guitar more in an act of showmanship than necessity.

He spoke into the mic. "Thank you all for coming. It's especially nice to see some familiar faces." His eyes darted in Maggie's and my direction before returning to the bulk of the crowd sitting front and center. "I'm a storyteller by trade," he said. "Some of the songs I'm going to play tonight are covers, and some are originals. But each one comes with a story, either personal to me, or within the song itself. This first one reminds me of a woman I used to know."

"Don't they all," someone in the audience heckled, drawing laughs, including one from Andrew in concession.

He began to play George Harrison's "Something." One of my favorites.

Maggie and I exchanged glances again, communicating nonverbally:

Coincidence?

Nuh-uh.

The song sounded beautiful on his twelve-string guitar. And although he sang a little sharp, his voice hadn't changed much over the years.

The set continued: John Mayer's "Daughters." Hall and Oates's "Wait For Me." Eric Clapton's "Change The World." John Lennon's "Instant Karma."

No Cat Stevens? No James Taylor? No Joan Baez? For chrissakes, he even threw in a Huey Lewis song.

"This is folk music?" Maggie asked at one point. I shrugged my shoulders in bafflement. He'd never played this many covers when I knew him; nor had he ever played this much pop. But he'd been right about one thing—he was never as talented as my brothers, and maybe the writing was on the wall. Or maybe he subscribed to the theory that when playing to a new audience, if you give them songs they already know, they'll always have something to applaud. We sat through the set, watching the sparse audience watch Andrew, and occasionally leaning in and making a comment to each other. Finally he interspersed a couple of original songs, new to me (I liked the second one), and ended with Harry Chapin's "Cat's in the Cradle," which, for some reason, audiences always liked despite its being so depressing, and they sang along with the chorus.

They showed their appreciation with boisterous applause; Andrew thanked them in return, removed his guitar and gently rested it on its stand before heading toward the bar, and was stopped along the way by tipsy patrons wanting to bestow a little more praise on him.

"I guess we can go now," I said.

"In that case, I'm going to the ladies' room first," said Maggie. As soon as she left, Andrew approached the table.

"So what did you think?" he asked.

"It was good," I said. "Although, I have to admit, it wasn't what I was expecting. Since when do you do pop songs? You were always a straightforward folk guy when I knew you."

"I've finally surrendered to the fact that pop songs draw a bigger audience. Besides, I confess I was trying to appeal to your tastes as well."

At least he copped to it, I thought.

"We're taking off after Maggie gets back," I said.

"I thought for sure your fiancé was going to be with you."

"Yeah, he wasn't feeling well," I repeated, averting his gaze as I said it. But when I reconnected, I was met with a hot stare of lust. And then Andrew leaned in so fast to kiss me that I almost fell off the chair trying to dodge him. Maggie's empty glass got knocked over in the process.

"*What are you doing?*" I yelled, drawing attention to us.

"Andi, I—"

"What part of 'I'm engaged' did you not understand?"

"Come on, Andi—we were good together. I screwed up before but I'm different now."

"Oh, really? So instead of breaking up your own relationship by cheating, you're breaking up someone else's by getting them to do it? Yeah, that's really evolved." I pulled on my coat and stood up. "I am such a fool."

"If you're so committed, then where is he? Where's your precious David? And don't tell me he wasn't feeling well. I spotted that lie a mile away the first time you said it."

"So you decided to take his place. Some friend."

"I made a little bet with myself. If David showed, then I'd walk away, fair and square. But if he didn't, then it would be your way of telling me that there was still a chance. Are you seriously telling me I misread this?"

A myriad of options flashed before me: slapping him in dramatic fashion; throwing what was left of my drink in his face; going up and smashing his guitar the way I had imagined David doing. I opened my mouth, but nothing happened. I froze.

Turn into the skid.

"You . . . *asshole*," I said through clenched teeth.

And then, in another second that warped into slow motion, David came into focus. At first, I thought he was a mirage. But then he grabbed me by the waist, turned and *dipped* me, and planted a kiss on me so smooth it practically tasted like chocolate. It even drew applause and woots.

I opened my eyes slowly, reluctantly. And when I did all I could see in the dim light were David's eyes—dappled, electric, transfixed. He pulled me to my feet. And he smiled his most dazzling smile. Devin's smile.

"Let's go, *cara*," he said.

From my peripheral vision I caught Maggie break into a grin of approval as she grabbed my purse for me and headed out the door.

Andrew, who had been rendered into a statue, watched us, gawking at David as if he were a celebrity or superhero or something. Which, of course, he was.

David stopped short and turned to him, pulling out a hundred-dollar bill. "Oh, hey. Good set, man. Next time throw something in there by the Killers." He held out the bill as if to show Andrew it was for him before dropping it on the table, then escorted me out, his hand barely touching my back in that sexy way.

chapter thirty-seven

Since Maggie had picked me up on the way to the pub, she and I said good-bye in the parking lot and I went home with David, who smelled of leather and secondhand cologne and beer and smoke.

"How long were you there?" I asked once we were in the car.

"Not long. About halfway through the set."

"I didn't see you."

"I didn't want to be seen."

We were almost to the house when I asked, "Why did you change your mind and come?"

"I guess I really am that asshole," he said, and I recalled one of our earlier fights.

"You didn't trust me?"

"I didn't trust *him*," he said, staring straight ahead at the road. Another minute of silence passed before he confessed. "And I didn't trust you."

My heart sank. He still wouldn't look at me, although he held my hand.

"I don't mean that I actually thought you would do something," he said. "I was afraid that you wanted to. I was afraid I was going to see it on your face."

"And what did you see?" Even though I asked him the question, I tried to go back in time, step outside of myself and see me from David's point of view. What would he have seen? Maggie and I were chatting a bit—would he think we were having a good time? Would he have seen how tense I was with each song? Would he have misinterpreted that as my being nervous because it made me feel tenderness rather than tension?

"You looked like you didn't want to be there," he answered.

"I didn't. At least not in the way you think."

"You looked like you were missing someone."

"I was," I said, and squeezed his hand.

"But when he came to your table, Andi . . . ," he started and trailed off.

"I was a fool to think Andrew could be a friend. To think that's all he wanted."

"Maybe that was all he wanted at first," said David in a surprising act of deference. "Maybe he took one look at you and decided to give it a shot. Not sure I can blame the guy for that. Happened to me, after all." This time he squeezed my hand.

"You never pursued me when I was with Sam," I pointed out.

He conceded. "I knew better. But in Italy . . ."

I flashed back to my trip to Rome, my first time abroad, on what was supposed to have been a second honeymoon with Sam, and seeing David for the first time in years. . . . I blushed at the memory of accidentally walking in on him in the men's room, and a smile escaped, as if having a mind of its own.

"I'm surprised you didn't punch him out," I said of Andrew.

"I could say the same of you," he said. "Besides, the alternative was better, don't you think? The way you called him an asshole . . . Suddenly you were the hottest, sexiest, feistiest version of yourself I'd ever seen. And I thought, *Holy shit, that deserves a kiss.* "

"It was a very Devin thing to do. Come to think of it, a very Devin way to *think* too."

He said nothing more until we were home and in the kitchen. I filled a kettle with water and put it on the stove.

"So we still haven't made a schedule for the painting-for-pizza arrangement," said David, out of the blue, as if trying to find something normal to discuss.

"Yeah," I replied, and added, "I changed my mind. I don't want to do it."

He stiffened. "Why not?"

I shrugged. "There's just too much going on. Plus, do we really want to keep trying to be something we're not anymore?"

"What do you mean?"

"David. Please. Lessons for painting in exchange for lessons in pizza? Are we gonna do it naked, too? A little Etta James in the background?"

"Andi, if I recall, it was your idea."

I leaned against the butcher-block table to face him. "No, it was *your* idea to do an exchange, propose an arrangement."

"So? What's wrong with that?"

"Look, you can't have it both ways. One minute you're soliciting sex from me in coffee shops; the next minute you're biting my head off for using our past against you. You insist on being David, but lately you've been taking Devin out for a walk. Like tonight, for instance. What was that really all about?"

"Sometimes I think you still prefer him to me."

I shook my head. "That's unfair. Don't lay it all on me."

"Why not? You're the one e-mailing, *seeing* your ex-fiancé. . . ."

"You make it sound like I was meeting him for sex on a regular basis."

"You might as well have. How do you think it made me feel knowing you were confiding in another man?"

"I confide in Jeff all the time."

"You know that's different. You weren't engaged to Jeff at one time. Jeff never cheated on you and then suddenly came back into your life."

"Dev, I wasn't pouring my heart out to Andrew. But he offered to listen, and no one else seemed to be doing that."

"Not even Maggie? Not *me*?" he said, wounded.

I wiped a tear from my cheek. "Especially not you."

He stared straight ahead at nothing, letting the weight of the reality sink in.

"My God, I practically drove you straight into his arms," he said after a long pause.

"No, Dev—it was *never* going to come to that. You know I wanted nothing but friendship with Andrew."

He shook his head. "Yes, it would've. If things kept up the way they have been between us, it would have. I'm not saying it would've been premeditated—at least not on your part—but the odds of it were likely."

"How could you think I would ever betray you like that? David, I want *you*. I've always wanted you."

"Not always," he said, and Sam's face appeared before my mind's eye. "God, I fucked up," he said more to himself than to me. "I fucked up ten years ago. Even before that. I fucked up the day I thought being an escort was a good idea."

I brought my hand to his cheek and caressed it. "David, no. You saved my life. You and Devin."

"And by the way, you've been happy to play along with our little game. Hell, Andi, you were salivating for it. You think I

247

didn't take note of the way you so voraciously looked at me? You haven't looked at me that way since—" He stopped short.

"Since we lived in New York, when I wanted and couldn't have you?" I finished for him. "Like *that* was so good?"

"On some level, it was. Face it. Some part of you liked having your nose pressed up against the glass. It meant no one could get to you."

"And what about *you*?" I zapped. "The glass my nose was pressed up against was yours."

He paced to the other side of the kitchen. "Fine. I admit it. I've been missing that guy lately. You know why? Because being Devin was the bomb. I was fucking Superman. I had women begging to get a piece of me, men begging to be me for a day, an endless flow of cash, and I was doing it all in the greatest city in the world. On top of that, I could stick it to my old man day after day."

In an instant, the fire in his eyes faded. He paused to collect himself. "Devin was fearless. But David is vulnerable. David's a mortal. He has weaknesses. He bleeds. He hurts."

And suddenly, it hit me: It was the *fearlessness* I'd been craving. We both were. That's why I—we—had been wanting Devin. That's what had drawn me to him back then, and now, why I ravished him that day he picked me up at Perch. Why the game was so invigorating. That craving for fearlessness, for control, started the day Wylie showed up, and it got progressively worse: first with my mother's illness, and then Andrew. Andrew set off David's fear of losing me to him, and my fear that I could possibly go. Strange, David never felt that way where Sam was concerned. But what if I was wrong? What if all this time Sam posed the same threat to David that Andrew did, and that Wylie posed to me despite my caring for her? And wasn't that what Andrew's resurgence meant to *me*?

Wasn't it more than just the attention he was giving me, more than a chance for healing and forgiveness? Wasn't his *not* being attached to anyone else appealing to me, now that David had someone else in his life, someone I'd have to share him with from now on?

Yes, it was.

I went to David, stood on my toes, and put my hand to his cheek.

"You don't have to be that guy to win me over. You don't have to sweep me off my feet to save the day. You do that just by being you. *David*. All those years ago, in your best moments, it wasn't Devin I was in love with, but *you*. The best of Devin was always you, inside and out. That goes for now, too."

He took hold of my hand, put it to his lips, and kissed it.

"I was wrong to go tonight, and I'm so sorry. My behavior was inexcusable. I gave you every reason not to trust me," I said.

He wrapped his arms around me.

"Will you forgive me?" I asked, my voice muffled.

He kissed the top of my head. "Of course," he said. "If you'll forgive me."

I kissed him, more intimately than I had in a while. We walked up the stairs, arm in arm, to our bedroom.

"So is it wrong of me to say I've never been so turned on by you in that oversized, rumpled up hoodie?" said David when we reached the top.

"You know," I said in a sly voice, "I still have that wig from when I went shopping with my mother."

He turned slick and cool and take-charge. And yet, not a trace of Devin to be found. *"Get it."*

chapter thirty-eight

Thanksgiving week

"I cannot believe you told your mother about my past," said David, more mortified than mad at me, as we packed to spend Thanksgiving week on Long Island. I'd finally spilled the beans to him. "For chrissakes, Andi, what possessed you?"

"I don't know. Maybe the chemo has vapors and they went into my brain or something."

"You know what's gonna happen the next time she sees me, don't you. She's going to try to picture it."

"I used to try to picture it all the time," I said.

"Yes, but you're not anyone's mother."

"Thanks for the reminder," I replied.

"So I was thinking," said David, "that maybe we can invite Wylie, for dessert. Just dessert."

I sighed. We'd already discussed why I didn't want to invite Wylie for dinner, didn't think it was a good idea to see her at all, didn't want to spend the day with anyone other than my immediate family.

"We've been over this, Dev. It's too soon. Wylie's been a part of our lives for two months. She's been a part of Janine and Peter's for fifteen years. What makes you think they're going to be OK with it? And besides, even if they were, you're going to drive all the way to Hartford from the East End of Long Island and back? The traffic will be murder. And all the ferries are booked up."

He looked down at his suitcase, like a boy who was just told he wasn't going to see the Yankees (or, in his case, the Mets). "You're right," he said. "Wishful thinking. Still, it would be nice to extend the invitation just as a courtesy."

"I'm sure you'll have future Thanksgivings with Wylie. Just be patient." I, on the other hand, was trying not to dwell on the reality that this was probably my last with my mom. For years I used to dread going home for Thanksgiving, loved when Sam and I made plans with his brother, or with our friends. And now I wanted a thousand more Thanksgivings with my mother.

David and I left Tuesday afternoon. We were quiet during much of the trip down, but while waiting to board the ferry, I finally brought up the long overdue conversation.

"There's something I've been meaning to discuss with you," I said. "My mother wants us to get married before . . ." I still couldn't bring myself to say it. "Well, she doesn't have a lot of time and asked if we could do it sooner than later."

David looked agitated. "Are you having second thoughts?"

"About what?"

"About getting married."

I practically gasped. "God, no, Dev. What made you think that?"

"I'm just wondering why it's taken so long for you to tell me."

I felt a kick in my gut. "It hasn't been that long. Since my mother broke the news to us."

251

"Well, considering that your mother brought it up to me on the phone almost two weeks ago, I'd say it's been a while."

My jaw dropped. "When did she call you?"

"I called her. You know, to tell her I was sorry to hear the news, offer my help. . . . Even she wondered why you hadn't said anything about it."

This gesture on his part should've touched me. But instead I became annoyed. "So why didn't *you* tell *me*?"

He shook his head. "Geezus, Andi. When are we going to get it together?" He was saying it more out of sadness than anger, desperation, even, and I felt ashamed.

✍

We decided to stay at a nearby bed-and-breakfast rather than at the house—too much chaos, and I knew Mom wouldn't be entirely comfortable with David there. It wasn't that she didn't like him—on the contrary, sometimes I thought she was more smitten with David than I was. We had stayed at the house before and she was cordial and hospitable. But although she never overtly disapproved, somehow our not being married and sharing a bed still rankled the part of her that had been raised to believe it was inappropriate to do such things. Then again, maybe I had just assumed that. Maybe she really had mellowed out over the years. Maybe she really was truthful when she said she didn't believe herself to be sexually repressed. If that was the case, then what other false assumptions had I made in the course of a lifetime? How much of our relationship could've been salvaged if we'd just found a way to directly communicate with each other?

David dropped me off at Mom's first so that I could begin the preparations, and he went to the bed-and-breakfast to check us in. Mom helped me make a shopping list and insisted on accompanying me to the supermarket. "I'm not an invalid, you know," she snapped. "I can push a grocery cart."

"Of course I didn't think that," I said. "I just didn't think you'd be up for the mayhem of King Kullen."

"I need to get out of here for a few hours," she said.

David came back to the house and gave my mother a kiss on the cheek. "It's good to see you, Genevieve. I love the wig. Love it. You wear it like a fine piece of jewelry."

My mother looked at me as if to say, *Do you believe this guy?* But I could see it in her eyes: David won her over yet again. And he wasn't buttering her up; she really did look chic and sophisticated as only she could, and I told her so. But the validation from a man, from *David*, I think meant more to her.

"Thank you," she said. "You look debonair, as always." She then slipped me a sideways glance, and I knew what she was thinking, or rather, what she was trying *not* to think. Her mind was conjuring an image of Devin the Escort, doing God knows what to God knows whom. And I cringed on the inside until I noticed something cunning in her expression, as if to say, *Well done for snaring the stud!* She seemed proud of me, and I couldn't help but laugh. David's cheeks flushed to a shade of zinfandel.

On the way to the supermarket, Mom goaded, "So tell me all about Wylie, David. Andi tells me you went to see her the weekend she was with me."

"Yes, that's right," he said as he turned onto the main road. "She's a good kid. Smart, funny, talented . . ."

"What does she do?"

"She draws and paints."

"Chip off the old block," I said.

"Do you two get along?" Mom asked him.

"It was a little awkward at first, but now we're getting along pretty well," he said.

"Must be difficult to know you missed all those years of her growing up," said Mom.

I saw him purse his lips as his eyes misted over. "Yes, it is," he said softly.

"I'm sorry Andi's father never got to see her grow up."

"He would've been proud of her, that's for sure," said David.

They carried on as if I weren't in the car. "He would've liked her being a professor," said Mom. "Probably would've preferred she taught someplace like Harvard than that liberal arts university, but that's just the way he was. Status was important to him. He would've liked that she got her PhD."

"Would've introduced her to all his friends as Dr. Cutrone, eh?"

"And called her that himself probably, yes."

I never considered that my father could've or would've been proud of me. He had spent way more time bragging about Joey and Tony playing music professionally at the ages of ten and twelve. I was just the kid with her nose in a book. Many years later, when we were well into adulthood, Joey told me that our father didn't know how to express himself around me, that he didn't want me to be some stereotypical Daddy's princess that *his* sister had been, that he didn't want me to be a prize to show off. However, the pendulum had swung so far in the opposite direction that he wouldn't let any other man take notice of me either.

"Do you really think so?" I asked.

"Why wouldn't he?" said David, although he knew all too well about how much my father had stifled me, especially when it came to expressing my sexuality.

"Andrea, you've got to get over this notion that your father and I hated you while you were growing up," my mother said.

"I never thought you *hated* me," I said. "But let's face it: There was a shortage on positive reinforcement back then. At least for me."

"I'm sure your husband more than made up for it," she replied, an edge to her tone. "And now David," she quickly added.

As I had predicted, King Kullen was a deluge of East Enders scrambling for last-minute food items, stock people building towers of canned cranberry sauce and boxes of instant stuffing, Butterball turkeys slashed fifty percent in price, and a produce aisle that looked like Armageddon. David and I navigated the aisles the way we used to the streets of Manhattan, zigzagging between shoppers and end cap displays, Mom doing her best to keep up. By the time we got to the checkout counter (each line queued with at least five shoppers), Mom had enough.

"I'm going to the car," she announced.

"You OK, Mom?" I asked. She was pale.

"I need some air."

David handed me the keys. "Both of you go. I'll stay and pay for the groceries."

"You sure?" I asked. Mom didn't object, a sign that she really wasn't feeling well.

He nodded. "Go."

I pecked him on the lips. "I love you, you know," I said for his ears only.

He grinned. "I'll meet you in the car," he said. But his eyes said, *I love you too.*

When we stepped out into the crisp air, I turned to my mother. "Why don't you wait here while I get the car," I suggested. The lot was so full that we wound up parking at least a quarter of a mile away.

"Actually, I'd rather just sit here with you for a few minutes." She pointed to a metal bench by the curb and sat down. "It's nice here in the sun."

She had a point. I joined her and squinted up at the cloudless sky. We sat and people-watched.

Mom spoke first. "Have you and David decided on when you're going to be married?"

"With everything going on, we've barely had time to discuss it."

"Please don't wait too long." I could hear the worry in her voice.

"Is there something you're not telling me?" I asked.

"Nothing you don't already know. It's just . . . it's not good to wait for things."

"OK, Mom. I'll talk to David about it tonight when we get back to the inn."

She nodded her approval, then waited a few minutes before changing the subject.

"Is there something you're not telling *me*?"

I hesitated. "We've been having problems, Mom. David and I."

"Because of this parental situation?"

"And other things—not you," I quickly added before she could jump to that conclusion. "Wylie's mother handed me an ultimatum. Either I stay out of Wylie's life or she keeps Wylie away from David."

My mother turned to me sharply. "What for?"

Tears began to well up. "I don't know. I came over to help her with her English assignment, and the next thing I knew, Janine was threatening me to stay away."

"Did you tell David?"

I wiped a runaway tear from my face. "Yes and no. He thought it would be best to placate Janine."

"I can't believe he would give in so easily," said Mom.

I shook my head. "Neither could I. But he's different since Wylie came into his life. She's become his priority."

We both seemed at a loss for words.

"He loves you a lot, Andi," my mother finally said.

"I love him a lot too."

"I can tell." She paused. "Did he like the wig?"

"Your wig?"

"No, *yours.*"

"Oh." Part of me was shocked by her boldness. But the other part, I discovered, was delighted. "He *loved* the wig," I said.

She lowered her chin and peered at me over her sunglasses. "He loved *you* in the wig," she corrected. Exactly what Mike told Gloria on *All in the Family.*

We watched a mother wheel a cart attached to a play car with her two kids in it, and I pointed in its direction. "Don't you wish they had those things when we were little?" I said, but she seemed not to hear me.

"Was it hard to be with him after Sam? I mean, is it different?"

Never had we talked like this before, and although the newness of it felt awkward, I drank it like water, parching a lifelong thirst. "Yes, it was. And that was with us already knowing each

257

other pretty well. It took me a long time to stop feeling like I was betraying Sam. God bless David, he was really patient with me. He had justification to dump me plenty of times."

"Does he ever feel like there's a ghost in the room?"

"He doesn't want me to forget Sam, if that's what you mean. We never shy away from talking about him. Sometimes he even brings Sam up, like if something reminds him of a story I told him about Sam. And he's not trying to be a replacement for Sam, nor does he think that's how I regard him. I don't think he feels like there's competition or anything like that. It's strange. Like I really am married to both of them. And David's OK with it. At least, he's never given me any hint that he's not."

"You're a lucky woman, Andi."

"I know."

"I couldn't do it. Couldn't stand to even think of a man other than your father."

"I understand. I used to feel that way about Sam."

"And the thing is, I don't think he would've been OK with the idea of me meeting someone else. If he had known he was going to die, that is. Maybe that's the other reason why I never remarried, never even considered it."

"Oh, Mom, I'm sorry," I said.

"For what?"

"I don't know. For your being alone all this time."

"I got used to it. Even got to like it after a while."

We people-watched a bit more.

"I like that we talk like this now," she said matter-of-factly.

I closed my eyes for a moment to savor her words. "Me too," I said.

My hand opened, and she placed hers into it.

"It's going to be OK, Andi," she said.

We sat that way until I caught sight of David exiting the store, hidden behind the cart loaded with plastic sacks full of groceries. Mom and I pulled ourselves to our feet.

"Wow," he said. "It's like Penn Station in there, only better smelling." I laughed. Mom smiled. "You two been out here the whole time?"

"It's a beautiful day," said Mom.

David squinted and looked around. "It really is. Wait here and I'll get the car," he said.

"I'll get it," I offered, and headed out to the parking lot, basking in the sun along the way.

We loaded the groceries and drove back to the house. When David and I got a moment alone, he pulled me to him in an embrace, and then let go to take in a view of me.

"I love you," he said.

"I love you too." It was a moment when everything in the world was OK. Yet behind it lurked a knowing that it wouldn't last.

He kissed me.

"Mom says I'm a lucky woman," I said.

"Funny, she said the same thing about herself while we waited for you to get the car."

"She did?"

He nodded. "Yep. After I told her she raised a wonderful daughter. You know what she said about you?"

I shook my head. "What?"

"She said, 'She has her father's eyes.'"

chapter thirty-nine

Joey, Tony, David, and I spent most of the day before Thanksgiving prepping, cooking, baking, cleaning the house, doing yard work, and washing Mom's car while she sat in the sunroom reading a book or closing her eyes, a blanket over her lap. Occasionally she would emerge to supervise.

I got into an argument with her when I found out she had canceled her chemotherapy appointment.

"This isn't some beauty parlor appointment you're canceling," I said. "This is saving your life."

"It's *prolonging* my life," she corrected, "and given that it's *my* life I can do whatever I damn well want with it. And I choose not to ruin what is likely going to be our last Thanksgiving together by spending it on my knees and retching."

David concurred. "She's right, Andi. Leave her alone."

I looked at him, incredulous. "I thought you of all people would be on my side."

"I am on your side," he said. "That's why I'm telling you to listen to what your mother is saying."

I tried to rally Joey and Tony, but they were aligned with her as well.

"I can't believe you two. Don't you want her around for as long as possible?"

"Not if she's sick as a dog and miserable all the time," said Tony. "Look at her, Andi. She's taking care of herself and she's content. I don't understand what you're so angry about."

And then it hit me: They were already preparing themselves to let go. I, on the other hand, was clinging to her for dear life, because I finally had the mother I always wanted. The realization smacked me in the face, hard, and I crumpled up in tears as if the pain had been physically inflicted.

"It's so unfair," I cried. "We finally . . ." I couldn't finish my sentence, and Tony took me into his arms and held me. "I hate that this is what it took," I said.

"I know," he said as he consoled me. "I'm sorry."

After I regained composure, I went to the sunroom and apologized to her.

"I'm sorry I yelled at you," I said. "I projected my anger on you. I should probably talk to someone about that," I said, making a mental note to call Melody Greene, the therapist who had helped me cope with Sam's death, after the holiday weekend.

"It's OK, Andrea. I understand. Thank you for the apology."

"Incidentally, have you considered joining a support group or something like that?"

"You know that's not my style," she said.

"You never know, maybe it'll help you. And why not try new things?"

"I am not joining a support group."

"OK, then how about a counselor, just one on one?"

"Andi, enough."

I put my hands up in surrender. Just as I left the sunroom, I heard her call out, "I appreciate your concern," and I smiled. Turned out she was trying new things.

Before David and I went back to the inn for the night, Mom said, "David, why don't you invite Wylie here for dessert tomorrow?"

Had he had been drinking something, he would've done a spit take. I was just as shocked. "Excuse me?" he said.

"I'd like to meet her. After all, she's going to be Andi's stepdaughter."

It was the first time anyone had used the word, and it felt completely inappropriate.

"That's very kind of you, Genevieve, and I'm sure she would appreciate the invitation. But Wylie's going to be with her family in Hartford for the day."

"I just thought it would be nice for Joey's stepdaughter–to-be—we hope—to have someone closer to her age to talk to." I caught her dart her eyes in my direction as she spoke.

"Perhaps for Christmas," he offered.

"Perhaps," Mom replied just as politely.

We were almost out the door when she asked me into the other room for a moment. I excused myself and followed her in, and she closed the door behind her.

"Listen to me: You have got to be a part of that girl's life," she said.

I folded my arms like an obstinate child. "She already has a mother, Mom. One who would probably get a restraining order on me if she could. And I've got a lot on my plate right now."

"Don't sit on the sidelines. You're watching David get close to her without you and it's tearing you up. Worse still, you're not telling him because you're afraid you're going to lose him if you do. And I'm telling you to stop it right now before the very thing you fear comes true."

I was astounded not only by her perception but also her clarity. This from the woman who had absolutely no advice for me when I first told her about Wylie! I recalled David telling me last year that he had experienced a similar transformation with his father. "Cancer gives you a lot of time to be still, and to think," David had said. "And not the stupid stuff like doing the dishes or your next appointment, but the hard questions. You start to put the pieces together in those moments of stillness. You figure it all out."

Mom added, "And if by 'a lot on your plate' you mean me, then you can cut that out as well. I will not be made the scapegoat for your poor decisions anymore."

I opened my mouth to protest, but cut myself off. She was right.

She didn't wait for me to respond. "Tell him, Andi. Tell him what you want and how you feel."

"I've *tried* to tell him."

"And?"

"And he says he wants me to be a part of it but he wants to keep Janine happy."

"Tell him again, and tell him everything this time. Tell him about this asinine ultimatum. Tell him you won't stand for it."

"What, you want me to issue him an ultimatum of my own?"

"You're on *his* side, remember? If you're in it together, then there's no need for ultimatums. But you've taken yourself out of it. So I'm telling you to get back in. He needs you. And apparently his daughter needs you too; otherwise that mother of hers wouldn't be playing dirty pool with you."

"Since when do *you* tell people how you feel?" I didn't meant this to be as cold and accusatory as it sounded. She didn't seem to take it that way, however.

"Since I got cancer. It's a sad reality, but there you go. It's probably how the damn tumor grew in the first place, because I bottled everything in for sixty years."

"You don't really believe that, do you?"

"We're talking about *you*, not me. And I'm telling you to talk to your husband-to-be, and get involved in that girl's life. Take her out to lunch. Take her shopping. Do *something.*"

"I'm sure her mother's going to love that," I said, deadpan.

"David will deal with her."

"Why is it so important to you that I have a relationship with Wylie?" I asked, more out of curiosity than argument. "I've never wanted children. Not even with Sam. And it never seemed to bother you that I didn't. Never bothered me either."

She paused for a beat. "Who's going to take care of you when you get older?"

I was startled by the question. "David," I said.

"And if he's not around?"

I couldn't bear the thought. "I'll take care of myself," I replied.

"And what if you can't?"

"I thought you said we were talking about *me*," I said. "Mom, I'm here. Joey and Tony and David and I are all here. And we're not leaving you. We are never, ever going to leave you. We'll be with you to the very last day."

She shook her head sadly. "You don't get it, Andrea."

I searched for understanding. "What? What don't I get?"

"I have no grandchildren. Is that your fate too? You need more. All of you."

I didn't respond because I didn't know what to say. I still didn't understand. More what?

Rather than explain, Mom gave in. "David's waiting for you. I'll see you tomorrow. Get some sleep."

"You too." We briefly hugged good-bye, and David and I went back to the inn.

"Everything OK?" he asked in the car as we drove away.

"Dev, I need to know what role I'm going to play in Wylie's life—and yours, for that matter. I need to know where I fit in. I don't want to be some *stepmother*," I said, the word reeking of condescension, "but I don't want to be on the outside anymore, either. I want in. Now."

"You were in before I was," he said, disappointment ringing in his voice.

"Not anymore," I replied. "We've got to work this out. All of it."

chapter forty

Thanksgiving Day

I had expected the day to be one of forced happiness, when you dig past the myriad of realities—a mother wearing a wig to hide the effects of chemotherapy, a fiancé missing a newly discovered teenage daughter, and a certainty that one would be here for the next Thanksgiving, and one would not. I thought my fears and sadness and anger would usurp any scintilla of gratitude.

The gratitude was that I was wrong.

I don't remember ever laughing so much with my family in the presence of my mother. Silly things, like making sculptures with our mashed potatoes and bringing the turkey back to life with a soliloquy about the virtues of veganism (to which the salad revolted). Things that forty- and fifty-somethings have no business laughing at. And Mom, shaking her head and rolling her eyes in feigned exasperation with our immaturity, a smile plastered on her face the entire time. She ate very little, picked around the edges of her plate while the rest of us were gluttonous, almost in an act of defiance. She seemed more content to watch each one of us, taking snapshots for the soul, something to carry with her into the afterlife. I imagined that if she could choose moment to live in throughout eternity, this would be it. Although I'm sure she'd somehow arrange it with God to get my father into the picture as well.

David called Wylie earlier in the day; their phone conversations were lasting longer with each call, I noticed. I thought about my conversations both with my mother and David the night before, about asserting myself more into Wylie's life and the situation, and at one point I asked David to hand me the phone, but he made an excuse that she had to get back to dinner, mouthing the word, *Janine*.

So much for me asserting myself.

After dinner, Joey went to pick up his girlfriend, Carmen, and her daughter, Lisa, and brought them back for dessert. Mom went into the living room, sat in her reading chair, and closed her eyes while Tony, David, and I cleared the dishes and cleaned up. When Joey returned, Mom attached herself to Lisa for the remainder of the evening. I'd never seen her so alight, so affectionate with anyone. She bombarded Lisa with question after question, and Lisa took it all in stride, basking in the attention, I could tell. She reminded me a little bit of David's niece Meredith when she had been Lisa's age.

Following dessert, Mom beckoned Joey and Tony to take out the guitars. "Are you kidding?" asked Tony. "I'm so stuffed even my fingers are bloated." But we all knew it wouldn't take further coaxing. Joey played Lisa's favorite first—"Blackbird" by the Beatles—followed by the usual suspects: the Doobie Brothers' "Long Train Runnin'," John Lennon's "Watching the Wheels," and another Beatles song, "Oh Darlin'."

"Play 'Two of Us,'" said Mom to Tony. "You and Andi." My heart moved into my throat. Ever since that awful night following chemotherapy, I had been singing it to her, just a verse at a time, either in person or on the phone before or even after she went to sleep. She avoided eye contact with me as she made the request. Tony and I exchanged glances as he finger-picked the opening bars, and I picked up the rhythm by tapping my foot on the floor. I took the melody while Tony took the harmony, and we laughed as we stumbled through the song, Tony forgetting some of the words or my throat closing up and missing a note. Mom seemed to appreciate the ineptitude more than if we had performed it flawlessly. And I was grateful for the levity; otherwise I couldn't have gotten through the song intact. I caught a glimpse of David watching me, his expression a hybrid of enchantment and pride and desire and wistfulness, and that, for some reason, unhinged me as tears pushed themselves to the surface. When we finished the song, he clapped, and I dabbed my eyes with the cuff of my sweater sleeve.

"Thank you, Andi," said Mom, not acknowledging Tony. "That was the best one."

I laughed and cried simultaneously, muttering, "You're crazy," to which she responded with a chuckle of her own.

"Dear, that's the nicest thing you've ever said to me," she said, a mix of sarcasm and affection, and she and I laughed even more, as if we'd just shared some private joke. I excused myself to use the bathroom, shut the door behind me, and burst into tears, covering my mouth to prevent myself from erupting into a wail.

~ॐॐॐ~

I didn't say two words during the ride back to the inn—just stared out the window at the scenic woods, on the lookout for deer and solace, sobbing quietly while David drove, no doubt his own inner cogs spinning. Later, when we were in bed, waiting in the dark for sleep, I felt for his hand and laced my fingers into his when I found it.

"Euro for your thoughts," he said his standard line softly.

My eyes were still wet. "I have a mother, Dev. Finally, after forty-three years."

"I know."

"And she's leaving me."

"I know."

"This is the way it felt when I lost Sam. Like I just found happiness, found a sense of peace and purpose and myself, and it was ripped out from under me."

He squeezed my hand, but didn't say anything for several minutes.

"I fell in love with you again while you were singing," he said, as if it were something routine. "You should sing more often. I so rarely hear you do it."

I fell in love with him again just for saying the words. I let go of his hand so I could turn to face him, and repeatedly caressed his cheek and hair.

"And I wanted . . ." He hesitated, but I somehow already knew what he wanted to say. "I wished Wylie was there. I know it's too soon, but I wished we were a family: the three of us, your brothers and Genevieve and Carman and Lisa, and my sisters and mother and—" For perhaps the first time, I realized just how much he longed for the same kind of love between his siblings as I had with mine. How much he longed for a family. "Two of us" was him and Wylie, I thought. I saw them in my mind's eye, standing side by side, those identical sienna eyes smiling. I couldn't stand between them. I could only stand on the outer edge.

I sat up in bed and flicked on the light. "There's something I haven't told you. The day I tutored Wylie, Janine issued me an ultimatum. If I made any trouble, tried to see Wylie, then Janine would forbid *you* from seeing her. And if I made any trouble about that, she threatened to out you as an escort."

David sat up as well.

"God, Andi, why didn't you tell me this? I mean, I knew she wanted you to back off, but I didn't know she blackmailed you."

"I tried to tell you. But you'd already taken her side. I understand that Wylie comes first now, and that everyone's better off without me in her life, but—"

David interrupted me. "How could you think Wylie would be better off without you in her life? How could you think *I* would be better off without you in Wylie's life?"

Something inside me snapped. "Stop it, Dev. We both have to stop this. We've done a crappy job at managing this situation, and managing *us*, too."

"Andi, I wasn't—" he stopped himself, and I wasn't sure if it was because he was censoring himself or because he didn't know what to say. "I'm sorry." His tone softened. "Janine had reservations about you from the start. That was one of the things we had talked about early on. She didn't want you spending time with Wylie alone, without me. You didn't put up much of a fight, so I figured you were OK with it. And when you were adamant about not inviting her for Thanksgiving . . . I guess I didn't know what to think anymore. Then there was everything going on with you and Andrew. . . ." He stopped himself there. I didn't say anything else either.

I turned out the light again and we lay in bed, silent and motionless. Our silence wasn't out of secrecy or resentment or worry; no, this time we were processing all that had transpired—not just then, but during the last twelve weeks. Perhaps even longer than that. He spooned me, his arm draped over my midriff in a protective clasp, locked by my own hand over his, and I felt warm and protected, like wearing a fur coat in the dead of winter.

"I don't want to lose my mother, Dev," I murmured.

"I know," he murmured back.

"And I don't want you to lose Wylie."

"I know."

"I don't want to lose her either. I care for her deeply. I did the moment I met her, I think."

"Me too," he said.

I said one more thing before drifting off to sleep: "I don't want to lose you either."

"Nor do I want to lose you," he said. "So let's make sure it never happens."

chapter forty-one

I felt guilty about leaving my mother so soon (I had originally promised to stay the entire week), but when I told her about David's and my plans to see Wylie and talk to Janine and Peter on Saturday, she practically pushed me out the door.

David called Janine the day after Thanksgiving to ask for a sit-down with her and Peter before we took Wylie out for lunch. To my surprise, she acquiesced. During the drive David and I planned how to approach the conversation—we didn't want to ambush Janine, and we didn't want to say anything that could irrevocably damage Wylie. I incessantly played out various dramatic scenarios in my head, few of them ending well. By the time we arrived I was a ball of nerves. David gently laid his hand on my back as we walked to the door, as if to anchor me. "It's going to be OK, *cara*," he said. "It's not us against them. Just remember that. We're a family now."

He was right. We were a family. All five of us. For better or worse. Expected or unexpected. And we were all on the same side.

Peter answered the door and greeted us cordially.

"Happy Thanksgiving," I offered. We had picked up a bouquet of flowers along the way, and I presented them. He seemed touched by the gesture, and for the first time in our presence, a receptive smile appeared.

"Thank you," said Peter. "Same to you. How was dinner with your family?"

"Very nice," I replied.

"Wylie told us your mom isn't doing well. I'm sorry to hear it."

"Thank you," I said.

"My father died of cancer a few years ago," said Peter.

"Mine too," said David. Peter turned to him, and in another first, looked at David not in a way that was guarded, but almost of solidarity.

"I'm sorry for your loss," said Peter.

"I'm sorry for yours as well," said David.

Peter called for Janine as he took the flowers into the kitchen. "Wylie went Christmas shopping with her sister first thing this morning. They're not back yet."

Janine entered the room. "Well, the gang's all here," she said without exchanging formal pleasantries. Instead she motioned to the seating area in the living room. "Shall we?"

We all took our unofficially designated places—David and I on the love seat, Peter and Janine on the sofa.

David took the lead. "I respectfully want to clear up some misconceptions and miscommunications." He turned to Janine. "What really happened following Andi's tutoring session with Wylie last month?"

I had warned David not to corner Janine, and was surprised he took this approach. And just as I had anticipated, her defenses shot up. "Are you accusing me of something?"

"I'm not accusing you of anything. I just want to get the facts straight."

Before he could go any farther, I jumped in. "Janine, can you show me your kitchen?" The three of them looked at me as if I'd lost my mind.

"Why do you want to see my kitchen?" she asked.

"Please?" I said again. "I'd really like to see it."

Janine shot me a skeptical glare; yet, in similar Wylie form, placated me with a "Sure, whatever."

As I stood up to follow her, David whispered in my ear, "What are you doing?" but I didn't answer him. Then I turned to the men. "Would you both excuse us?"

Peter and David exchanged awkward glances, as if to say, *What in hell are* we *supposed to do while they're in there?* But they allowed us to go.

The kitchen was open and spacious, with an island and two bar stools in the center, and the bouquet of flowers resting comfortably there. I took in the surroundings. "It's lovely," I said. I pointed to the island and asked if I could sit; she gave me her permission and I invited her to join me.

"I'm not a mom," I started. "And that was by choice. I didn't have a good relationship with my mother. In hindsight, I gave her a raw deal. I didn't understand her, misinterpreted a lot of her treatment of me as unloving."

"It must be difficult to live with that, knowing you don't have much time left with her," she said. I surmised her delivery of words to be more jagged than her intent behind them.

"It is," I said. "But here's the thing: I was always a good teacher. And I love doing it. Especially for college kids. They're at an age where they're learning to think for themselves, figure out their place in the world. And I get to help them make sense of that with words. Better yet, they let me in on that process. Sometimes we end up being counselors to our students, sometimes mentors. It's both an honor and a responsibility."

I wondered if I was rambling.

"I want to be a part of Wylie's life. But not just as a teacher or a mentor, and certainly not as a counselor. I want to be more."

Janine stiffened. "Andi, I know I was harsh the day you came here, and I'm sorry about that. Especially after Wylie told me it was the anniversary of your first husband's death. I should've apologized to you myself, but I was too angry. You have to understand what Wylie's actions—her seeking out David and bringing you both, these two strangers, into our lives—has done. It's put quite a strain on our family. On my husband and me."

Tears came to her eyes, and I restrained myself from offering some physical gesture of comfort, like taking her hand, that I would've extended to Maggie or Miranda.

"Us too," I confessed. We both fell silent as the truth consumed us. I could almost see the fights Peter and Janine probably had in their bedroom at night, after Wylie and Trish went to bed. The days of not speaking to one another, of tension thick as a forest, of being on the same side yet acting as if in opposite corners. And I felt such compassion for them, given what David and I went through.

"You know," I started, "I knew David when he went by Devin. Knew what he did for a living. In fact, that's sort of how we met. By then he was—how shall I say this?—withholding certain services. But we got to know each other, and became friends. And let me tell you, I was quite taken with him. He was rather aloof, however. Would only let me in so far, then kicked me right back out."

I could see Janine going back to that time and place, a twisted grin, no doubt remembering that charismatic guy turning on his charm.

"I thought he wanted *me*," she said. "You know what it's like to be young and stupid, thinking you'll change 'em after one night."

I nodded in validation. "Hell, yes."

"I know I should've told him about Wylie," she said. "Believe me, I have felt guilty about that."

"But you didn't think he would care?"

"Maybe. Maybe I was afraid of being rejected twice. Worse still, that he'd reject my child. *His* child."

"I can understand that," I said. "But David's so not that guy anymore. He's present and loving and committed. He's *vulnerable*. He goes to church and always strives to be a better person."

Janine seemed to be trying to conjure an image of David on his knees in prayer. "I'm glad to hear that," she said. I could hear the trepidation in her voice, however.

"You and Peter are Wylie's parents. We don't want to insert ourselves and take over as her parents. But we do want to be a part of her life. Both of us. And we want her as part of ours."

Janine paused for a beat, taking everything in. "Ever since Wylie found out Peter wasn't her biological father, she stopped trusting me. I just want my daughter back—the one who believed in me."

"I think she does. In fact, I suspect she gets her best qualities from you—her tenacity, her honesty. . . . And just from the few conversations we've had, I can tell that you're the most important person in her life."

"Wylie and Trish were both too young to remember what it was like when Peter and I blended our families. And Trish's mother was a nightmare to deal with. I guess we didn't want to go through it again."

"And here we came in like gangbusters, or so it must have seemed to you both," I said. "I'm sorry."

"I'm not a bitch, Andi," said Janine.

"I *never* thought you were," I said. "Look, I'd like for us to start over. I'm not saying we can all be one big happy family, but at least know we're all on the same side."

Janine deliberated before speaking. "I won't restrict you from seeing or speaking to Wylie anymore. I know she likes you. But if you both could just slow down a little," she said of David and me. "Give her time to breathe, and us too. I don't think Wylie has had a chance to process this. She's thrown herself in without stopping to think of the consequences."

"I think you're right. That's something we can all talk about," I said.

With that, we both returned to the living room to rejoin David and Peter. When we got there, however, the room was empty. A puzzled look came across Janine's face. "Where did the guys go?" she asked, She went into another room to look for them, calling out Peter's name. I followed her. We returned to the kitchen when, at the same time, we heard voices outside. I followed Janine out the side door to find Peter and David in the driveway, involved in a game of hoops. It was the male equivalent of what Janine and I had been doing in the kitchen, I realized. She and I watched them for a couple of minutes; they were unaware we were standing there. We then looked at each other, and I could've sworn we were thinking the same thing: *Men.* We even smiled and rolled our eyes in agreement.

chapter forty-two

Just as I had asked David for one-on-one time with Janine, I made the same request regarding Wylie when she got home from Christmas shopping. I suggested the two of us take a walk around the block. She seemed hesitant, perhaps even a little scared. But when Janine gave her a nod of approval, she agreed.

We were about fifty feet away from the house when I broke the ice.

"I want to apologize for breaking communication with you. I know you were hurt by it."

Wylie crossed her arms and looked at the houses we passed. "I know why you did. It was because of my mom. We had a big fight after you left, and I'm still really mad at her for it. I just don't understand why you caved so easily."

"Because I knew how important it was for David to have a relationship with you, and I didn't want to get in the way of that happening. I also thought disrespecting your mother's wishes and talking to you behind her back would only make more trouble for everyone."

"So, what, you don't want a relationship with me?"

"I absolutely want a relationship with you, Wylie. In fact, your mom and I just had a really good talk about it. I'm so sorry you thought otherwise. I'm sorry I let you down."

She pursed her lips and watched her footsteps on the pavement. "It's OK," she finally said.

I didn't expect to be overcome with emotion. "It took a lot of courage for you to do what you did—finding your biological father, I mean. Tracking him down that way. I didn't have that kind of moxie when I was your age."

"What's moxie?" she asked.

I smiled. "Pluck," I said. "Sass. Guts. You're never afraid to speak up for yourself. In fact, I wish I were more like you."

"Really?" she said. "My mother says I tore the family apart. Sometimes I think she's right."

"It may feel like that right now, but I think you did something much bigger. You gave David, and yourself, the gift of getting to know each other. You gave everyone a second chance."

We got to the end of the street and turned around.

"Is your mother dying?" she asked.

"Yes," I replied. "She has cancer." I wondered if this was something I should be discussing with a fifteen-year-old. But I found that I wanted to. "We've gotten really close in such a short amount of time. I spent most of my life being mad at my mother, and I regret every single minute of it now. I know you're mad at your mother for certain things, but you've got to keep the lines of communication open with her."

"OK," she said in a contemplative way. As we approached the house, she confessed, "I wasn't just mad at my mother. I was mad at you too. I'm sorry for that."

"You had every right to be mad at me."

She waited a moment before asking, "Are we OK now? You and me?"

"Yep," I said with a smile. "We are."

And in that Wylie way, she changed the subject when the moment was over. "I got an A on that English paper, by the way. It brought my average up to a B."

I practically hooted as I pumped my fists in the air. "That is *fantastic*, Wylie. I am so proud of you!" And without thinking, I put my arm around her. And without warning, she stopped in her tracks and started to sob. I didn't ask why, didn't need to know. But I put both my arms around her, she took hold of me, and the two of us cried together.

chapter forty-three

When we got back to the house, Wylie asked David and me for a rain check on lunch. We rescheduled for the following week, said good-bye to and thanked Janine and Peter, and walked back to the car. I stood on my toes, reached up to David, and kissed him; his face felt so warm against my own.

"You're cold," he said.

"You're hot." I winked. And then I blurted, "Let's elope."

He blinked in rapid succession. "What?"

"Let's get married right now. Just the two of us."

"Are you crazy? Do you know how many people you're gonna piss off, your mother being at the top of the list?"

"We can still have the ceremony she wants us to have, but we'll do this one first, just for us and no one else."

"What about Wylie?"

"She can come to the other one too. C'mon, where's your sense of adventure?"

He took hold of my hands as if to steady me. "I'm chalking this up to the stress of recent events temporarily freezing your brain." I didn't reply. Just looked at him in a sort of mischievous, seductive way. Then he broke into a smile—the electric *Devin* smile. He was *considering* it. "Hmmmm . . ."

We talked about it during the ride back to Northampton—laughing like campy villains planning our coup: getting a justice of the peace, to tell or not to tell the families, to honeymoon or not to honeymoon. . . . The closer to home we got, however, the increasingly quieter we became. When we pulled into our driveway we looked at each other, and you could hear the momentum *whoosh* out of us, like a deflating balloon.

"Face it: your mother would've known," said David. "And she would've killed us."

I concurred. "So would everyone else. No way I could keep something like that a secret."

"And the real wedding would feel anticlimactic. Like cutting into a cake after someone's already put their fingers in it."

"It probably wouldn't even feel like the real wedding. It would feel like we were fooling everyone."

We sat in the car, silent and sad.

"But the idea of having something just between the two of us is so appealing to me right now," I said. "Why is that?"

"Because it's not the two of us anymore, I guess," he said. "There's Wylie now."

"Am I wrong to want it, though?"

"I don't think so."

"Do *you* want it?" I asked.

He stared straight ahead. "I don't know what I want right now." He looked pensive, wistful, searching.

"What is it?" I asked. "You can tell me."

David cut the engine, and we sat like still lifes.

"That's not my house," he finally said.

My heart stuck in my throat.

"It never bothered me until now. And that scares me a little, because I know what it means to you."

I stared at the house too, and for the first time could see what he was seeing: Sam. Larger than life, casting some kind of dome over us.

"I now know why you sometimes feel threatened by Wylie. It's how I've been feeling about Sam lately. Maybe it'll pass, but, Andi, he never leaves. I've always been OK with it, but right now, right this moment . . ." His eyes misted over.

"Let's go to the Cambridge house tonight," I suggested.

He shook his head. "That's not home either."

"David," I said, putting my thumb and pointer finger to his chin, gingerly turning it to face me, "I wanted to marry *you* today. Just you, with no one else there. Doesn't that tell you something?"

He didn't answer me.

"Sam's not here right now," I said. It was the oddest feeling, but it really was as if he'd suddenly stepped out of our aura, left the space, and for once I didn't feel guilty, didn't feel as if I was turning my back on him. It was OK to close the door on him once in a while, I reminded myself. In fact, it was imperative, for David's sake.

"If Sam were here right this minute, in the flesh, and you had to choose between the two of us, who would you choose?" David asked.

He was asking the impossible. He was asking me to sacrifice one of my children, save a Rembrandt versus a Monet. He was giving me an ultimatum. He knew it. I knew it.

I also knew that I had to give him an answer, and whatever answer I gave him was going to change our lives forever. When I watched the second tower crumble to the ground on television on September 11, 2001, watched it disappear into its own cloud of ugly dust, I had a numbing realization: *We now live in a world without the Twin Towers. The skyline is never going to be the same.* And ever since, when I saw the gaping hole in the Manhattan skyline, I instantly felt the same gaping hole in my heart. As a New Yorker, I lost a piece of home. I lost a little piece of me, perhaps. God knows how it felt for people who actually lost a loved one that day.

Sam was my Twin Towers.

I never did like the Freedom Tower. I didn't like its look, didn't like its shape and its purpose. It didn't seem to fit in that space. It didn't fill the hole. It didn't belong.

But David did. He belonged.

I never saw it coming. Never believed it was possible. He wasn't a replacement. He wasn't a runner-up or a stand-in. He was neither better nor worse. It wasn't that enough time had passed, or I'd finally gotten over it, or shed the mythological image of Sam I'd formed over the years. But now was now, and nothing else mattered.

I looked at him, and spoke with more truth and conviction than I ever had in my entire life.

"You."

And sure enough, life changed on a dime.

"Let's get married and sell the house," I said. "Let's start over completely, reinvent ourselves."

His face glowed, as if he just saw an angelic vision. And then it turned devilish and playful.

"And I know just how to do it," he said.

chapter forty-four

Wylie, David, and I sat at a table in her neighborhood pizza parlor with our slices and Cokes.

"So," David started, and he looked about to burst, "Andi and I would love to see you for Christmas. We're going to be on Long Island with Andi's mother, and we thought either we could pick you up on Christmas Eve and then drop you off at your grandmother's in Commack on Christmas Day, or pick you up on Christmas Day. We already spoke to your parents, and they were agreeable with either-or, but of course it's your decision."

Wylie looked away, and I somehow knew what was coming.

"I figured you were going to invite me," she said. "And I'm really, really sorry, but I can't."

David's glow was doused. "Why not?"

She took in a breath. "I totally love you guys, but it's weird. Like, you guys aren't quite my parents, but you're more than just friends. My mom and I had a long talk, and what she said . . . about my tearing the family apart, and being afraid that I'd choose you . . . well, that got to me, especially since I really did want to spend Thanksgiving with you."

A wave of guilt crested over me. "That was my fault, Wylie. With my mother being sick, I didn't want to invite—"

She cut me off. "It's OK. No way my parents would've allowed it. Anyway, it made me realize that I might be rushing things a bit. And when I thought about Christmas—you know, like, all the things we do—our traditions and stuff—I realized I'm not ready to let those things go."

I understood all too well, and I told her so. David, however, couldn't speak.

"I know you're disappointed, David, and I know you want to be all father-daughter, and I kind of want that too, but, I don't know, I just want to slow down for a bit."

David looked crushed. I'd seen that look before. Hell, I'd *caused* that look before. It reminded me once more of how vulnerable he could be sometimes, what a sharp contrast it was to the invincible Devin the Escort.

Wylie took notice of it too. "Are you mad? Please, please don't hate me," she begged.

David smiled wistfully. "I'm not mad, Wylie. And I'll never, ever hate you, so please don't ever think that, and don't ever be afraid to tell me anything, even if you think it'll hurt my feelings."

I brought my hand to his back and rubbed it.

"I'm disappointed, that's all," he said. "Not in you," he quickly added. "Just in general. I guess I pushed too hard."

"You didn't mean to," she said. "And it's not like I never wanna see you again. Just not for Christmas. Not *this* Christmas," she clarified.

As bad as I felt for David, I was also secretly relieved. Even though David and I had both discussed it, both wanted to see Wylie for Christmas, I couldn't help but not want to lose even one extra minute with my mother.

David didn't respond, so I piped in. "We understand about Christmas, but would you consider New Year's Eve instead?

We're having a party, and we really want you to be there. We've invited our family and close friends."

"Please?" said David. "It would *really* mean a lot to us if you came to this party."

"I'll think about that one," she said. "And I'll ask my parents."

After Wylie excused herself to use the restroom, David looked at me. "What if she doesn't come?"

"Don't worry," I said, giving him a quick kiss of assurance. "She will."

After lunch, we brought Wylie back to her house. When she went inside, I leaned over and hugged David in the car before he put it in gear again. "I'm sorry," I said. "I know you're more than disappointed."

He held me close. "You know, isn't it funny that I was the one who was so resistant at first? I was afraid of being a father. Scratch that—I was afraid of being *my* father. Now all I want is to be her dad."

"You are," I said. "And you will be. You heard her. Just not *this* Christmas."

chapter forty-five

Christmas week

Joey, Tony, Mom, and I decorated the tree together. With every ornament we hung, we told a story: last-minute shopping trips; caroling in the neighborhood, complete with kazoos and matching Santa hats—we blew all the other neighborhood carolers away; cookie-baking with my playmates and their mothers; staying up as late as we could, sitting at the top of the stairs, waiting for Santa to come; and more. And we reminisced about how every year we found a new ornament in our stockings: miniature guitars, books, action figures, pop-culture reminders of the times—Rubik's Cubes, Millennium Falcons, Coke bottles, and baubles with names and dates.

We played all Mom's favorite Christmas music: Bing Crosby, Nat King Cole, Andy Williams, and *The Nutcracker Suite*. We watched *Miracle on 34th Street* and *It's a Wonderful Life* and the Baryshnikov version of *The Nutcracker* and all the classic cartoons and stop-animation. I made tins of cookies for Wylie's family, David's mom and sisters, Jeff and Patsy Baxter, Maggie, Miranda and Kevin, my students, and Sam's brother. I even offered to take Mom shopping but she said she already finished. Moreover she insisted, practically threatened, that we not buy her anything. But she had made a request of me in private, shortly after Thanksgiving.

"I'd like for you to write about three times in your life in which we shared something good. And not just recently. And I don't want anyone else to read it. Just keep a copy for you and me."

I worked on it almost every day since. When it was finished, I uploaded it to a publish-on-demand website and printed two bound copies, using a photo of my mother holding me when I was born on the cover. I titled the memoir *Daughters*.

Mom's house smelled like pine and nutmeg, and even my happiest childhood Christmas memories couldn't compare to how good this Christmas was with my mother. The underlying notion that this was our last Christmas together, omnipresent as it was, didn't hamper our spirits, although we cried a little bit longer and a little bit harder throughout *It's a Wonderful Life*.

Mom asked David and me to take her to Christmas Eve mass, and I couldn't help but watch her throughout, couldn't help but try to read her thoughts, especially as a solitary tear rolled down her cheek. I kept my arm locked in hers for most of the service. And when it was time for the sign of peace, I turned to *her*, not David, first. We looked at each other, took hold and held on tight.

"I love you, Mom," I whispered in her ear.

"I love you too, Andrea," she whispered back.

I don't remember us ever saying those words to each other with so much sincerity. They were filled with remorse, with forgiveness, with appreciation. They were full of joy and sadness.

We didn't let go until the priest and congregation said, "Lord, I am not worthy to receive you, but only say the word and I shall be healed."

chapter forty-six

New Year's Eve

Tony drove my mother to Northampton with him, and both were shocked to find the FOR SALE sign on the lawn.

"You're selling your house?" Mom asked.

I nodded. "Yep." For a moment, the panic of David's and my decision barreled through me like a freight train.

"I can't believe it, Andi. You told me you could never sell the house. You said it would be like leaving Sam," she said.

"I know," I said, this time overcome with sadness.

"Then why?"

"David and I need a place of our own."

"But you said he always loved it. *He* said it felt like home to him."

"It did."

"So what changed?"

"Everything changed," was all I could say.

"Think about what you're doing, Andi. Once it's gone, you can't get it back."

"Do you regret selling the old house, Mom?" I asked.

"Sometimes," she said. "The worst was packing it up, cleaning it out, going through every item and memory. Your father haunted me every day during those months."

"I'm sorry," I said. "I never knew that. I never even considered that it would be so painful for you. I just assumed that it was something you wanted and were ready for."

"Don't misunderstand me—I like where I live now. And it's much easier to take care of than the old house. But sometimes I wish I could've kept it. Even if no one lived in it. Just keep it the way you keep a photo album. I know that probably sounds ridiculous to you."

"Not at all," I said. I thought about Sam's and my house as something I could occasionally visit, like a summer or winter house, or David's Cambridge apartment, which he had also decided to sell. Perhaps on days I wanted to be close to Sam. But I didn't need a house for that, I thought. And I knew it was time.

David and I were delighted when Wylie showed up at the door, overnight suitcase by her side, poinsettia in hand, and wearing the sweater set I sent her for Christmas. Peter was with her. "Thanks for inviting Janine and me," he said as she stepped inside and made her way upstairs to her room. "I hope you don't mind that I'm just dropping Wylie off and not staying."

"It's OK," said David. "And we'll take her home tomorrow."

"I'd appreciate that," said Peter.

"Would you like to come in for a cup of coffee or something?" I offered.

"Some other time."

I believed him. Peter then extended his hand to David, who took it in a firm grasp and shook hard.

"Thank you," said David. "Thank you for being her father. Thank you for allowing me to get to know her."

Peter pressed his lips tight and choked back his emotion. "You're welcome," he said. "I think Wylie's fortunate to know you too." And with that he bade us a Happy New Year and went back to his truck.

Wylie came back downstairs. I smiled and put my arm around her. "I'm really glad you're here." She smiled back. "Come meet my mom," I said. Together we walked to the living room and found my mother sitting on the sofa, upright, looking stylish as always, but I could tell she was tired.

"Do you want to lie down for a bit?" I asked her. "We can wake you before the party."

"I'll be OK," she replied.

I straightened my posture. "Mom, this is David's daughter, Wylie," I said. "Wylie, this is my mother, Genevieve Cutrone." Never had I spoken with such pride.

"Hello," said Wylie.

My mother took her in and switched her gaze from Wylie to me. "Her eyes."

"I know," I said.

Mom looked at Wylie again. "You have your father's eyes."

"I know," said Wylie.

Mom continued to marvel at her, and finally said, "It's very nice to meet you, Wylie."

"Same here," said Wylie.

"How do you like your new parents?"

I worried that Wylie would be bothered by the term, but she seemed to take it in stride. "Oh, they've been really nice to me, especially considering that I totally turned their lives upside down."

Before I could say anything, my mother said, "Don't you dare say something like that. A good parent, a parent who loves you, will gladly turn their life upside down, inside out, backward and forward for you without batting an eye. Consider your father and Andi among them."

I put my arm around Wylie again and pulled her to me. "Of course she knows that, Mom," I said, hoping I wasn't coming off as scolding. "She was just joking around. I'm going to introduce her to Tony next. You sure you're feeling OK?"

"I'm fine," she said more forcefully. "No p—"

"Yeah, yeah, I know. No pussyfooting," and whisked Wylie away. When we were out of earshot I said, "My mother has a way of making something nice sound like something you did wrong. I hope you didn't take it that way."

"Oh, I didn't think that," said Wylie. "I'd love to know more about her."

"I'm sure she'd love to talk to you," I replied.

Our families and closest friends, including Sam's brother, all showed up to the party. I appreciated that they all were so willing to come, even though they only had a few weeks' notice. I spotted Sam everywhere I turned—the wainscoting in the den; the butcher-block table in the kitchen; the hours we spent in front of the fireplace; the warmth and woodsy smell that was so Sam. I tried to gather and store it somewhere inside of me, a permanent keepsake box for the senses, as if it were all going to disappear at midnight.

At eleven forty-five, David and I rounded everyone up and squeezed them all into the living room. David clinked his glass with a swizzle stick and the chatter quickly dissolved into a hushed silence. He cleared his throat.

"Everyone, I know we've still got fifteen minutes till midnight, but Andi and I have an announcement to make."

The room grew silent. I caught a glimpse of Maggie slowly mouthing the words, "Oh my God, are you pregnant?" to me, and I tried to inconspicuously shake my head no. Wylie was grinning like the Cheshire cat, although no one seemed to notice, probably because she was the last person anyone would guess to know our secret.

"We're really, *really* glad all of you could come tonight," I said slowly, delaying the rest of the sentence, "because . . ." and when I knew they couldn't take it anymore, I blurted, "this is our wedding."

chapter forty-seven

The room erupted into a collective yawp, followed by applause as both Maggie and Miranda rushed and nearly tackled me with their hugs, while my brothers slapped David on the back and shook his hand, taking mock sucker punches at him for not letting them in on the surprise. Wylie, my mother, and Sam's brother were the only people we had told. I had called him and asked for his blessing, and I was even more touched that he not only approved, but wanted to be here.

Mom was seated on the sofa, but I could see a mix of satisfaction and sadness on her face: relief that we'd granted her request, yet aware that an ominous clock was ticking, and not just until midnight. My eyes already wet, I sent her a signal with my body language: *Is this OK? Do you approve?* She responded by holding up her glass in a toast. Tony caught the gesture, and he went to help her stand—she clearly was fighting to stay awake—and brought her over to us. David and I stood in front of the fireplace. Wylie stood by his side, and Mom by mine. David's friend Jim, a notary public, agreed to preside over the exchange of rings and vows.

David and I had written our own.

"Andrea," he began, "I promise to honor our love, and the loves that have come before us. I promise to cherish you, and the people that made us who we have become. I promise to always reread and revise. I promise to listen, to look at the light, to paint in fleeting brushstrokes, to be your student, your teacher, and your partner. I promise to be your best friend."

"David," I replied, willing my voice not to get caught in my throat, "you are both my prologue and my epilogue. You are my co-writer, my reader, my teacher, and my student. You are my best friend. I vow to be all that to you and more. I vow to be yours and yours only. I vow that wherever we go, we'll be home, and we'll be a family." I caught a glimpse of Wylie and winked at her.

The moment Jim pronounced us married, the grandfather clock chimed. David kissed me in a tornado of an embrace swirling with whistles and congratulatory cheers.

Tony held up a glass and toasted us. "To David and Andi," he said. Our friends and family followed suit. We clinked glasses, a melody of bells ringing in the first day of the rest of our lives. And when I looked at my mother, I'd never seen her so proud of me.

chapter forty-eight

Six months later

I was outside tending to the flower beds. Since I never had a green thumb, I had asked Mom to give me a crash course in what seeds to plant and when, when to water and weed them, and what kinds of flowers she liked. I started with orange lilies, planting them in April. Weeding and feeding time became quality time with Mom; working methodically, rhythmically, having conversations with her in my mind, I imagined her standing over my shoulder, correcting me, instructing me, even praising me.

I missed her something fierce.

She had deteriorated sooner than any of us had expected. Maybe David's and my wedding was the last thing she'd held out for. Maybe the cancer had been worse than she'd let on, or than the doctors had anticipated. Maybe she simply didn't want to put us through the agony. She had requested in-home care rather than hospice, and we accommodated, David and I paying for anything Mom's insurance didn't cover. Joey and Tony and I sat vigil throughout the month of March, all three of us moving in, singing three-part harmony to her, and me reading *Daughters* to her when they weren't around. She liked the three events I had chosen: my eighth birthday, when she took me to Carvel, just the two of us; the near bicycle accident I'd mentioned during that first chemotherapy session; and the recipe box she gave me as a wedding present—not quite an "event," but for that piece I put together a profile of sorts, based on recipes that were passed down from her mother and grand-mother. The unifying theme, I decided, was "connection." More specifically, three moments that had brought us together, bonded us in ways we'd never taken the time to notice.

I promised I'd plant a garden, and that I'd try to take care of it.

I promised I'd sing more often.

I promised I'd be a good parent. And a good spouse.

I don't know what she told Joey or Tony when they sat with her alone, each saying their good-byes in their own ways, but to me she mostly gave advice: "Just be there for Wylie. Don't worry about being a mother or a stepmother or whatever you think you're supposed to be. Be yourself. And do it differently from me."

"You weren't so bad, Mom. I was wrong all those years."

"I could've been better. We both could have. Be better with Wylie."

"I will," I said, my voice breaking. "I promise."

She even asked me to give her copy of *Daughters* to Wylie one day, when she was older. Her wedding day, perhaps.

She passed away at the end of March, two days after her wedding anniversary. It seemed fitting. On the particularly difficult days, I would take out the letter she wrote to me—she gave one to each of us for Christmas, along with a framed photo and a keepsake. The photo she gave me was of the two of us in front of the Fontana di Trevi in Rome, almost two years ago. It was one of those candid shots, the kind you don't pose for, are hardly aware of. One of my brothers caught us in a moment of sharing something pleasant, the two of us facing each other and smiling. We had too few of those moments. I placed it on the end table next to my side of the bed. The keepsake was the program from my doctoral graduation; she highlighted my name. In the letter, she explained that she had been very proud of me that day.

> *It was one of those days I missed your father terribly. I knew how proud he would have been, to see you in cap and gown, the first and only one of our children not only to complete a college education, but at the highest level possible. I was proud too. I just didn't know how to tell you.*

The letter explained other things too.

> *When I saw you take your life into your own hands by going away to college, advancing your education, working in New York, and more, I believed you were exerting your independence. I didn't realize that your independence was really the result of your feeling as if you'd been abandoned by me as a parent. Your brothers were so attentive to you that I didn't feel needed by you. Maybe that's why I couldn't understand why you resented me so much. I didn't realize how much you really did need me, wanted me to be there for you.*

I always cry at that part, careful not to smudge the paper.

Wylie and David entered the yard. I squinted at them and waved before turning my attention back to the soil.

"Looks great," called David.

"Thanks," I said.

"It's really coming along," said Wylie as she took in the surroundings of our new house. We considered moving back to Long Island permanently, on the East End, not far from where my mother lived. Mom left her house to my brothers and me. "Use it as a summer home or something," she said. "But I beg of you, don't sell it." We also considered moving closer to Hartford, but I loved Northampton University too much to leave, and David had too many business contacts in the Boston area. We wound up selling our house to Sam's brother. Maybe Sam was meant to stick around. David and I found a plot of land not far from Smith College and hired a contractor. Thanks to the generous bonus we offered, the house went up in record time. We officially moved in two weeks ago.

I got to my feet, dusted the dirt off my hands and knees, and went inside to clean up. The house still smelled of fresh wood and paint. David and Wylie were already setting up the easels in the studio.

"I thought we were doing the pizza lesson first this week," I said.

"We figured we'd work up an appetite first," said Wylie.

"Did you do your homework?" David asked in a stern professor's voice.

Wylie and I rolled our eyes and made huffing noises. "Yes," we both said in mock exasperation.

"Well, let's see it," he instructed. We each pulled out our sketchbooks, and the three of us began a critique session. When David saw my sketches—swing sets, lilies, and my brothers' acoustic guitars (I could draw those from memory), he reached behind Wylie and took my hand. I could feel the sturdy wedding ring on his finger as it nestled with my own fingers, and it was like a battery that plugged into the rest of me. Being married to Dev felt right. Comfortable. Familiar.

As Wylie and David explained and analyzed her sketches, I almost couldn't remember what life was like before she came into our lives, and didn't need to. I commented on the fluidity of one of her drawings, making a comparison to the freewriting process, and she laughed, saying, "I knew you'd say that!"

Maybe this wasn't motherhood, but it was better, as far as I was concerned.

Wylie pointed to one of my sketches, calling attention to the roughness of the line and the balance of contrast. As she did, our eyes connected, and she winked.

acknowledgments

My gratitude cup runneth over for the following people:

Terry Goodman, for falling in love with the manuscript in its early draft form.

Tiffany Yates Martin, for helping me develop the manuscript into a full-fledged novel and doing it with sensitivity, insight, and humor.

Jessica Poore, who answers every stupid question I have (and makes me feel smarter in the process) and always lets me know when a Duran Duran song comes on her iPod.

The entire team at Amazon Publishing, including overseas, for their unwavering support and awesomeness.

Ru, for our Monday afternoon Skype meetings as well as that day in Burlington, Vermont, when she introduced me to those wool socks and that kick-ass hot chocolate.

Rob, Kel, Steffan, Greg, and all the fabulous AP authors who make me proud to be their colleague.

Pam Mottola, for being an early beta reader and assuring me I was on the right track.

My parents, siblings, nieces, nephews, in-laws, and extended family for their love and support.

My North Carolina friends, whom I miss.

The Undeletables, for their love.

Uncle Jon's Coffeehouse, for the delicious vanilla chai.

And to all my readers for loving Andi and David as much as I do, enough to want to spend more time with them. I hope I didn't let you down.

JOJO'S CHOCOLATE HOPE was started in memory of Jo Ensanian, a dear family friend who lost her life to cancer in 2012. Please go to _www.jojoschocolatehope.com_ to place an order of delicious chocolate bark and make a difference. Proceeds go to cancer research.

Follow Jojo's Chocolate Hope on Facebook or on Twitter @ ChocoForACure.

Follow Elisa on Facebook at Elisa Lorello, Author or on Twitter @ elisalorello.

Elisa's website: www.elisalorello.com

about the author

Elisa Lorello was born and raised on Long Island, the youngest of seven children. She earned her bachelor's and master's degrees from the University of Massachusetts-Dartmouth and eventually launched a career teaching rhetoric and composition. Elisa spent six years in North Carolina, where she split her time between teaching writing to university students, and publishing her own work. She has since returned home to the Northeast.

Elisa is the author of Kindle best-selling novels *Faking It* and *Ordinary World, Why I Love Singlehood* (co-authored with Sarah Girrell), and *Adulation. Faking It,* translated in German as *Vorgetäuscht,* also spent three consecutive weeks at #1 on the German Kindle Bestseller List. In 2013, Elisa published a memoir titled *Friends of Mine: Thirty Years in the Life of a Duran Duran Fan.*

When not writing, Elisa is an unapologetic Duran Duran fan, Pop-Tart enthusiast, walker, and coffee shop patron, and she can sing two-part harmony.